"I don't deserve to inherit any of Winston's holdings. You're his son. His blood relative. And I'm—"

"Not up to the challenge?" Crofton asked.

"But Winston would have wanted you to have it," she said with an exuberant amount of passion. "I know he would have."

Crofton ran both hands over his thighs. When she got all emotional, he wanted to wrap his arms around her, but couldn't. If he did that, he might kiss her. Not a peck on the cheek, but really kiss her. Where the hell had these yearnings come from? He'd never been known for his chivalry and had kissed more than his fair share of maidens, but this was out of the ordinary even for him. As was the misery it provided. She was a young, innocent girl with more on her plate than she could handle, and all he could think of was her. Kissing her. Holding her. Protecting her.

Author Note

Ideas for stories come to me in many ways. I dedicated this book to one of my granddaughters because she was behind my inspiration for *Unwrapping the Rancher's Secret*. While she was at our house one day, we watched a cute cartoon about a little girl whose mother married a king, turning the little girl from a commoner to a princess overnight. I found that concept intriguing, and that gave birth to Sara Johnson Parks, a girl who was born in a dirt dugout in Kansas and didn't own a pair of shoes until she was five, when her mother married a lumber baron. Upon the death of her stepfather, Sara becomes the richest woman in Royalton, Colorado, but that is also when Crofton Parks appears. The stepbrother she believed had died as a child.

I hope you enjoy Sara and Crofton's story!

LAURI ROBINSON

UNWRAPPING THE RANCHER'S SECRET

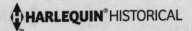

Recycling programs
for this product may
not exist in your area.

ISBN-13: 978-0-373-29904-1

Unwrapping the Rancher's Secret

Printed in U.S.A.

www.Harlequin.com

A lover of fairy tales and cowboy boots, **Lauri Robinson** can't imagine a better profession than penning happily-ever-after stories about men (and women) who pull on a pair of boots before riding off into the sunset—or kick them off for other reasons. Lauri and her husband raised three sons in their rural Minnesota home and are now getting their just rewards by spoiling their grandchildren.

Visit laurirobinson.blogspot.com, Facebook.com/lauri.robinson1 and Twitter.com/laurir.

Books by Lauri Robinson

Harlequin Historical

Daughters of the Roaring Twenties

The Runaway Daughter (Undone!)
The Bootlegger's Daughter
The Rebel Daughter
The Forgotten Daughter

Stand-Alone Novels

Christmas Cowboy Kisses
"Christmas with Her Cowboy"
The Major's Wife
The Wrong Cowboy
A Fortune for the Outlaw's Daughter
Saving Marina
Her Cheyenne Warrior
Unwrapping the Rancher's Secret

Harlequin Historical *Undone!* ebooks

What a Cowboy Wants
His Wild West Wife
Dance with the Rancher
Rescued by the Ranger
Snowbound with the Sheriff
Never Tempt a Lawman

Visit the Author Profile page at Harlequin.com for more titles.

To my granddaughter Hayley.
Love you to the moon and back!

Chapter One

Royalton, Colorado, 1885

There were several ways to play the hand that had been dealt to him. All of them would benefit him. That, of course, was the main object—benefitting him—and he would play it right. Not could. *Would.* Just as he always did.

Crofton Parks lit the cigarette he'd been twirling between his thumb and forefinger and leaned against the side of the building to ponder his options. Smoking wasn't a habit he partook of regularly, but a man with a smoldering stick between his lips could stand around doing nothing but dragging in smoke and no one would give him a second look. While a stranger staring at the mortuary across the street would catch attention. He wasn't ready for that yet. Attention. It would come later. At the moment, anonymity would benefit him the most.

White with a black door and shutters framing the windows, the mortuary was new, as were most of the buildings in town. Not surprising. Becoming a railroad hub, the town had doubled in size the past couple of years, and would keep growing. The lumber mill would continue to prosper, supplying all the houses and businesses the newcomers would build.

Crofton flicked off the ashes and lifted the cigarette to his lips for another draw. Through the smoke that swirled in the crisp air, he witnessed a woman open the door of the building she'd entered a short time ago. Leave it to Winston Parks—his good old flesh-and-blood father— to throw yet another boulder in his pathway. Another loop around the ankle. As if all the others hadn't been enough. At least this one wasn't an eyesore, or not from a distance anyway.

Disgusted by his own thoughts, Crofton dropped the cigarette to the ground and smashed the smoldering end deep into the dirt with the toe of his boot.

A man twice the woman's age, which Crofton knew to be twenty as of October, climbed down from a buggy to meet her as she walked down the steps of the mortuary. Once he arrived at her side, she leaned her head against the man's shoulder for a brief moment, and then straightened. With a shake of her head, as if that gave her fortitude, she squared her shoulders and marched forward. The man lagged behind momentarily, but then quickly caught up with her.

With the sole of one boot braced against the wall behind him and head down, fiddling with the tobacco pouch as if preparing to roll another cigarette, Crofton peered from beneath the brim of his hat to watch the man help the woman into the buggy.

The man climbed in, but Crofton remained still, waiting until the buggy turned the corner and disappeared. Then he glanced both ways, tucked the tobacco pouch into his pocket and crossed the street. It was time he said goodbye to his father. This time it would be for good.

* * *

"There will come a time, child, when you'll remember this day, not with pain and sorrow, but with peace."

The aching inside her was so profound that every movement hurt, yet Sara managed to nod in response to the bittersweet words Reverend Borman whispered in her ear. She understood that life went on, despite death and hardships. She'd lived through it before. Perhaps if she'd been older when her father had died she'd be able to remember how long the numbness lasted. For how many days tears would burst forward without warning, or how long the emptiness inside would remain.

She squeezed her eyes shut against the burning sting and bit her lips together. There were no memories to assure her the pain would ease. No memories of her real father. All that came forward were the things her mother had told her about that time in their lives. How little they'd had, and how far they'd come—all because of Winston Parks.

Older now, and in many ways wiser, Sara knew that no matter how long the pain, how deep the loss or how the numbness lingered, there was no time for her to mourn. A child born in a dirt dugout on the Kansas prairie, who hadn't owned a pair of shoes until she was five, was now the richest woman in town. Along with the wealth bequeathed upon her by the deaths of her mother and stepfather came responsibilities. Ones she couldn't ignore even long enough to grieve their passing.

That's what her mother would have wanted. For her to continue to pay homage to Winston for the life he'd provided them, and so many others.

She knelt down and laid the bouquet of yellow mums, that despite the cooler weather, were still blooming in her mother's garden, on top of the large mound of dirt.

Beneath were two coffins, side by side, in one grave. As soon as the stone arrived from Denver, there would be one granite marker, bearing the names of Winston and Suzanne Parks, describing them as loving husband and wife.

Years from now, looking upon the headstone, people wouldn't know both Winston and Suzanne had been married before. No one would know the anguish and loss they'd each suffered prior to finding one another. Or the strength of the love they'd shared.

Fresh tears formed. Winston had not only loved her mother, he'd loved her, too. He'd treated her as a daughter from the day she'd moved into his home, and in many ways, he'd transformed her from a pauper to a princess. That's how her mother had described the changes that had happened because of Winston, and why they needed to behave properly—to be women he could be proud of— and the importance of remaining grateful for everything he'd done at all times. The only way she could return his love now was to assure his dream came true.

After adjusting the white ribbon tying the flower stems together, Sara rose, and with a nod in Reverend Borman's direction, stepped back to stand amongst the few townsfolk who'd traveled up the steep mountainside from the church in town to the grave site on the homestead Winston had settled upon years ago. The service had been beautiful, and the pews packed with people, but Bugsley had suggested this part of the service should be private, that the last thing Sara needed was a house full of mourners. She'd agreed with him, even though it had left a knot in her stomach. The townsfolk had loved her mother and Winston as deeply as she.

Once the final prayer was recited, Sara turned and started walking down the hill toward the house, pausing now and again to accept a hug or word of comfort as people meandered toward their buggies and saddled mounts.

Hilda Austin's heavy sobbing forced her to remain in the woman's embrace a bit longer than most, and offer comforting words of her own.

"Hush, now," Sara whispered, recalling how her mother had responded to such situations over the years. "They are at peace, and together."

"I'm just going to miss her so much," Hilda sobbed. "I'll never have another friend like her."

"We've both suffered great losses." Sara's gaze went to the three-story brick house that still had the ability to awe her as it had the first day she'd seen it. From that day onward, she'd never wanted for anything. Her throat threatened to close up, and she had to swallow in order to say, "Keeping happy memories close these next few weeks is what we must do. It'll help."

Hilda sniffled and stepped back to wipe her nose with an embroidered hanky. "Look at me. I'm blubbering away when you're the one's who's lost her momma. You poor child—you're all alone now."

Sara's throat swelled shut. Blinking back tears, she nodded and started for the house again. Bugsley was right. She didn't need a house full of people. There wasn't time to dwell on the fact that she was completely alone. She wasn't. Mrs. Long wouldn't leave. Amelia Long had been managing Winston's house for decades and this morning promised to continue working here until she was too old to knead bread. Bugsley was here, too. He'd worked for Winston for years, and promised he'd help her with everything. She'd forever be grateful to him for being at her side the past few days. He'd kept her strong, and she'd needed that.

It was Bugsley who appeared at her elbow before she

was all the way down the hill. Sara didn't have to offer him a smile. He wouldn't expect it, and that felt good.

"Come," he said softly while tucking her arm through his. "You've had a rough day."

His wool suit was as black as her gabardine dress and his boots recently shined. Something that probably hadn't happened since the last funeral he'd attended.

Sara took a deep breath, drawing strength and resolve in understanding that she wasn't the only person who'd experienced such devastating pain. The Williams children had lost their father just last week. Bugsley hadn't gone to the funeral, but she and her mother had, and Winston, who had slipped into the recent widow's hand an envelope containing a sum of money to help the family through their hard time. Sara was grateful that part wasn't an issue for her. Just the opposite in fact. She had more money than she knew how to handle. That would soon change. She'd learn how to handle the money, and invest it for the future of Royalton.

Not entirely sure how she'd complete that daunting task, she said, "It was a lovely service."

"Yes, it was," Bugsley said. "I'll have a donation sent to the church tomorrow."

"I already made a donation for the services," she said. "Yesterday, when I gave Reverend Borman the selection of songs for today."

"I told you I'd take care of things for you," Bugsley said.

"I know," she answered. "And I appreciate your help, but there were some things I wanted to do myself. Needed to do."

"All right," he said, patting her arm. "But I'm here to handle everything else."

There was no doubt she'd need his help. She didn't

have the knowledge it would take to run the lumber mill and negotiate the contracts with the railroad, but she was astute and a fast learner, and wasn't going to shy away from any part of her duties. She'd stayed up late the last two nights, studying maps and contracts, and a plethora of other paperwork in Winston's office, but she now felt she knew less about what to do rather than more. She wasn't about to give up, though, or ask for help. Not yet. One couldn't ask for help until one knew what help was needed. "You'll be the first person I seek when I need assistance," she said. "I promise."

He stiffened slightly but held his silence until they arrived at the house and she looked up. His cheeks were ruddy from shaving off his scruffy whiskers for the day. He'd gotten a haircut, too. White skin showed where his brown hair had been snipped short around his ears. He wasn't what most would call handsome, but he was dedicated and that was what she needed above all else.

"You need some rest," he said with a gentle smile. "I'll see you tomorrow. Unless you want me to stay—maybe you don't want to be alone?"

Her gaze roamed to the house. To the flower bushes beside the steps, the set of white wicker furniture situated in the corner of the massive front porch and the wide front door complete with a screen door to let the air in on warm days. It could be warm today. She couldn't tell. The chill that had settled inside her, clear to her bones, was too encompassing, even wearing the heavy black dress and cape. Fighting off a shiver, Sara answered, "I won't be alone. Mrs. Long is here."

"She's still up the hill," he said. "Talking."

"But will be along shortly." Pulling her hand out of the crook of his elbow, Sara drew a fortifying breath. Mrs. Long had been upset about not hosting a gathering after the funeral, giving people the opportunity to mourn and share memories. Looking at the empty house, Sara had to wonder if she should have sided with Amelia rather than Bugsley. Perhaps entering the front door would be easier with others nearby. The decision had been made, though, and she had no choice but to abide by it. To go forward. Alone. "I'll see you tomorrow," she told Bugsley.

She entered the house without looking back. It would be easy to ask him to step in and see to everything. Too easy. Turning, she closed the inside door, thankful it provided a barrier, making it harder to change her mind. Winston had never let her or her mother down, and now she couldn't let him down. There was no law that said he had to be her father, that he had to feed and clothe her. But he had. Along with so many other things. Therefore, she would do what no law said she had to do. Take up where he had left off. Make sure the railroad had enough timber to build the line from the pass to the border. Farther even, all the way across the Utah Territory and into Nevada.

The ache in her chest became all-consuming. Winston had been so proud of this project. He'd been committed to it, too. Needing to diminish the pain, center her attention on something other than her loss, Sara focused on walking past the sweeping staircase that led to the second floor. The very steps she'd loved to run down and jump into Winston's arms when she'd been younger. He'd laugh and twirl her about before hugging her tight and then setting her down to run off, giggling and dizzy.

Removing the black gloves that matched her funeral dress and cape as she walked, she held them both in one hand when she arrived at Winston's office door. The contracts were in there, and maps and statements and correspondence with railroad men. Reading through them would take her mind off other things as well as prepare her for her next steps. She'd make sure of it this time. Really focus. Living with Winston all these years had left her with considerable knowledge already. Just a few years ago the railroad had been at a standstill in Colorado. The two largest companies attempting to build a line through the southern part of the state had taken each other to court. The Santa Fe had won out, being a standard gauge. Winston had said, and many others had agreed, that the narrow-gauge rails of the Denver & Rio Grande were far better when it came to laying track through the Rocky Mountains, but not beyond, and he'd said that was the important piece. Running tracks beyond the mountains, clear to the ocean.

Winston had won the bid to provide lumber for the Santa Fe and their standard-gauge rail, and that's what she needed to research. She would spend the rest of the day reading and taking notes so this time she'd remember things. Understand them. She needed to know what was expected of the lumber mill better than she knew the recipe for her famous cinnamon cookies. Made famous by her stepfather who ate them two at a time as soon as she took them out of the oven.

The smile that memory evoked froze on her lips as she opened the door to Winston's office. Her heart momentarily stopped, too. For a split second she could have sworn she was staring at Winston—how he'd looked fifteen years ago when she and her mother first met him back on the Kansas prairie.

The man behind the big desk that sat angled in the corner swiveled the chair around and lifted a dark brow as his gaze met hers. "Well, hello, little sister."

A shiver curled around her spine. "E-Excuse me?"

"I said, hello, little sister."

She'd dropped a glove, and used the time it took to bend down and pick it up to gather her wits. A cold and frightening lump formed in her stomach. One that left her hands trembling. "I do not have any siblings," she said, straightening as tall as possible and squeezing her gloves with both hands. "And you, sir, are trespassing."

Crofton Parks almost cracked a grin. Might have if the situation had even an ounce of humor surrounding it. It didn't, and neither did he. Have an ounce of humor that is. Her black cape didn't disguise her hourglass figure and her chestnut-colored hair had just enough red to make it shimmer like gold in the sunshine. The sight of Sara Johnson—or Parks as everyone referred to her— confirmed he'd been right. She wasn't an eyesore. Not from a distance or up close. If her mother had looked anything like her, with eyes that big and blue and skin that lily-white, he could almost understand why his father had deserted him and his mother back in Ohio. Almost, because to his way of thinking, no man should discard one family for another. Not for any reason.

He leaned back in the big leather chair and stretched his arms overhead before threading his fingers together and lowering them until the back of his head rested against his palms. Even after all these years, he could remember how his father had used to sit like that. All he'd have to do was kick up his feet to rest his heels on the desk and his memory would be complete. He didn't kick up his feet for several reasons, including that he wasn't here to relax. "I'm not trespassing, little sister. I'm just here to collect what's mine."

She was wringing the gloves in her hands so hard they were practically tied in knots, and her eyes were darting around as if she couldn't let them rest on him. He knew why. From the time he'd been born people had said he looked exactly like his father. At one time he'd taken pride in that. That was no longer the case. Hadn't been for years.

"Stop calling me that, and there's nothing here that could be—"

"Mine?" he interrupted. "Yes, there is, and you know it." He dropped his hands and leaned forward to wave a finger her way. "Don't bother lying. I can see by the fear in your eyes that you know who I am." Crofton stood and straightened the bottom of his vest before reaching behind him to gather up the jacket that completed the suit he'd purchased for the occasion, his father's funeral. He also attempted to keep the scorn out of his tone when he added, "I've always been the spitting image of my father."

One arm was in his jacket sleeve when he paused, waiting for her reaction.

Her fair skin had turned whiter. Colorless. He dropped the coat just as her blue eyes disappeared behind her eyelids.

"Damn!"

Crofton made it around the desk in time to catch her before she hit the floor.

He'd picked up and carried calves that weighed more than she did. However, none of those critters ever smelled liked flowers and sunshine. She did, and all the other things women were supposed to smell like. Ignoring that, for it made no difference, he carried her to the long sofa covered in cowhide and situated near a massive stone fireplace on the other side of the room. There he set her down. On her bottom. She hadn't passed out, not completely and was already squirming to get out of his hold.

As soon as she was free, she scooted along the seat, farther away from him. "You're—you're dead," she whispered. "Dead."

"I could apologize for that, but since I wasn't the one to put that idea in your head, I won't. As you can clearly see, I'm not dead. Never was." A shred of guilt laced his gut at the way she trembled. He tried to ignore it, but in the end, he told himself she wasn't to blame and holding his father's faults against her wouldn't be fair. Despite his parentage, that was one thing he did pride himself on: being a fair man. An honest one, too. It had taken him a long way in this life.

"How can that be?"

Crofton stopped his inner musings and shrugged. "Because it never was."

"Fa—" She pinched her lips together for a second. "Winston said you died as a small child, back in Ohio, in a fire. He was devastated over it."

"Was he?" The scorn slipped out before Crofton had a chance to conceal it.

"Yes," she said. "He spoke of you often, especially—"

Her lips pinched tight and her thick lashes held teardrops when she lifted them. The sight was as unique as it was touching.

Once again Crofton had to detour his thoughts. "Especially when?"

"Before my little brother died. He was only four."

"Your little brother?"

Looking up at him with moisture filled eyes, she nodded. "Yes, my little brother. Hilton. He died of the fever six years ago."

Why that felt like a gut punch, Crofton wasn't sure, but either way, he sat down. It would make sense that his father had gone on to have more children, but he'd never contemplated that aspect. Probably should have. "How many other children are there?" Wrestling a stepdaughter would be a simple enough feat; another blood son might not be. It wouldn't stand in his way, though. Nothing would stand in his way of finding out why the railroad had pulled out of running a line south into New Mexico. He'd made promises on it, and he never broke a promise. There, too, he was nothing like his father.

"Other—" She shook her head. "None."

"None?"

She wiped aside a teardrop sitting on her left cheek. "No, there were no more children, not before or after Hilton."

Crofton withheld a grin, kept it hidden deep inside where only he knew it existed. "So it's just you and me."

After a lengthy hesitation, she met him eye to eye. "Yes. Just you and me."

Chapter Two

The walls were closing in on her. She unbuttoned her cloak and shrugged it off her shoulders, but it didn't help. The heavy black dress was just as suffocating. So was his nearness. Willing her legs to cooperate, she pushed off the sofa. She stumbled slightly, but caught herself. This was all impossible. Crofton Parks was impossible. He'd died years ago. Winston would never have lied about that. Not something that important. Actually, he wouldn't have lied about anything. He was a good, honest man.

Gaining inner strength, she turned her attention to the stranger. He certainly resembled Winston. Dark brown hair, hazel-rimmed green eyes flecked with specks of gold. Tall. Broad at the shoulders and lean at the waist. He even had a dimple in the middle of his chin. However, he couldn't possibly be Winston's son. More like an impostor who was simply after her stepfather's money. Winston's wealth, the lumberyard he'd spent a lifetime building and his work with the railroad were well-known, perhaps nationwide or even worldwide.

Sara lifted her chin and tightened her neck muscles to keep her voice from quivering. "You, sir, are an impostor and I insist you leave immediately."

He leaned back and swung a foot up to balance on his opposite knee. "I'm not an impostor, Sara—"

"I gave you no invitation to use my first name," she snapped, unwilling to listen to anything he had to say. "If you don't leave immediately, I'll summon the sheriff."

"And how will you do that?" he asked, crossing his arms. "You got a little bell you ring or something?"

His comment was so arrogant and smug that Sara wished she'd asked Bugsley to stay, or that Mrs. Long had returned. Something deep inside said she didn't want to be alone with this man. He couldn't be trusted, that was a given, but his uncanny resemblance to Winston was confusing her usual good sense.

Alvin Thompson who saw to the horses and other chores around the property lived just down the hill, but not within shouting distance. Nonetheless, she said, "I have men I will send to town." A bluff, but he wouldn't know that. "As a matter of fact, I have men who will take you to town. See you jailed for trespassing."

Relief washed over her as he planted his foot back on the floor and stood. Without a word, he crossed the room and gathered his suit coat. She moved toward the open doorway, prepared to walk him all the way to the large front door, and lock it after he left.

Rather than putting on the coat, he pulled something out of a pocket and turned, holding an envelope out to her. "The sheriff's out of town."

Knowing Sheriff Wingard was out of town, and not wanting to dwell upon it, she asked, "What's that?"

"An affidavit proving I am indeed Crofton Parks, son and heir of Winston Parks." Still holding the envelope out for her to take, he added, "And Alvin won't be any help. He's at his job at the lumber mill."

"How—" She bit down on her bottom lip, angry for allowing a word to slip out before she'd thought it through. Alvin did work at the mill, and had returned there upon leaving the church, so therefore, was not home.

"How do I know about Alvin? And Sheriff Wingard?" He laid the envelope on the desk as if it made no difference whether she read it or not. "I've made it my business to know." Walking toward the windows framed by long olive-green drapes held back to let the sun in with gold rope ties, he said, "I also know everything about my father's company and his deal with the railroad. And you. And your mother."

The disdain in his voice was strikingly sharp. Out of defiance, Sara lifted her chin. "Why?"

"Because I'm his son."

She wasn't ready to believe that. Might never be. She did however want to know what he was doing here. "Anyone can have a piece of paper written up. That's no proof whatsoever. Besides, if you truly were his son, you would have come to see Winston while he was alive. Any decent man would have."

His back was to her as he stared out the window. The lumber mill was a distance down the mountainside, but large and visible from where he stood. So was the town of Royalton. Winston had often stood in that same spot, watching the hustle and bustle below. She'd stood there plenty of times herself.

"How do you know I didn't?" he asked.

Sara didn't know for sure, however there was one thing she knew for certain. "Because I knew Winston Parks. If his son was alive, and had contacted him, he would have told me. He would have told my mother. He would have shouted it from the rooftop."

He turned. The smile on his face was false; the dullness of his eyes said so. Yet, at the same time, she couldn't help but see Winston in him, and that was frightening.

"Maybe you didn't know him as well as you thought," he said.

Sara was saved from responding by the sound of the front door being opened, as well as someone saying her name.

"Mrs. Long is calling for you," he said. "The housekeeper."

He was attempting to intimidate her—something she refused to let happen. "Anyone in town could have told you who lives here, including Mrs. Long, and that the sheriff is out of town, and that Alvin Thompson lives next door so there's no need to pretend you're full of family secrets. There aren't any."

"You're wrong, Sara," he said softly. "There are lots of family secrets when it comes to Winston Parks."

As much as she didn't want to believe his words, she couldn't ignore the clarity of his gaze.

"Oh, there you are," Amelia Long said. "I—Oh, I didn't know we had company."

Sara didn't turn around to where the woman was obviously standing in the doorway. Instead, she kept her gaze on the man, and held her stance. "We don't," she said. "He was just leaving."

"Land sakes," Amelia gasped. "It can't be. Can it? Lord have mercy! Is it? Is it you, Crofton? Crofton, oh, sweet Lord! Tell me it's really you! Tell me! Please, tell me!"

The smile that appeared on his face was as bright as sunshine. "Yes, Amelia, it's me."

Sara had no time to react, not even when the man rushed past her and caught Amelia as she slumped.

Crofton once again carried a woman across the room,

questioning if every woman in Colorado fainted on a regular basis. This one was much older, heavier and not nearly as firm or sweet smelling as the younger one he'd carried mere minutes ago. But, this one had carried him around when he was little, and he'd never forgotten her.

Placing Amelia gently on the sofa, he told Sara, "Get some water. Unlike you, she's not pretending. She really fainted."

"I—I didn't pretend."

Crofton knelt near the sofa. "Just get some water, would you?"

She hurried out the door, and Crofton laid a hand on Amelia's cheek. Her face was soft, full of wrinkles, and her blond hair streaked with gray, but she was as lovely to him as she had been twenty years ago when he used to wish she was his mother. Amelia had always had time for him. Never shooed him from the room or scolded him for getting dirty. She even helped dig worms and would drop whatever she'd been doing to take him fishing. At least that was how he remembered it. Just like he remembered her cooking had been the best he'd ever eaten. Especially her fried chicken. Of all the people, all the things he'd missed when his mother had whisked him off to England, it had been Amelia Long and her fried chicken.

Amelia stirred, and Crofton leaned closer. "Shh," he whispered. "Just lie still for a moment. You're fine."

"Here."

He took the glass of water Sara held out and as Amelia's eyes opened, he gently raised her head up with his other hand. "Take a sip," he said. "It'll help."

Watching him closely, Amelia took several small sips, and then shook her head. He handed the glass back to Sara before asking, "Are you feeling all right?"

"Yes," Amelia answered. "I was just so shocked to see you. She told us you were dead."

"I've heard that," he said. "But as you can see, she was wrong."

Amelia popped up with all the speed of a spring chicken. "Why would she have done such a thing? Oh, if only Winston could have seen you." Sniffling, she wiped her nose with the tip of one finger as tears dripped down her wrinkled cheeks. "Oh, Crofton, he would have been so joyous. He never got over your death. Never."

Damn, she was making his nose burn, and his chest. He bit the inside of his bottom lip. He'd never gotten over his father's death, either. That hadn't been possible for an eight-year-old who'd believed his father had been the bravest, strongest man on earth. His father had been his hero, up until he turned eighteen and learned the truth.

"Oh, that Ida," Amelia growled. "I'd like to give her a piece of my mind. I tell you that. She always was nasty, but this—you—it's downright evil. Evil I say."

"She had her reasons, Amelia," he said quietly.

"Oh, and what would they be?" Without waiting for a response, she added, "Pure selfishness is what she had. No reason is good enough for what she did—for this. Not a single one. Winston was so sick over your death, so lost and…" Sniffling again, she shook her head. "We all were. My heart is breaking all over again. For Winston. Oh, your poor, poor father. He loved you so much."

To his surprise, Sara sat down next to Amelia and put her arm around her.

"Hush, now," she whispered. "He knows Crofton is here now. He knows."

Crofton pretended he hadn't heard her words, but he had, and it appeared it had taken less convincing for her to believe he was Winston's son than he'd expected.

"I expect he does," Amelia said. "He was probably searching all over the pearly gates for his baby boy. Just like he did back in Ohio all those years ago." Wiping at the tears on her cheek, she whispered, "He didn't believe the news and went back to see for himself."

Crofton couldn't take much more. Of course Amelia would side with his father. Nate, her husband, had been in on Winston's first lumber deal. Nate had died during the railroad wars, back in '78, when both companies had brought in hired guns to settle their dispute over laying westbound tracks out of Colorado. A judge finally settled things, but there was still plenty of fighting going on. Both sides had gained ground. The narrow-gage line was working its way west through the mountains, and the standard-gage was running along the south end of the state. That was the set to run a line down into New Mexico, give ranchers a way to ship cattle. A way for him to ship his cattle, but the railroad had withdrawn for no apparent reason. He knew the reason. His father.

The silence in the room tickled his neck, and Crofton lifted his head to find both women looking at him expectantly. Having no idea what they'd asked, yet noting they were clearly waiting for an answer, he shrugged and turned it back on them. "What do you think?"

"I think she's dead," Amelia said with more hatred than he'd ever have expected to hear from her. "Otherwise, she'd have been trying to get money out of your father. Just like she did when you di—when she claimed you'd died."

So the topic was his mother. He'd expected that. There had been no love lost between her and anyone left on this side of the ocean. With a nod, he stood and walked over to the fireplace. The mantel was massive, as was the hearth, with a large area to stack wood built right in the stone.

It was an impressive design, something his father had been good at. Anyone who knew Winston said he was a visionary, could see what he wanted and didn't stop until he got it. That, too, Crofton had inherited.

"That's you."

He frowned at Amelia's statement, and then scanned the mantle, wondering what she referred to. A photo of a child sat in the center, in a polished frame.

"The one next to it is Hilton, taken shortly before he died."

Sara had said that, and he took a moment to examine the other picture of a boy child, no more than a baby actually. There was a certain family resemblance, which caused an odd pang inside him.

Turning about, he said to Amelia, "I'm assuming my mother is still alive, but I can't say for sure. I haven't seen her in eight years."

"Eight years?" Sara asked, biting her tongue as soon as the words were out. Although Amelia was convinced of this man's heritage, she wasn't. But, even if he was Winston's son, he wasn't to be trusted. Any man who hadn't seen his father in over twenty years, and his mother in eight, had to be a scoundrel. A selfish, no-good rascal.

"Yes," he answered. "Eight years. Since I left England." His cold stare turned to Amelia, where it warmed slightly. "I left the day I learned my father was alive."

"Alive?"

Sara was glad Amelia asked that. It had been on the tip of her tongue, but the years of being told to only speak when spoken to had returned.

"Yes. Just as my mother told him I was dead, she told me he was dead. That you all were dead."

"Oh, that bitter woman," Amelia hissed. "She'll have her judgment day. Lord forgive me, but she will."

He turned away from the fireplace, and after gazing at both her and Amelia for what seemed like an eternity, he gave a subtle nod. "I have an appointment I must see to now. Good day, ladies."

Amelia shot to her feet. "You can't leave, Crofton, you can't."

"I'll be back," he said, patting the hand she'd used to grab his arm. "I just have to see a man about a horse."

His answer struck Sara to the core. Winston had always used that saying. Crofton obviously knew that and was trying to get a rise out of her. So was Amelia, the way she turned a set of sad eyes her way.

"Sara, tell him he mustn't leave," Amelia pleaded. "Tell him."

That was the last thing she'd do. "Mr. Parks..." She let her words linger, telling him she didn't completely believe that was his name. "Can most certainly leave." *And not return*, she added silently, but knew he understood. ·

"No, he can't," Amelia insisted. "We have so much—"

"I'll return for the evening meal," he said, drawing Amelia's attention. "If I can wrangle an invitation."

The look he gave the older woman was enough to make Sara throw up, or see red, which she was doing.

"You don't need an invitation," Amelia said. "You're family." With a sigh, and while hugging his arm, she added, "It's a miracle. A pure Christmas miracle having you here. Sara needs family right now. We all do."

His gaze, which went over Amelia's head to meet her stare, was as clear as the words written in the Good Book. Just as she was reading his mind, he was reading hers, and neither one of them considered the other family, nor did they believe this was a Christmas miracle.

Amelia followed him out of the room, and Sara moved to the window, waiting to see him leave. Her stomach was churning and her mind was spinning. His arrival could change everything. Winston's dream. The railroad's success. The town of Royalton. She had no right to fight him, no claim to all that Winston had left behind, but he wasn't here to further Winston's dream. Intuition told her that, and her allegiance to Winston said she couldn't let his dream die. Couldn't and wouldn't.

During the years since Winston had built his lumber mill, over a hundred buildings and homes had been built in Royalton. The town had been transformed from a lumber camp to a bustling city, complete with stage coach service, and more important, a railroad depot. The entire town depended upon Parks Lumber. Jobs. The railroad. Prosperity for all.

It was all up to her.

The air in Sara's lungs burned as Crofton appeared outside the window. He made a point of stopping the big roan he rode at the top of the hill, and turned around to tip his hat directly at the window. At her.

She didn't respond, or move, other than the sinking of her stomach.

He nudged the horse and rode away. Once again she was reminded of Winston. Of all the times she'd watched him ride down that hill.

When Crofton, if that truly was his name, disappeared amongst the bustle of Royalton, Sara turned and walked to the desk. Rather than anything of Winston's, the item that caught and held her attention was the envelope Crofton had left behind. Burning it would be the smart thing to do, but her curiosity was too strong for that. Taking up the sharp knife Winston always used to slit open the mail, she eased it beneath the flap.

"I can't believe it," Amelia said from the open doorway. "Just can't believe it. All these years we thought he was dead. All these years."

Sara set the envelope and the knife down. "Don't you find it odd that he learned Winston wasn't dead eight years ago, but never once visited? Never once tried to make contact?"

With eyes sadder than they had been this morning, Amelia shook her head and sat in the chair in front of the desk. "We have no way of knowing what she told him."

"Who?"

"Crofton's mother. Ida."

Sara wasn't willing to believe there was anyone to blame except Crofton. "He doesn't seem like the type of man to take someone else's word." *Or orders*, she supplied completely for herself.

"I'm sure he's not, just like Winston wasn't, but Ida had a way about her."

"What sort of way?" Sara asked.

"A sneaky, conniving one. That woman wouldn't stop until she got her way. Ever."

Amelia's tone held more scorn than Sara had ever heard her use, and that alone would have been enough to make her jittery, if she hadn't been already. Like mother, like son.

Slapping her knees, Amelia jumped to her feet. "I'm going to go fetch that hen that's been pecking at the others. Crofton always liked fried chicken. Oh, that boy could eat like no other. I think I'll bake a pie, too."

"A pie?"

"Yes. Make us a real celebration dinner."

"We just left a funeral," Sara pointed out. "A celebration dinner wouldn't be appropriate."

Waving a hand at the desk, and the rest of the room, Amelia asked, "Do you think Winston would mind? Or your mother? They wouldn't want us sitting around moping. They'd expect us to get on with life. And they would expect us to give Crofton a proper welcome home. It truly is a Christmas miracle."

"Christmas is weeks away."

Amelia shrugged. "So it is." While heading for the door, she added, "And we both have to eat. Fried chicken is your favorite, too."

Sara waited until Amelia left the room before mumbling, "It won't be after today." The letter lying on the desk, the one she'd been prepared to slit open moments ago mocked her. She was still curious, but did she really want proof Crofton was Winston's son? Did she need proof?

The answer was obvious. Amelia would not say he was if he wasn't. Furthermore, he was too much like Winston not to be his son. Besides looks, he had the attitude, the swagger, even sat upon a horse the same way. Straight and tall. The only notable difference was that Winston had had a softness about him. He'd been loveable. Crofton wasn't even likable.

Chapter Three

Crofton rode into town with a chip on his shoulder. It had been there for years, but today it felt like a boulder. He popped his neck and arched his back, but the weight didn't shift. He hadn't expected it to. What he did expect was to get a pair of blue eyes out of his mind.

"Damn it," he muttered. "Why couldn't she have been homely?" That was another trait his father had given him—the inability to ignore a beautiful woman.

It wasn't Sara's beauty that worried him. It was the intelligence in those blue eyes. She'd been sizing him up since the moment they met, and that told him being Winston's son wasn't going to be enough.

Burying those thoughts as much as he could, Crofton pulled up his reason for being here tackling all these old memories, and rode up the main street of town. Buildings of all sizes lined the street on both sides of him. Not a one was as large as the home he'd just left. Leave it to his father to build a home larger than even the hotel. It was only two stories. His father's brick house had three, plus a basement. Imagine that, the owner of the lumber company building himself a brick house. Ironic.

There was plenty of wood in his father's house, too.

The trim, windows, door and large porch were all painted white, making it look even more impressive. So were the balconies off the second floor, and the two round turrets on the third.

It had taken plenty of wood to build the town. Businesses, the same as most towns, offered customers goods and services. As he scanned the stores—a mercantile, feed store, blacksmith, hotel, saloon, nothing out of the ordinary—he thought of other boom towns he'd seen. Here today. Gone tomorrow. Royalton didn't have the look or feel of the others he'd seen, and he wasn't sure whether he appreciated that or not.

He'd already visited the dry goods store, that's where he'd purchased his suit yesterday, and this morning he'd bought a bath and shave. While scraping his face, the barber had seen exactly what Sara had: his resemblance to Winston. Others would, too. He'd planned on using that to his advantage, and now was as good a time as any. Actually, the sooner the better.

Riding to the edge of town, where the lumber mill was located, Crofton maneuvered his way through the busy yard. The noise was immense, and he couldn't help but be impressed. Two huge water wheels provided some of the power needed for the numerous saws, but there was also a large steam shed that generated other saws. The heat was intense, but it didn't slow down the workers. The mill was a town in itself, with traffic, wagons empty and full, maneuvering about, and men, far more than he could quickly count, went about completing various jobs. Laborious jobs. A locomotive whistle sounded where it slowly chugged its way down the hill behind the mill. The long logs it carried were so large only three fit on the flat car behind the engine.

His father had never done anything on a small scale,

but this lumber mill went beyond that. He'd been young, but Crofton remembered the mill in Ohio, the one his father had built there to supply wood for the railroad expansion back then. He also remembered how his father had waved a hand at that mill, saying someday that it all would be his.

This may not be Ohio, but that day had come.

Crofton frowned at his own thought. He wasn't here to inherit a lumber mill. Why was he thinking that way? Because, no one but him needed to know that. That's why. Convinced, he made his way toward the door on a large wooden structure that had the word *Office* painted in red. There he dismounted, tethered his horse and made his way to the open doorway. He entered the building, and took a deep breath.

The smell of fresh-cut wood filled his nostrils, and his mind, invoking more memories. Ones he'd long ago buried. How he'd loved visiting the mill with his father, and how the pride of walking beside him had puffed out his small chest back then.

The attention his slow ride through the yard had aroused wasn't just outside, and Crofton pushed aside his childhood memories. The man standing before him was the one he'd seen with Sara at the mortuary yesterday and at the funeral today. Bugsley Morton wasn't as old as Winston had been, but he was middle aged, maybe forty or so, and from the looks of him, considered himself in charge.

"If you're here to place an order, Walter can help you," Bugsley said, gesturing toward a counter.

Though he tried not to show it, shock was written all over Bugsley's face. Much like the man standing behind the wide counter. Walter. He was as stiff as a corpse with eyes so wide they nearly popped out of his head.

Crofton glanced back to Bugsley. The man knew full
well he wasn't here to place an order, and was attempting
to disguise his nervousness. He'd stuck his hands in his
pockets and rocked on his heels. The man saw exactly
what Crofton wanted him to see. Exactly what Walter
saw. A clear resemblance to Winston.

"We aren't hiring, if it's a job you're after," Bugsley
said.

Crofton let a hint of a grin form while shaking his
head. He didn't know much about Bugsley Morton. The
man hadn't been a part of Winston's pack back in Ohio,
but Mel's letters had said Morton was Winston's right-
hand man, had been for the past decade or so. That didn't
bother him. Neither a right- nor left-hand man meant anything compared to flesh and blood, and that was a card
Crofton was more than prepared to use.

"I said—"

"I heard you." Crofton kept one eye on the man while
moving toward a set of stairs that led to the second floor.

"You can't go up there."

Crofton gave the man a solid once-over, from his shiny
boots to his newly trimmed hair, but never detoured from
walking toward the staircase. "Who's going to stop me?"
he asked. "You?"

"Matter of fact, yes. Me." Bugsley stepped closer, but
didn't block the stairway.

Crofton had noticed the gun hanging on the man's
hip, and how Bugsley's right hand hovered over the well-
worn handle. That gun had known plenty of use, and the
thought it may have been the one to end Mel's life crossed
Crofton's mind. Briefly, for he knew that couldn't have
been possible. Mel had been shot from a distance, with
a rifle.

"Go ahead then." Crofton stepped onto the stairs and

started to climb. Bugsley was far too curious to draw the gun or pull the trigger, and shooting a man in the back with witnesses nearby was the best way to get hanged.

A hallway led off the top step, was lit by a tall window at the far end and contained four doors, all closed. Crofton knew which one would have been his father's, the last one on the left. It would host windows that not only looked over the back side of the mill, but up the hill, to where the view would show the big brick house.

He was right of course, but the room surprised him. There was the usual desk, shelves, table and chairs, a long sofa along the interior wall, a small stove in the outside corner and other necessities here and there, but things were out of place. Although it had been years, certain things about a man rarely changed. His father had been meticulous with his paperwork, and everything had always been put away, under lock and key when he left a room. That's how his office back at the house had been.

Granted he had been dead for a few days, and it was expected someone else would need to take over the running of the business, but if that person respected the man Winston had been, they would have continued his practices.

A stack of maps were haphazardly spread across the table and several open ledgers sat on top of the desk, almost as if someone was searching through them for something particular, but had yet to find it. Whatever it was.

Bugsley was on his heels, so Crofton barely paused upon entering the room. He strode over to the sofa and took a moment to examine the pictures hanging along the wall. Family portraits of Winston, his wife and Sara, and again, there was the grainy photo of him as a child. It didn't stir him as strongly as the one of Sara did. She'd been little, maybe five or six and looked like a cherub with her softly painted pink cheeks. The big picture hanging front and center had her in it, too, taken at the same time. In this one, she sat upon Winston's lap while her mother stood behind them.

He let his gaze linger on his father in that portrait for a few minutes before he turned to Bugsley. "Uncanny resemblance, wouldn't you say?"

"Who are you? What do you want?"

Crofton took another glance at the picture before he moved toward the desk sitting at an angle in the corner. "You know who I am."

"But that's impossible," Bugsley answered.

"Evidently not." He walked around the desk to the window. It provided a spectacular view of the brick house on the hill. With the right eyepiece he'd be able to see inside the windows of the house. When thoughts of Sara, of which room was hers, attempted to wheedle their way into his mind, he shifted his gaze to the hillside.

"Winston said you were dead."

"Perhaps I was," Crofton answered. "To him." He walked to the window on the other wall. This one overlooked the train tracks leading up the hill and into a thick forest. The trees were tall, and went on for as far as he could see. Winston had certainly picked out the right spot for his lumber mill. The mountainside appeared to have a never-ending supply of timber.

"Did he know?"

Crofton turned. Bugsley appeared more nervous. The truth must be hitting him, and he wasn't liking it. "Know that I was alive?" Crofton asked.

"Yes."

Shrugging his shoulders, Crofton took a step to the desk and flipped through a few pages of one of the open ledgers, not really seeing what was written on the pages, but pretending to. He'd wondered if his father had always known that he was alive. His mother claimed Winston knew and didn't want anything to do with him, but she'd say most anything, truth or lie, depending on what suited her best. He'd long ago learned to never lay much on her word.

"I guess we'll never know, will we?" Crofton closed the book, letting the snap of the cover echo through the room. He knew. Winston had known.

Bugsley stiffened. "Well, you can't just waltz in here—"

"Yes," Crofton said. "I can."

Squaring his shoulders, Bugsley shook his head. "Winston left me in charge, every time he went out of town he left me in charge."

"He's not merely out of town this time, is he?" Crofton had seen enough to know what he was up against when it came to Bugsley Morton. The man was afraid of losing and wasn't about to go down easily. The black hat that hung on the hook near the door was the same one he'd been wearing at the funeral. Winston may have left Bugsley in charge when he went out of town, but he obviously didn't let the man in on every detail of his business. Some things never changed. Crofton had been counting on that.

Holding back a grin, he walked to the open doorway. "My lawyer will arrive later this week. Until then, business should continue as usual."

"Whoa up there. You can't—"

"Yes, I can." Pausing long enough to tip the brim of his hat, Crofton said, "Good day, Mr. Morton." Just because the opportunity was there, he added, "I expect you to put everything back where you found it."

On the ground floor he nodded at Walter, who was still standing behind the counter, board stiff and staring at him like he was a ghost. In a sense he was. He hadn't been Winston's son in a long time, but it was time to re-enter that role.

The weight on his shoulders seemed to lessen a bit as he stepped outside. The crisp mountain air was filled with the sweet smell of freshly cut wood, and more memories returned. For the first time in a long time, they didn't make his gut tighten. The past no longer mattered nearly as much as the future.

Considering December had arrived, he'd expected snow this high up, and had appreciated the weather's cooperation during his trek here. He hoped the warmer temperatures held out a while longer as he mounted his horse.

His next stop was the livery. He'd paid a few extra coins the past couple of nights to bed down in the hay-loft. The owner had been more than happy to oblige, just as Mel had said in his letter.

While climbing the ladder into the loft, Crofton once again questioned if his father could have been behind Mel's death. He'd gone back and forth with the idea for some time, and after meeting Bugsley Morton face-to-face, was leaning toward the possibility. Or maybe he was thinking Bugsley could be behind it. That would mean his father had been, too. Winston had always called the shots and that wouldn't have changed.

He, however, had changed. He was no longer a kid being dropped at one school after the other, wishing his father hadn't died. He was no longer a young man wondering why his father had abandoned him and why his mother lied about it, either. He was older and wiser, and knew his path had little to do with either parent. Once this railroad fiasco was over that is.

Crofton gathered his bundle of dirty clothes. He hadn't worried about leaving them here, figured if someone took them, they needed an old shirt and pair of pants more than he did. But, he'd never left messes for others to clean up, and wasn't going to start now. Perhaps because he'd been a product of someone's mess his entire life.

After thanking the livery owner for his hospitality, who stared at him as if seeing double now that his face wasn't covered with scraggly whiskers, Crofton made his way up the main street to Buster's Saloon. Mel's letter had said he was meeting a man there and would write more afterward. Of course, more never came. Instead of a letter, a week after his last post, Mel's horse had wandered into the yard, still saddled. Gun still in the scabbard. A day later, Crofton had found Mel's body. Halfway between home and Royalton. Shot in the back.

After tethering his horse to the hitching post, Crofton entered the saloon. Someone had preceded him. The silence that fell upon the crowded room told him who even before he saw Bugsley Morton at a table with three men dressed in suits. They could have been at the funeral, but his gut said they were dressed in suits because they were railroad men not mourners. The fourth stranger at the table wasn't a mourner, nor a railroad man. He was a gunslinger. A well-known one. If rumors were correct, Woody Wilson was on the Santa Fe Railroad payroll.

Here for only one thing at the moment, Crofton walked to the bar and ordered a shot of whiskey. Holes were burning in his back, but he paid them no mind as the man behind the bar took the money he'd laid down and poured amber-shaded whiskey into a shot glass until it sloshed over the rim. After downing the whiskey in one gulp, Crofton set the glass down. "I'd like to buy a round."

The barkeep frowned. "For who?"

Crofton twirled a finger in the air.

Frowning so deep his forehead had crevices, the barkeep asked, "The entire room?"

Crofton nodded.

"Why?" the man asked over the mumbling that circled the room.

Crofton slapped several bills on the counter, and pointed to his glass. "Line them up," he said. "Just like that one."

The barkeep shrugged and started setting out glasses. Like horses smelling water, men gravitated toward the bar. Crofton took his glass and stepped aside, making more room as the bartender poured whiskey into glasses from bottles in both hands.

"Step up, gentlemen," Crofton said loudly. "I'd like to make a toast."

Bugsley and the men at his table hadn't moved. Crofton hadn't expected them to, and made no point in singling them out until every other man in the saloon had made their way to the bar and now held a shot of whiskey.

"I'd like to make a toast." Crofton held up his glass and looked at Bugsley. "To Winston Parks, may he rest in peace."

Men shouting, "Hear, hear!" held up their glasses.

"He was one hell of a father!" Crofton tossed down his drink in one gulp again, and while others were choking and coughing, half because of the whiskey, half because of his toast, he walked over and set his glass on the table in front of Bugsley and then walked out the door.

Chapter Four

"Surely you aren't going to wear that to dinner."

"Of course I am," Sara answered. Given a choice, she would have changed out of the black gabardine dress, but considering their dinner guest, she felt the dress she'd worn to the funeral was more than suitable.

Amelia opened her mouth, but must have changed her mind. After a heavy sigh, she muttered, "Suit yourself. Crofton should be here shortly."

Glancing at the clock on the top shelf of the buffet that held the set of delicate china Winston had purchased for her mother several years ago, Sara said, "We'll eat at six whether he's here or not."

Amelia finished setting the silverware on napkins beside all three plates before she glanced up. "It's not his fault, you know."

"I never said anything was his fault," Sara pointed out. "I never said anything was anyone's fault."

"You're acting like it is."

"I have no idea what you're referring to," Sara said, stepping forward to move the place setting from the head of the table to a chair on the side. Winston was not here, and no one, not even his son, would sit at the head of the table. "But I will tell you what I'm acting like. I'm acting like someone who just attended the funeral of her parents this morning and does not feel like having company for dinner." The plate in her hand clattered against the table as she set it down. "Company of any kind."

Her throat had thickened and no amount of swallowing helped ease the stinging. The pain inside wasn't due to Crofton's arrival, but blaming him for it would be easy. Anything would be easier than coming to grips with the idea of never seeing Mother again, of never seeing Winston.

The gentle touch of Amelia's hand on her shoulder was more than she could take. The tears she'd been fighting to contain spilled forth. Sara spun around and hurried from the room. The air in her lungs burned as if she was suffocating, and no matter how hard she tried, she couldn't take a breath. She stumbled across the foyer, toward the door, needing air.

She opened the door, but blinded by tears, wasn't sure what stopped her, not until firm hands gripped her upper arms.

"Hey there, slow down."

The greeting and hold were so familiar that her knees wobbled and the tears came faster. Winston always said *"Hey there,"* and more than once he'd stopped her from running down the steps, telling her to slow down before she fell and broke something.

"Here, let's go back inside."

She shook her head against the tug on her arms. Air was once again entering her lungs, but her legs were too weak to move. The need to escape had left, but the pain hadn't. So full of loss, she just wanted to collapse and cry. Cry until she couldn't any more.

"Sit here then."

She didn't fight the help to move forward enough to step down onto the first step and sit on the porch floor. Wiping at the tears didn't stop them from running down her cheeks, so she just covered her face with both hands and let them flow. At that moment in time, she truly didn't care what Crofton Parks thought of that. Of her. Of anything.

He said nothing, but didn't move, either. Just sat there beside her.

Eventually the heart-wrenching pain turned into a hollow ache, and her tears eased. She lifted her head, wiping at her cheeks with both hands. After blinking several times she could make out the barn and farther up the hill, the fenced-in area that held the fresh mound of dirt. The wave of sadness that washed over her was heavy, but she was too numb to react.

"It gets easier."

"I know," she replied. "Time heals."

"In some ways," he said quietly, "it does."

Glancing sideways, just enough to see his profile, she said, "In other ways it doesn't."

He nodded.

She looked back over the yard and without the energy to do much more, simply stared up the hill. "I know that, too." Not having anything in common with Crofton would have suited her, but not having an accident, a stupid, unbelievable accident, take the lives of her mother and Winston would have suited her, too. But she hadn't had a choice, and still didn't. In other words, this is what she had. A mound of dirt and a man who wanted Lord knows what.

The sigh that left her chest was thick and rather hopeless. However, her life had been worse. She and her mother hadn't even had hope when Winston had arrived

at their place back in Kansas. Although she couldn't remember much about that time, her mother had said that
with no money and very little food, they wouldn't have
made it through the month. Winston had been their miracle.

Squeezing her eyes shut, she told herself she did not
need a miracle. Not like her mother had back then. The
last thing she needed was a husband. She'd dreamed
of getting married someday. Having children. But her
mother had told her to be careful with those dreams.
With her heart. That a wife's duty was to be completely
dedicated to her husband. To give up everything to follow
him wherever he may lead her. That's how she'd ended
up in Kansas, alone, with a small child.

Sara had thought about that long and hard, and
couldn't imagine leaving home. Leaving Royalton, her
parents, Amelia.

On that thought, she gave her face one final swipe
with both hands and then slapped her knees. She had
money, food, a home, and wouldn't be giving any of that
up. "Dinner's getting cold."

Without waiting for his help, she stood and stepped
up onto the porch. He was just as quick, and was already
holding open the door. Even that, his manners, irritated
her. His presence did, too. Winston would have been so
happy to see him, so happy to have him here, and knowing he'd prevented that happiness from ever happening
went beyond irritation.

As soon as he walked in, he asked, "Is that fried
chicken I smell?"

"Your favorite," Sara seethed between her teeth. This
would be a lot easier if Amelia didn't welcome him so
fully. Blame is what he deserved. Amelia should see that.

"That it is," he said, pretending to sniff the air. "That it is."

He wasn't pretending. The smell of fried chicken filled the house. Amelia had probably stood over the pan with a towel, waving it about in hopes the scent would have made it all the way to town, telling him the meal was ready.

In the dining room he greeted Amelia with a hug, and if he thought it odd that they'd all be eating together, he didn't comment. Amelia had eaten with the family ever since her husband Nate had died. Before then, the two of them had lived in the house between here and the mill. The one Alvin now lived in.

Sara took her seat on the one side of the table, and again, if Crofton found it odd that no one sat at the head of the table, he didn't comment. He took the chair next to Amelia, and surprisingly, offered to say grace. Sara wasn't sure why that surprised her, or why his heartfelt blessing, which wasn't a rote one, was as equally surprising. Winston had never been a churchgoing man, but he had been God-fearing, so it was believable that his son was as well. If she wanted to believe such things, that is.

They'd no sooner passed around the platter of fried chicken and bowls of potatoes, gravy, beans, and bread when a knock sounded on the door.

Amelia set down her fork, "I'll get it."

Sara stood. "No, I will." The other two had been visiting like old friends, which it appeared they were, and she'd already heard and seen enough to tell her there would be no convincing Amelia to agree with any notions of sending Crofton away. Back to where he came from, wherever that was.

With those thoughts filling her mind, Sara felt a

scowl pulling on her brows by the time she opened the front door.

"Hello, Miss Parks," Samuel Wellington said as she pushed open the screen door. "I do hope I'm not interrupting anything."

For years everyone had assumed her last name was Parks instead of Johnson, and she'd never corrected them. Now wasn't the time to start. "We have just sat down to eat," she said. "Is there something you need, Samuel?"

He nodded, but didn't apologize for the interruption. Instead, he shifted from foot to foot, much like he did when delivering things ordered from the general store his father owned.

Normally congenial to all, she wasn't in an affable mood today. Might never be again. "Well, what is it?"

"Well...uh...I—I." With a nod he spit out, "I've come to talk to you."

His face had turned almost as red as his hair and his shuffling had increased.

"About what? Did Mother or Winston order something from your father? I can come by to pay for whatever it is tomorrow."

"No, no, that's not it. Not it at all."

Growing frustrated, she asked, "Then what is?"

"Well, I...uh...well...uh...I've come to offer you my—my hand in marriage."

He'd spit the last four words out so quickly it took her a second to decipher what he'd said. Once she did, a rattling shock raced through her so fast she didn't have time to engage her brain before repeating, "Marriage?"

Samuel seemed to remember his hat at that moment and with a jolt, pulled it off his head to hold over his chest. "Yes, m-m-marriage."

She recalled what Winston had told her about marriage—that any man trekking up that hill to ask for her hand had better be the best of the best. Samuel was not that—not at any stretch of the imagination. Except of course his mother's. All Sara could think to say was, "Why?"

"Well, b-because folks are t-talking. Now that M-Mr. Parks is dead, y-you'll n-need a husband."

Winston's statement about the best of the best had not been a guarded secret, and steam replaced her shock. "Folks are talking, are they?"

Tall and gangly, Samuel's entire body seemed to nod, not just his head.

Although he was a couple years older than her, she'd always looked upon him as being much younger. Plenty of folks did. Therefore, she willed her nerves to remain calm. Drawing a deep breath helped. Gossipers had been talking since the accident, but she hadn't imagined their topics would turn to her. Not in the sense of marriage. "Thank you, Samuel, but I can't marry you. And…" She let the word stretch out while reminding herself to remain in check. People would naturally wonder what was to happen with the lumberyard and the railroad upon Winston's death. The entire community depended upon them for their livelihoods. She couldn't blame anyone for being anxious, or curious, however, her material status was not of their concern. "If you hear people talking, feel free to mention that I do not need a husband, and assure them they have no need to worry."

"But you can't—"

"I assure you I can." Although she had no idea of what he'd been about to say she was unable to do, she was perfectly capable of many things. "And most certainly have no need for a husband."

The way his shoulders slumped, she wasn't sure if he was disappointed or relieved.

"I—I'll let you get back to your supper, then," he said with barely a stutter. "B-but if you change your mind, I'd be obliged if you'd consider my offer."

She bit the end of her tongue to stifle a promise she'd not be considering his offer now or ever. The fact Winston's son sat at the dining room table did cross her mind. Briefly, for if by some cruel act of fate, Crofton did end up inheriting everything, she would not remain in Royalton. Watching him blunder Winston's dream would be as devastating as the deaths she'd just experienced. A shudder made her tense her shoulder muscles. She had not considered that aspect—of what might happen to her if Crofton got what he came after. Where would she go? What would she do?

She hadn't considered it, because it would not happen. "Goodbye, Samuel," she said, spinning around to return to the dining room with the momentum of urgency. She would need to find a way to appease the townsfolk until she got herself on solid footing with the lumber mill, and despite Bugsley's assurance that there was no need for her to speak with Winston's lawyer, Ralph Wainwright, she would set up an appointment with him. Of course Bugsley hadn't known about Crofton when he'd told Mr. Wainwright all was under control when the lawyer had come to the house to offer his condolences. None of them had known about Crofton.

Word traveled fast, and by morning she had no doubt everyone would know about Crofton. He had, after all, gone into town.

"Who was it?" Amelia asked as Sara entered the dining room.

"Just Samuel," she said, taking her seat and waiting

until Crofton sat back down before lifting her fork. His manners shouldn't surprise her—he was Winston's son. Maybe they irritated her more than surprised her. For that exact reason. That he was Winston's son.

"What did he need? Had you ordered something?" Amelia asked.

Not answering, Sara turned a cold stare to their guest. "Where did you go this afternoon?"

He finished chewing and swallowed, before stating, "I told you, to see a man about a horse."

This time around, hearing him use the line Winston often did lit a fireball in her stomach. Although she knew neither was the case, she asked, "What man? What horse?"

His stare remained steady. "The owner of the livery. I had to pay for my accommodations the past few days."

"Your accommodations?" Amelia asked. "Surely you haven't been staying at the livery stable."

He offered Amelia a smile along with a glance. "I didn't want to intrude, considering the circumstances."

"Intrude?" Sara spat. "Circumstances?" Anger rarely got the best of her, but today was far from normal. She'd just buried her parents. "Do you think you aren't intruding now? Do you think the *circumstances* have changed?"

"Sara!"

She didn't so much as blink at Amelia's admonishment. His eyes were locked on hers and she would not be the one to look away first.

"The *circumstances* changed the moment I rode into town and heard about Winston's death," he said.

Fully prepared to get to the bottom of his arrival, she asked, "Oh? Were you coming to see him?"

Leaning back in his chair, he crossed his arms and

eyed her quizzically before eventually saying, "I was sure our paths would cross once I arrived."

"Your paths would have crossed?" She repeated his answer as a question to let it roll around in her head for a moment. If he hadn't been coming to see Winston, what had he come here for?

Amelia was more straightforward. "If it wasn't to see your father, why did you come here?"

A smile tugged at Sara's lips. It was about time Amelia questioned something about him. Sara lifted a brow, as he had earlier, and waited to hear his response.

His silence lingered so long she was just about to concede he wouldn't answer when he opened his mouth.

"I came here to discover who murdered my friend."

Regardless of the anger still fueling her system, the stone-coldness of his eyes and the gravel in his voice sent a chill up Sara's spine.

"Murdered?" Amelia asked. "Here in Royalton? When? Who?"

The naturalness of how he laid a hand over the top of Amelia's made Sara's stomach churn. There was a clear connection between Amelia and Crofton. It might have lain sleeping beneath the surface for years, but had returned the moment the two had seen one another. Expecting anything less from Amelia would be impossible. She cared about people, even those she didn't know, and inside Sara's troubled mind, she knew Amelia more than cared for Crofton. She loved him. She'd spoken of him often, as if he'd been her own child. His death, or supposed death, had been as painful for Amelia as it had been for Winston.

That realization made Sara's churning stomach sink. She would have no ally in Amelia when it came to fighting this man for Winston's dream. Then again, she had no right to fight him. She had no claim to anything of Winston's. Although she'd loved him like a father, and he'd loved her like a daughter, she wasn't his rightful heir. Had no legal place to stand.

"Mel's murder didn't happen in Royalton," he said, "but this was the last place he'd been."

"Mel who?" she asked.

"Barton," he said meticulously, almost as if it hurt. "Mel Barton."

"I don't know of any Bartons in the area," Amelia said. "Do you, Sara?"

Never taking her eyes off Crofton, for his were still leveled on her, she shook her head. "No."

"He wasn't from around here," Crofton said. "He was my partner. We share—shared several thousand acres of rangeland."

Knowing the mountainous region around Royalton fairly well, Sara asked, "Where?"

"Arizona Territory," he answered.

"Arizona!" Amelia squealed. "You live in Arizona and never once came to see me? How long have you been there?"

"About two years," he answered. "I never came to see you because Winston didn't want me to."

A shiver rippled up Sara's neck at the hint of anger in his tone, but it appeared Amelia didn't notice it, or at least didn't care. How could she be so blind to this man and his actions? He clearly didn't care about her, or his father. He didn't care about anyone but himself.

"That's not true. Winston would have been overjoyed to see you," Amelia said. "Purely overjoyed."

Although no one had touched their food the last few minutes, Crofton pushed his plate toward the center of the table, as if signaling his appetite had left him. There was a twitch in the center of his cheek as he turned to look at Amelia. "Evidently not. I know you were committed to Winston, and don't want to believe certain things about him, but my father did not want to see me. Did not want to acknowledge I was alive."

Sara had her own opinion on that, but this conversation was clearly between Crofton and Amelia, so chose to remain silent. In her mind, though, she couldn't ignore the fact that Winston would never have denied seeing his son. When Hilton had died she'd seen Winston cry and mourn the child's death deeply. It had to have been that way when he'd heard of Crofton's death, too.

With an unusual show of anger, Amelia threw her napkin on the table. "That's impossible. I won't believe it for a minute. Not a single one, I tell you. Your father loved you and would have wanted to see you. Don't you dare sit here and tell me otherwise. I saw the anguish that man went through all those years ago, how it hung with him, and I know how happy he would have been to know you were alive."

Crofton had remained quiet during Amelia's fiery outburst, but had pulled a pocketbook out of the suit jacket hanging on the back of his chair, and as soon as she'd closed her mouth, he handed something to her.

Itching to know what was on the slip of paper, Sara leaned closer to the table. From the looks of the tattered edges, Crofton had been carrying it with him for some time.

"What's this?" Amelia asked.

"Open it."

She unfolded the paper and frowned as she read whatever it held. Slowly lifting her gaze to Crofton, she opened her mouth and then closed it.

"Speaks for itself, doesn't it?"

Sara balled her hand into a fist to keep it from shooting across the table to snatch the paper from Amelia. Crofton must have sensed that because he waved a hand in her direction. Following his unspoken command, Amelia handed the piece of paper across the table. Suddenly apprehensive, not overly sure she wanted to know what it said, Sara took the paper gingerly.

Western Union Telegraph Company was printed in large letters across the top along with a paragraph of rules and regulations in much smaller print. Below that, someone had written on the printed lines, noting that the message had been received at 6:48 p.m. on the twelfth of April 1879—more than six years ago—in Baltimore, and that it had been sent from Royalton.

She had to swallow at the lump forming in her throat before letting her eyes go lower. The ink on the well-tattered and thin-at-the-folds note was faded, but readable. It was to M. Hammond, and the message below that was simple.

Impossible. Crofton Parks died years ago. Do not contact me again.

W. Parks.

Handing the paper back to Crofton, she said, "I'm assuming this is a telegraph in response to one sent to Winston. Who is M. Hammond?"

"A judge in Baltimore."

"Why did a judge in Baltimore send a telegraph to Winston?"

Crofton was in the midst of reasoning how he wanted to answer that question when once again a knock sounded on the front door. He wasn't so deep in thought he missed a flash of disgust in Sara's eyes. She could have been disappointed to have their conversation disrupted, but he sensed it was more than that.

"Is that Samuel returning?" Amelia asked. "Did you order something from Wellington's?"

"No," Sara answered. "I didn't order anything from Wellington's."

Wellington's was the mercantile, but that didn't explain why her hands shook when she laid her napkin on the table.

"I'll go see who it is," she said with a ragged sigh.

Crofton waited until she rounded the corner of the dining room before pushing away from the table. He paused in the arched doorway and everything inside him hardened at the sound of a man's voice. Extending one arm, he braced himself against the narrow wall of the dining room archway and willed his muscles to relax while deliberately capturing Bugsley Morton's gaze as the man entered the house.

Chapter Five

Upon spying him, Bugsley turned a crimson shade of red, and Crofton almost cracked a smile. Instead, to prove who was in charge, he gave a single nod. "Morton."

Bugsley's nostrils flared, but he managed to hide anything else as he turned to Sara. "I wanted to see how you're doing."

"We're fine," she said.

"I see you have company," Bugsley said.

Crofton caught a chortle before it expelled. If Bugsley thought that attitude would get, or perhaps keep, him on Sara's good side, he was a buffoon. From what he'd encountered so far, a man would have better odds going up against a cross-eyed bull with a lasso than using that condescending tone with her.

"Yes, we do," she said coldly. "Have you met...Crofton?"

He didn't miss the pause before she said his name, almost as if saying it grated her nerves down to the last one.

"I've had the...pleasure," Bugsley answered.

Crofton did let out a laugh. Turning to Sara, he explained, "Mr. Morton was at the lumber mill when I stopped by there earlier, and I saw him again at the saloon."

Her frown let him know what she thought of Bugsley being at the saloon. The only woman he'd ever met that didn't mind a man stopping by a saloon was June. Thinking of her made him think of Mel, June's brother, his best friend, and that brought his full attention right back to where it should be. "I hope my toast to my father didn't interrupt your business with those railroad men and their gunman."

While Bugsley glared at him, Sara glared at Bugsley. "What railroad men?"

"They were in town for the funeral," Bugsley answered with an annoyed tone.

Crofton knew all about being annoyed, and this man increased every ounce of it in him. He also knew a liar when he saw one.

"I didn't see them at the funeral," she said.

"Perhaps they didn't want to intrude," Crofton offered, knowing that would get even more of a rise out of her.

He hadn't realized Amelia was nearby until she jabbed him in the back.

"We've just finished eating, Bugsley," Amelia said, skirting around Crofton as she walked out of the dining room. "But are about to have dessert if you'd care to join us."

"Thank you," Bugsley answered. "But I just need to speak with Sara for a moment and will then be on my way."

Like the mother hen Crofton remembered, Amelia stopped directly in front of Sara and shook her head. "Not tonight. Sara just buried her mother and father. There is nothing you need to speak to her about that can't wait until tomorrow, or the next day."

Crofton was holding his breath, waiting for Sara to spout off, but as the seconds ticked by he realized that wasn't going to happen. Surprisingly. Then again, perhaps not. Amelia's hand was only heavy when it was loaded with love. He remembered that, and the woman's words caused an inkling of guilt to tickle his stomach. Sara had loved her mother and Winston, and the day had to have been a hard one for her.

"Now, as I said," Amelia continued, "you're welcome to join us for dessert if you'd like."

That clearly was not what Bugsley would like, and Crofton never took his eyes off the man.

Bugsley was staring back, and a challenge appeared in his eyes when he said, "Thank you, dessert sounds wonderful."

"Right this way, then," Amelia said, hooking her arm through Bugsley's.

It was clear the other man would much prefer to escort Sara, but obviously had no choice. With a nod toward Morton, Crofton pushed off the wall and moved forward, making a clear point that he would assist Sara into the dining room. Anticipating she might not approve, he walked around her and closed the inside door, and then rather than take her arm, merely waved toward the dining room.

She gave him a solid glare, and then with her chin in the air, walked toward the arched doorway. He lagged a step behind. In this instance, he'd rather have her for an ally than an enemy. His gut had signaled an instant dislike of Morton from the first time he'd seen the man leading Sara down the steps of the mortuary. If you asked him, Morton could easily be behind Mel's death, but a gut feeling wasn't proof, and that was what he needed. Proof.

When Sara paused in the dining room doorway, he gently laid a hand against her back to move her forward. Understanding the reason for her hesitation, he stepped around her and grasped the back of the chair Bugsley was about to pull out. The head of the table had purposefully been left empty while they ate, and would remain so. Call it respect for his father, or empathy for Sara, either way, Crofton placed a foot against the chair leg, making sure it wouldn't be pulled out.

There was a brief showdown of eyes only before Bugsley stepped to the side of the table. Amelia hustling through the door to the kitchen with a tray may have been the reason, but Crofton preferred to take pleasure in the fact the other man had conceded because of him.

Sara had entered the kitchen and returned with a second tray. Hers contained a silver coffeepot, four cups with saucers, cream and sugar containers. Amelia was already setting out the four plates holding slices of pie. Crofton stood on one side of the table, with Bugsley straight across from him. They were still sizing up one another. The man may have been Winston's right-hand man, but something said he hadn't been as welcome in the family home as he had been in the lumber mill. Or at least he hadn't had free rein in the home. Perhaps he hadn't at the lumber mill, either. Until lately that is, which, in itself, was interesting.

Amelia pulled out a chair next to the other man, and though Crofton could tell Sara wasn't impressed, she walked around the table. He held her chair, and once she was settled, sat down next to her.

"I must say, Amelia," Crofton started while she poured coffee for all four of them. "Your fried chicken was even better than I remembered, and I'd lay bets this pie is going to be beyond that even."

Her cheeks flushed as she scooted his cup closer to him. "I've had practice. Fried chicken is Sara's favorite, too."

He lifted a brow as he glanced toward Sara. She made no comment, in fact, barely glanced his way.

"Apple pie is her favorite, too," Amelia said.

He picked up his fork. "I guess we have a lot in common."

"I'd surmise that fried chicken and apple pie are favorites for many people," Sara said. "Including Winston."

If she was trying to get his goat, it didn't work. He remembered many things about his father, including his likes and dislikes. "Did he still sprinkle a teaspoon of sugar over the top of his pie?"

He'd addressed the question toward Amelia, and the way she giggled and glanced across the table had him turning toward Sara in time to see her drop the spoon back into the sugar dish. "Go ahead," he said. "I'll take it when you're finished. It always adds the perfect touch, don't you think?"

She quickly took the spoon and sifted sugar across the top of her pie before setting the spoon back in the dish and passing it to him.

"I don't believe Sara needs such reminders this evening," Bugsley said.

"Oh, I disagree," Amelia piped in. "Wonderful memories are exactly what she needs."

Crofton didn't take the time to consider whether he agreed that's what Sara needed or not. His mind was set on disagreeing with whatever Bugsley said or did. The man needed to understand who had the upper hand. "Did Winston still like his beef red, not pink?" he asked Amelia.

"Oh, yes, the redder the better, and that was hard sometimes, timing things so precisely," Amelia answered.

"Did he alter his six o'clock meal time?" Crofton

asked, slicing off the end of the triangle-shaped piece of pie with his fork.

"No," Sara supplied. "The evening meal was always served at six."

"And lunch at noon," Crofton added before lifting his fork to his mouth. The pie was as good as he remembered, just as the chicken had been. He hadn't been exaggerating about that, nor had he forgotten Amelia's cooking. The first few years in England he'd thought he might starve. Nothing had compared to the meals she'd prepared. He gave an inflated groan, just to let her know his appreciation.

Amelia giggled and turned toward Bugsley. "Is the pie not to your liking?"

"No—yes," he said, taking a bite. "It's very good. I just haven't had much of an appetite."

Crofton bit back a grin at how Amelia frowned.

"Not eating isn't good for the body, or the mind, no matter what the circumstances," she said.

Perhaps he hadn't given Amelia enough credit all these years. He may have been only a child, but he never recalled Amelia speaking ill of anyone, nor openly reproofing them. Hearing how she'd spoken about his mother earlier today had surprised him, except for the fact his mother deserved the scorn considering her actions. However, it appeared Amelia had a bushel of contempt for Bugsley Morton, and that increased his curiosity.

While taking another bite of pie, he let his gaze wander to Sara, wondering what her feelings were towards Bugsley. They had appeared friendly toward one another at the mortuary yesterday, but considering the circumstances, she'd needed a friend. Bugsley would have put himself into that roll as easily as he had put himself into Winston's office at the lumber mill.

Counting on Amelia to put him in an even closer position, Crofton asked her, "Remember when you brought Sampson home for me?"

Her eyes lit up. "Yes, but I didn't exactly bring him home. He followed me. Poor thing was practically starved to death."

"Who was Sampson?" Sara asked.

"A dog," he answered. "The best one ever."

"And biggest," Amelia said. "He ate more than Crofton, which I didn't think was possible. And goodness but that dog had hair. Long black hair that stuck to everything."

Crofton laughed. "Good thing it was black and not white, otherwise we'd never have made it to church in time." Turning to Sara, he explained, "She used to pick the hair off my clothes the entire way to town."

"I swear that dog slept on your Sunday clothes—it was as if he thought that might keep you at home come Sunday morning." Glancing at Sara, Amelia continued, "That dog went everywhere with Crofton. He'd walk him to school every morning, and then come home and lie on the porch until it was time to go back and walk him home. But I put my foot down when it came to church. He was so big he scared the daylights out of people."

"He was big," Crofton said. In all his years and travels, he'd never seen another dog as big as Sampson had been.

"And thank goodness he was," Amelia said. "You would have drowned if not for that dog. Remember that?"

With his mouthful of pie, he could only nod.

"I should never have agreed to take you fishing. That river was much too high." Once again including Sara in the conversation, Amelia said, "His hook got caught in the weeds and rather than break the line, he jumped in the water to unhook it. You know I can't swim, and was scared to death. Crofton was only about seven. He was a good swimmer, but the current was strong because of the high water and before I knew it, he was heading downstream. Sampson ran along the bank until he was ahead of Crofton and then jumped in, swimming out for Crofton to grab a hold of him."

"I did more than grab a hold," Crofton said, having forgotten the incident until she brought it up. "I leaped onto his back."

"He must have been a large dog," Sara said.

"He was," Crofton assured.

"Winston claimed the dog was bigger than a pony," Amelia said. "He always joked about putting a saddle on him."

Crofton had forgotten that, too. "We did once," he said. "Father said not to tell you because you'd take a switch to both of us. Sampson wasn't impressed so we never did it again."

"Oh, you two," Amelia said with a giggle. "What one of you didn't think of, the other did. I said it was like having two children at times." Shaking her head, she added, "No wonder that dog wouldn't sleep in the barn."

"That and my bed was far more comfortable."

"Oh, and did your mother go into a tizzy over that. Every time she returned home, she'd have a conniption fit over that dog being in the house," Amelia said.

That was something else Crofton had forgotten about. His mother's ire at Sampson. All of a sudden, he could hear his father's voice, *Leave the boy and his dog alone, Ida.*

"Return home?" Sara said with brows knit together. "Where was your mother?"

Crofton shrugged, he didn't remember much about his mother back then, considering she was never around, but he had heard her side of things. "Baltimore, usually," he said. "Her father worked for the B & O Railroad, the Baltimore and Ohio, and was ailing. She had to make several trips to see to his care."

Though she hid it well, Crofton heard the huff that Amelia let out and saw the tightness of her lips. Bugsley, who had remained quiet the entire time, saw it, too, and Crofton was sure the man made a mental note of that.

The man pushed away from the table. "The pie was excellent, thank you."

Amelia rose to her feet at the same time Bugsley did. "You two finish your coffee," she said. "I'll see Mr. Morton to the door."

Crofton waited for Sara to protest, while considering if he should offer to walk Morton to the door. Amelia hadn't changed much over the years, and he could tell she wanted the man gone without speaking to anyone. He wondered if that included him.

When Sara offered no protest, Bugsley said, "You and I will need to discuss a few things, Sara. Perhaps I could stop by tomorrow?"

"That will be fine," she answered.

The other two left the room, and though his plate was empty and his coffee cold, Crofton didn't attempt to rise.

"More coffee?" she asked.

"No, thank you," he replied, wondering what his next steps should be. In his mind, he'd planned on being offered lodging at the house, but at the moment was feeling a bit intrusive. Perhaps it would be better if he got a room at the hotel. However, considering he wanted the entire town to view him as Winston's son, staying here was an important factor.

The subtle silence that hovered over the table was broken when Sara asked, "What happened to Sampson?"

Crofton had wondered about that for years. He'd felt

utterly abandoned that day all those years ago. Hadn't understood why his father had taken Sampson. With a shrug, he said, "He came West with my father and Amelia and Nate."

"No, he didn't." Having wasted no time in seeing Bugsley to the door, Amelia was already walking back into the dining room. "We left him with you—your father insisted upon it."

Memories flowed stronger than they had in years, and he clearly remembered coming home from school that day to find Sampson gone. He also recalled that his father had driven him to school in the buggy that morning, telling him all about Colorado during the ride. How they were going there to start another lumber mill, larger than the one in Ohio, and that as soon as the house was built, he'd be back to get him and his mother. Sampson had trotted along beside the horse. The memory of the last time he'd seen his father and Sampson was as clear right now as it had been back then. He'd stood in the school yard, watching his father drive away with Sampson running alongside the buggy. From then on, he had few memories. Sadness had clouded his young mind, along with train rides and hotels, and eventually the long ship ride to England. After arriving there, he'd chosen to forget more than he chose to remember. He lifted a shoulder. "I guess he must have died. I don't remember."

"You don't remember?" Sara asked.

He shook his head.

"Did he die in the fire?" she asked.

Having learned his mother had informed Winston he'd died when their Ohio house caught fire, he shook his head. "There was no fire. At least not while we lived there. I did stop by the old place on my way West. The barn was the same, but the house wasn't."

"Yes, there was a fire," Amelia said. "It burned the house to the ground. Winston traveled back there and spoke to people about the fire. He also saw your grave, had a big headstone made for it."

Having seen it himself, he told Amelia, "The headstone is in Baltimore."

"Because that is where Ida claimed you were buried. She said you'd been burned in the house fire and she sent you to Baltimore for medical help, and that's where you died. She buried you next to her father. Your grandfather." Amelia sat back down at the table. "Where were you during that time?"

Crofton only had fragments of memories during that time, and his mother hadn't enlightened him even when he'd asked. "I honestly don't know." Having strolled down memory lane—a place he rarely liked to visit—long enough, Crofton stood. "I thank you ladies for a wonderful," nodding toward Amelia, he added, "and delicious, evening."

Frowning, Amelia asked, "Where are you going?"

No longer wanting an invitation, he said, "I must acquire accommodations for the night at the hotel."

"You will not," Amelia stated. "You'll be staying here. We have plenty of room, don't we, Sara?"

She'd risen and was gathering dishes from the table. "Mr. Parks may find the accommodations at the hotel more hospitable."

"He will not," Amelia said. "There are three extra bedrooms upstairs, and he will use one of them. No arguments." Piling dishes on the second tray, she added, "From either of you."

Sara felt Amelia's glare and Crofton's curious stare on her back, and ignored them both as she carried the tray into the kitchen. She also heard Amelia continue insisting

Crofton stay at the house. At the moment, her mind was too full of other things to care where he slept. He was part of what was dancing about inside her head—especially why his mother would have told Winston he'd died when he hadn't. The other part of her was wondering about Bugsley. He'd seemed nervous tonight, and subdued. Of course the conversation and Amelia's attitude could have been part of it. Amelia hadn't liked Bugsley since he'd taken Nate's place as Winston's right-hand man.

Bugsley had worked for Winston before Nate had died during the rail road wars, but had become more essential afterward. Therefore, Sara could understand a small portion of Amelia's dislike, but she'd never made it quite as obvious before.

Scraping clean the plates, her mind shifted once more—to that of Sampson. She'd often thought having a dog would be fun, but had never asked for one. Mother would never have approved. Life should focus on what was needed not wanted.

It was still that way.

"Well, that's settled," Amelia said, setting down the other tray. "Crofton will stay in the room at the end of the hall."

Sara crossed the room to the stove to dip hot water from the reservoir into the washing bowl. Arguing wouldn't solve anything; furthermore, he had more right to be in Winston's house than she did, a fact that truly didn't settle well.

"Now who could that be?"

Lost in thought, Sara hadn't heard a knock until it sounded again. "Here," she said, handing over the wash-bowl, "I'll go see."

"If it's Mr. Morton, tell him you're tired, and—"

"I'll tell him," Sara interrupted. Or talk to him.

That might help clear her mind a bit. It was so full of Crofton Parks that thinking straight was becoming difficult. Rather than wondering what had happened to a long-haired dog and why someone would lie about the death of their child, she needed to be thinking about the amount of wood promised to the railroad, and by when, and assure it was delivered. If she'd paid more attention she might know how much it took to build trestles and bridges and tunnels. Different types of wood were needed for each, and also for the ties. That much she remembered from one of Winston's conversations, but unfortunately, he didn't believe in talking about work at home.

Her mind was well and focused on such details when she arrived at the front door, and the knocking on the other side caused a hint of irritation. When she'd asked Bugsley about those details, he'd said not to worry about it. That he'd handle everything.

Expecting Bugsley, seeing Elliott Cross on the porch confused her. He'd already interviewed her for the article he'd published in his paper about the accident.

"Good evening, Sara," he said while removing the glasses from his face with ink-stained fingers.

"Mr. Cross," she greeted, before asking, "Is there something you need?"

He tucked the glasses in his shirt pocket. "Why, yes there is, Sara."

Baffled, she opened the screen door. "What would that be?"

He waved a hand toward the chairs on the porch. "Perhaps we could sit out here. It's a particularly lovely evening for December. Usually we have snow by now."

She wasn't interested in how lovely the evening was for December, or the lack of snow, but a thud overhead from the second floor had her crossing the threshold. The news of Crofton staying here would spread fast enough without Elliott Cross's help. "What is it you need?" she asked once they were both seated.

Squinting, as if he couldn't quite see her without his glasses, he leaned a bit closer. "It has come to my attention that you are now open to seeking a suitable partner, and—"

"Partner?" She shook her head. "The lumber mill does not need a partner."

"I do not mean the lumber mill, my dear Sara. I'm speaking about you. Now that Winston has passed on, God rest his soul, you—"

"No," she growled through clenched teeth. "Mr. Cross, I am not interested in a *partner* of any kind."

"Well, now, hear me out, dear—"

"No," she said, jumping to her feet. "I will not hear you out." The look of shock on his face had her taking a deep breath. From the time they'd moved in with Winston, her mother had been extremely clear on how they had to behave. Actually, she'd insisted on being polite to everyone even before then, and those manners had been instilled deep. "I do not wish to be rude, but in this instance, I may appear so in order to make it clear that I am not interested in marriage to anyone. Not today, not tomorrow, not next week or next month, or even next year. Now, if you will kindly take your leave."

He snatched his glasses from his pocket and hooked them over both ears before standing. "How will you manage?"

"I will manage just fine."

"Not with Winston's son in town," he said.

Her intention had been to leave him standing on the porch, but his statement froze her feet to the porch boards.

Pulling a little notepad out of his pocket, the exact

kind he'd used to take notes for the article about the accident, Elliott said, "He was at the mill and the saloon, and the barber shop and livery. As a matter of fact, he's been in town for a few days."

"I'm well aware of that," she said.

"If he truly is Winston's son, as many already believe due to his uncanny resemblance, then you must realize anything bestowed upon you because of Winston's death will be taken away, unless of course, you have the wherewithal to go against this man in court. By wherewithal, I mean the financial backing and support of a husband. You must understand, Sara, whether the people of this town thought of you as Winston's daughter or not, the fact is that you weren't and this will be held against you in a court of law. You, my dear, are Sara Johnson, not Sara Parks."

"I am well aware of that as well."

"Then you must also realize that married to a man of the community, a well-standing citizen who could vouch for the years you lived with Winston, your chances of inheriting at least a portion of Winston's holdings will be greatly increased."

Her head was spinning and her stomach was turning the pie she'd eaten into applesauce.

"The timing of this man's arrival was quite perfect, don't you agree, Sara? Winston's long-lost son, believed to be dead for years, arrives in town the day after Winston dies in a tragic accident? It sounds rather fictional, don't you agree?"

She didn't want to agree with anything he'd said, and had to squeeze her hands together to stop them shaking. They'd done that earlier today, when she'd walked into Winston's office and found Crofton sitting there.

"I see you have a lot to think on, Sara, including my

proposal. A union between the two of us would be very beneficial, because you see, I would not only be able to obtain the legal assistance you will need, I will be able to unearth the truth behind Crofton Parks and Winston's untimely accident—or timely, depending on who's perspective one sees it through."

The hair on her arms was slowly standing up, making her skin shiver as if a goose had just walked over her grave. Fighting to remain calm, she lifted her chin. Defying Elliott, as badly as she'd like to, could have consequences she didn't need right now. Though he proclaimed to only report the truth, plenty of people disagreed. Unfortunately, they never seemed to fare well. With a nod, and a deep breath, she said, "Good night, Mr. Cross."

She didn't wait for his response, or to see him down the steps, but once she'd shut the front door, she moved to the side window to watch and make sure he left. Which he did, strolled along the walkway and then down the road to town as if he hadn't a care in the world.

Maybe he hadn't.

They were all on her shoulders.

Chapter Six

By noon the next day, Sara had received over a dozen marriage proposals. Some from men she'd never met, and hoped never to see again. The responsibility of telling them she wasn't interested in marriage had been lifted from her shoulders. Amelia had seen to that. Sara questioned whether she should be upset, or at least uncomfortable, but she wasn't. Grateful was more what she felt, and that didn't settle well, either. Being grateful to Crofton for anything was not what she wanted.

She didn't want to be married, either. Elliott Cross had barely disappeared down the road when others had started walking up it. Amelia had handled the first knock after Elliott's, which had flustered her to the point she'd called Crofton downstairs to make the suitor leave. He'd done so, and had done the same to several others after that, including the ones who'd started knocking upon the door shortly after the sun rose this morning.

Crofton was polite enough not to mention them at breakfast, but she had a feeling lunch would be different. He'd positioned himself on the front porch all morning, stopping would-be suitors before they had a chance to knock. Not wanting to know who they were or how many had made the trip to the house, Sara had closed herself in Winston's office to focus on the contracts. That hadn't happened. There was no opportunity to focus on anything with Amelia opening the door every few minutes to tell her Crofton had just shooed away another one. Elliott Cross's words still echoed in her mind, too. Crofton's arrival was suspicious, very suspicious.

Closing the leather-bound ledger that Winston had used to record each load of lumber sold to the railroad, Sara leaned back to look out the window. Puffs of steam rising into the air proved the mill was processing lumber just like it had last week, and the week before, and the week before that. Nothing had slowed, not even the day of the accident, or yesterday during the funeral. It was as if Winston was still here, but he wasn't.

She closed her eyes and leaned her head back. If only he was still here, then none of this would be her problem. There would be no men knocking on the door, no Crofton sitting on the porch, no—

"Amelia asked me to remind you lunch is almost ready."

Sara opened her eyes and stood. "I know. I was on my way."

"Really?" Crofton said. "You looked like you were taking a nap."

"I was not napping." Pushing the chair up to the desk, she said, "I was resting my eyes."

"Winston's handwriting was that bad?"

"No." She sighed. "I was grasping all I'd read." It was a lie. The entries had been a blur, and her mind too full of other things to soak up what it should be absorbing. How was she going to assure his dream was kept alive if she couldn't decipher what it would take to achieve it?

"I'll help you go through it, if you'd like."

That was the last thing she'd like. "Bugsley has already offered to help," she said, exiting the office.

Walking beside her, Crofton asked, "Do you trust him?"

"Bugsley?"

"Yes."

"Of course. He was Winston's right-hand man."

Crofton said no more as they walked into the dining room, but she read his silence as clearly as if he'd spoken. He didn't like Bugsley any more than Amelia did, which considering how they felt about each other was easy to understand. If she was in an understanding mood, which she wasn't.

They sat at the table much like they had the night before. With Crofton and Amelia on one side, her on the other. Once again, with a grin that could charm the hair off snakes, he complimented Amelia on her cooking, claiming it was far better than he remembered.

"I told you I've had practice," Amelia said. "You'd never know by the looks of her, but there were days that Sara could have eaten you under the table."

Snakes of course didn't have hair, and his charm didn't affect her, but the way he turned that grin in her direction, Sara felt a blush heating her cheeks.

He lifted a brow, which she tried hard to ignore. If possible, he looked even more like Winston when he did that, and that had her mind going back to Elliott, and the rest of Royalton. Winston had made it no secret that he'd had a son who had died back in Ohio. Besides what Elliott had pointed out, Crofton's appearance could make some believe Winston had lied about his past. Elliott could even have created that story himself. Although he claimed otherwise, she was sure he'd made up a story or two in order to sell more papers.

"So…" she said slowly, trying to gather coherent thoughts, "when did you hear about Winston's death? Were you already in town?"

He set his fork down and wiped his lips with his napkin before speaking. "The livery owner told me as soon as I arrived in town," he said. "It was late, but he was still up, and several others were gathered at his place, talking. The accident had happened that day."

She understood what they were talking about. The entire town had worried what would happen to the mill. Bugsley had put them at ease by announcing Winston would want things to continue just as they would if he'd been alive, which he would have. People had seemed to be satisfied with that, but they'd had to wonder how long things could go on as they always had. She certainly did.

"Come now," Amelia said, "we don't need sad thoughts surrounding our meal." Turning to Crofton, she pointed out, "Your father never liked to talk business at the meal table, just like back in Ohio. Said meals were to be enjoyed."

Crofton nodded and continued to eat, but Sara doubted he felt like eating any more than she did.

They'd no sooner taken their last mouthfuls, when a knock sounded on the door.

"I'm starting to hate that sound," Amelia said.

Crofton was already standing, and Sara made no attempt to dissuade him. She didn't want to face another suitor now any more than she had earlier.

When he returned a few moments later, with Bugsley, Sara found herself wishing he'd sent the man away as quickly as he had the others. That made her angry at herself. She'd never been cowardly, and now wasn't the time to start. Finding resolve in that, she pushed away from the table.

"We can talk in the office," she said.

Amelia's tsk echoed in the room before she said, "We've just finished lunch, Mr. Morton, but there is plenty and it's still warm if you are hungry."

"No, thank you, though I appreciate the offer, Mrs. Long," he answered. "I won't keep Sara long."

"See that you don't. She's already had an exhausting day."

As Bugsley lifted both brows, Sara wanted to tsk herself. "No, I have not," she said to Bugsley. "However, I do have several questions for you."

Crofton watched the eye exchange between Amelia and Morton as closely as he had last night. He'd learned a lot from the would-be suitors showing up at the door, and had to wonder who was to blame for the rumors circulating Royalton. His money was on Morton.

There was more to it, though. Amelia didn't like Morton, and in order for that to have happened, there had to be a good reason.

"Go," Amelia hissed in his ear as soon as the other two left the room. "Follow them."

Even though he would like to know what Morton and Sara would discuss, he wouldn't stoop to eavesdropping. "There's no reason for me to follow them."

"Yes, there is," she said. "I don't trust him."

"I've sensed that." Crofton started gathering dishes off the table.

"I'll do that," Amelia said. "You should be in that office with those two."

"No," he said, continuing to clear the table. "I should be right here helping you. I'll have you know, I know my way around a kitchen. I've been doing my own cooking and cleaning, and laundry, for a long time now."

She took the plates from his hands. "Why'd she finally tell you? Your mother, why did she tell you Winston wasn't dead?"

He gathered more dishes. "She didn't. I overheard them in the study."

"Who?"

"Her and Thomas, her husband." He'd never thought of Thomas Bennett as his stepfather, certainly not in the way Sara had Winston, but on that day, he'd been grateful for what the man had done. "I overheard Thomas telling Mother that I had the right to know, therefore I stepped into the room and asked what he was referring to."

"Did she tell you why? Why she did it?"

"No." He led the way to the kitchen. In truth his mother hadn't been the one to say Winston hadn't died all those years before, Thomas had, and when Crofton had asked her if that was true, she'd refused to answer. "She just said she'd done it for me." His mother had shouted that out the door as he was leaving. That she'd done it for him, to save his life. Save him from dying in the wilderness his father had wanted to drag him into.

Dishes clanged as Amelia set them down on the cupboard. "It was not for you. It was for her. Everything that woman ever did was for herself. I suppose she got remarried as soon as you got to England."

"No." Crofton returned to the dining room for the rest of the lunch dishes. "I can't say exactly when she married Thomas. I was at school."

"School? She sent you off to boarding school?"

Amelia sounded about as appalled as he'd been when his mother first dropped him off at the Cheshire School for Boys, and in the years that followed. There had barely been a night when he hadn't lain awake wishing his father was still alive and would come rescue him. He'd grown to hate America at that time, believing his father had died while traveling West, as his mother had told him. Later, it had become that same hatred that had put the yearn inside him to return to America, to fulfill his father's dream of holding a bit of that untamed wilderness in the palm of his hand. Oddly enough, somewhere along the road, he'd forgotten that little tidbit.

"Yes, I was at boarding schools. Several of them," he answered. "It was less than a week after graduation that I learned that Winston hadn't died."

"What did you do?"

Carrying the last few dishes into the kitchen, he answered, "I left. Came to America." His answer sounded much simpler than it had been. He hadn't had a pound to his name. Thomas had offered him money, but he'd refused. Stubborn and full of hate, he hadn't wanted anything from anyone. Not for a long time. Still didn't.

A bit of the animosity his memories were sprouting had him stating, "It appears Winston wasted no time in getting remarried." All the while he'd been lying in a cold cot surrounded by identical cots holding other boys who did have fathers who came to get them regularly, Sara had been receiving all the love and attention he'd been wishing for.

"No, he didn't," Amelia said. "It took us a long time to get here. Trains didn't go as far then as they do now. It was a long and grueling trip, which was why your father didn't bring you with us. He would have though, if your mother would have allowed it. They'd argued about it. She'd refused to come West, or to let you, until there was a decent home for you to live in. That took time. We barely managed to get a cabin roughed in before the snow came. Besides a few that had come with us, your father had hired men along the way, and they worked all winter building the lumber mill. By spring it was running and he started building this house, just as he'd promised your mother. That's when her letter arrived—stating the details of your death. Winston left right away for Ohio, on horseback. Nate and I stayed here, and your father returned that fall. I thought he'd lost his will to live. He was a broken man that winter. Real broken."

Crofton hardened his insides against the pain that wanted to fill his chest.

"He didn't stop, though," Amelia went on. "Hardly slowed down, he just didn't have the gusto he'd had before. Understandably. It had to have been two summers later, or more, it's been so long now, I can't remember, that he headed East again for meetings with the railroad. He was on his way back here when the train he was on was robbed and he was shot. That was in Kansas. The folks that came out to rescue the passengers didn't think Winston would make the long trek back to town, so they dropped him off at the nearest farm. That was Sara's place, well her mother's, Suzanne. Suzanne's husband had died the year before—dragged to death by a wild horse he was attempting to break. Your father claimed Suzanne had saved his life. Once he was up and about, he loaded both Suzanne and Sara up and hauled them home with him."

A serene smile had settled upon Amelia's face. "She was a good woman. Suzanne, that is, you'd have liked her, and she'd have liked you. She loved your father like no tomorrow, and he loved her back. They were just what the other needed. She was soft-spoken and gentle and kind, but most of all, she believed in him. With that kind of love and support, he couldn't fail. And he didn't."

Crofton had buried his teeth in his bottom lip to keep from interrupting. He didn't need to know what kind of woman his father had married. Didn't want to know if they'd been happy, or in love or anything else.

With her hands in the dishwater, Amelia barely paused with the washing as she continued, "And of course he adored Sara from the moment he saw her. We all did." She laughed. "She wasn't like you. She barely made a peep, never asked for anything, but boy did that little girl aim to please. She'd haul in chunks of firewood so large her little arms would be trembling from the weight. But that never stopped her from going and fetching another one, without being asked, mind you."

He did mind. Given the opportunity, he would have hauled in firewood, too, without being asked, and anything else he could have done just to have had one more day with his father.

"Which is why you should be in that room with her right now," Amelia said. "All Sara knows is how to please people. She's not as strong as she thinks she is, and Bugsley Morton knows that."

Bringing his focus back to things that matter, Crofton asked, "Why do you dislike him so much?"

Amelia sighed and her hands stilled in the soapy water. Turning slowly, in order to look at him, bitterness filled her eyes when she said, "Because he got Nate killed." Disgust wrinkled her face as she continued. "You gotta fight guns with guns, that's what Bugsley told Winston when that silly railroad war was happening, and sure enough, Nate was the one to pay for it. With his life." Sniffling, she shook her head. "He'll convince Sara of something just as stupid, and you've gotta stop that. Winston wouldn't want that girl getting hurt. He'd expect you to stop that from happening. You know that as much as I do."

Although a part of him could sympathize with Amelia, Crofton shook his head. "I'm not here to fulfill what Winston would have wanted." Knowing she'd argue that until time stopped, he turned and started for the door. "I'll be back in time for supper."

"Where are you going? You can't leave with…"

He walked out of the kitchen and through the dining room, trying to tell his ears not to listen. He wasn't here to save Sara from Bugsley Morton or any of the other men who came knocking upon the door. Why he'd taken up that role this morning was beyond him. He should have told the first one to go fetch the reverend, then maybe his thoughts could focus on Mel. If Bugsley had been the one to convince his father to draw guns during the railroad wars, he could have also convinced him to pull the southern line, and to stop Mel from protesting it.

The one thing he'd never forgotten about his father was his passion. When Winston had wanted something, he'd become obsessed with it, and hadn't let anything stand in his way. Crofton had that passion, too. He'd put it into ranching, and wasn't about to let anyone stop him, either.

That thought was enough to change his direction. Instead of heading toward the front door, he walked past the sweeping staircase to the closed office door. Upon arrival, he knocked once before grasping the knob. Swinging the door open, he offered no apologies before stating, "Sara and I have an appointment."

She didn't respond, but Bugsley asked, "Where? With who?"

Although Crofton had claimed as much yesterday, he didn't have a lawyer who would be arriving next week, didn't even know one he could contact, but it was time he did.

"It's a family matter," he said.

"I'm handling—"

"You aren't handling this," Crofton interrupted before Bugsley could say more. Turning to Sara, he asked, "Do you need to change? There's enough time while I hitch up the buggy."

The glare in her eyes said far more than her lips ever could have, and the way she rose from the chair behind the desk, with her chin out and her back square, made him wonder if Amelia knew Sara as deeply as she thought she did.

"We can finish our conversation later, Bugsley," she said, never turning her gaze onto the other man. "As Crofton said, he and I have an appointment."

"Now, Sara, I just finished telling you—"

Snapping her gaze toward the other man, she said, "I heard what you told me. And I said we'll finish this conversation later."

Bugsley's ears turned red enough to spark flames as he grabbed his hat off the desk. "I'll return this evening."

"Tomorrow would be better," Crofton said.

With steam practically hissing from his head, Bugsley turned to Sara, who simply nodded. Crofton wasn't exactly sure why that delighted him, but it did. They weren't on the same side, him and her, probably never would be, but Morton didn't need to know that.

Sara waited until Bugsley had left the room before saying, "Close the door please." Her temper hadn't exploded as it had wanted to, at least not in front of Bugsley. However, she wasn't certain how much longer she could keep it under control.

Crofton closed the door, and the smug look on his face as he crossed the room was almost her undoing. Remembering her manners, and all sorts of other things her mother had taught her, such as that a woman should never lose her temper, she closed her eyes for a moment of fortitude.

Once her shoulders relaxed a touch, she said, "I understand that being Winston's son gives you certain rights, however, interrupting a meeting is not one of them. Furthermore, it's rude."

He merely lifted a brow while glancing her way as he walked toward the window.

Mother had never met Crofton Parks, and as a result of that, her lessons weren't sticking as well as they had in the past. This morning, while getting dressed, she'd considered wearing the black dress again, but had chosen a subtle gray one instead. Yes, she was in mourning, and would be for some time, perhaps forever, but questioning whether others would see that as weak and needing assistance—or a husband—had made her put on something other than black. She wasn't weak, and Crofton needed to know that as much as everyone else. "It's also rude to set up appointments for me without my knowledge, and to suggest that I may not be properly dressed for said appointments."

The chuckle he let out grated on her final nerve.

"It's not funny, Mr. Parks, nor will I allow such bad manners. Guest or not."

Turning from the window, he rested against the sill and crossed his legs at the ankles. "As you just pointed out, being Winston's son provides me with certain rights, one of those being that I'm not a guest, but family."

"You are not family."

"I'm more closely related to Winston than you'll ever be."

She swallowed against the burning sensation in her throat. He was making her madder than she could recall ever being. "That may be true, but you didn't have the decency to attempt to see your father in years. I, on the other hand, lived with him for fifteen years."

He tapped a finger against his chin. "That may be true, but, blood is thicker than water."

"Oh, for heaven's sake," she muttered. After listening to Bugsley insist they find a way to claim Crofton was an impostor, she didn't need him standing there repeating quotes Winston used on a regular basis to convince her he was indeed Winston's son. What she needed was one person focused on the mill. The railroad contracts. That's what the people of Royalton needed. She'd told Bugsley that, but he'd said that wasn't her concern. That the mill and railroad weren't her concerns. "What appointment did you set up?" she asked.

"Giving up so easily?" he said. "I was just starting to have fun."

"Fun? Is that what this is to you?" Flustered, she slapped a hand on the desk. "Nothing about any of this is fun. My parents are dead. Bugsley doesn't care about that, or the town, which will shrivel up to nothing without the mill, which you know nothing about, nor do you seem to care about it. If you want fun, you've certainly come to the wrong place."

"I don't know about that," he said, pushing off the windowsill. "I had fun this morning sending those men away, once it was two at a time."

She held her breath to keep from spouting off about that.

"And I know far more about the lumber mill than you give me credit for." He flipped open the ledger sitting atop the desk. "See these numbers right here? That's where Winston was figuring his cost per tree harvested in relationship to the price charged to the railroad, including variants due to the thickness of the different types of lumber needed. When a tree is cut down, the amount of lumber it will provide is estimated through surface and lineal calculations. Meaning its diameter and height. These are rather simple, both surface and lineal feet are calculated without regard to width. Some believe the taller the tree the longer the boards and therefore the more lumber it will provide. That's not always the case. Long narrow boards do not have the strength needed for the major construction the railroad is doing. Bridges and trestles take thick, solid boards, and railroad ties are very specific in length, width and density. For them, surface and lineal measurements won't provide the estimates needed. Therefore," he flipped the page to the next one. "Winston was using board measurement calculations to make those estimates. Thickness, times width, times length."

For the first time since she'd opened the ledgers something made sense. "No wonder there are so many pages of calculations."

Crofton leaned against the desk and crossed his arms. "For each tree cut down, Winston had to calculate the cost of harvesting that tree, of sawing it into lumber, of transporting it, and his margin of profit."

She hadn't been so naive as to believe the railroad had simply said they needed a certain number of trees, but she hadn't thought it was quite so complicated, either.

"Of course, he also had to be able to estimate how long it would take him to harvest the trees, have them produced into lumber and hauled to the corresponding location at the precise time the railroad would need it," Crofton said. "The railroad doesn't want their men standing around waiting on lumber, nor is there a way to stockpile it. They are building on the move. They want what they need, when they need it. One miscalculation can break even the best deal."

A lump formed in her throat, and she was almost afraid to look at Crofton, and to ask, "Is that why you are here? To break the deal he had with the railroad?"

Rather than answering right away, he walked back to the window and looked out of it for a stilled moment. She had no idea what she'd do if he said yes, or, in truth, what she'd do if he said no. Although the explanation he'd provided about the calculations had given her an insight she hadn't had, it also made the task at hand more complex.

"Is that what Morton told you?" he asked. "That I was here to break Winston's deal with the railroad?"

If she wanted the truth from him, she had to provide the same. "No, he told me you were an impostor."

"What did you say to that?"

"That you aren't an impostor." She let the air out of her lungs slowly, for it still seemed hard to admit, to understand. "That you truly are Winston's son."

He turned around and folded his arms across his chest, and once again she was reminded of just how much he was like Winston.

"It appears, Sara, for the first time, we have agreed on something."

She wasn't certain that had ever been a disagreement. From the moment she'd seen him, she'd known the truth. She just hadn't wanted to admit it, because she didn't know what to do about it. Still didn't.

Considering there weren't a lot of options, she leaned back in her chair. "Bugsley says you have a lawyer coming to town to prove you are Winston's son. When will he arrive?"

"I have no idea," Crofton said.

"You have no idea?"

He shrugged. "I don't have a lawyer."

Totally confused, she shook her head. "What?"

"I just told Morton that." He turned back toward the window. "I came here to discover who killed my friend, not to prove my parentage."

Compelled by something she couldn't quite name, she stood and walked to the window. Gazing out at the mill and the puffs of white steam rising high into a sky that appeared bluer because of the white peaks on the mountain ridge on the other side of the valley, she stood silent, unsure what to say. A moment hadn't gone by since the accident that she hadn't wished Winston and her mother hadn't died, and right now wished it more than ever. Not just for herself, but for Crofton. She didn't have to like him in order to know it was unfair that he and Winston had been separated for so many years. No matter who was at fault, it wasn't right. Just wasn't right.

"Winston built quite an empire, didn't he?"

"Yes," she answered. "Was the mill in Ohio this large?"

"No."

"The mountains around here are full of mines," she explained, "not big ones, but large enough they needed a way to get their ore to the smelters. The mill provided most of the lumber for the railroad from Denver to here, and now it's providing the lumber to build it West. The tracks will reach the coast someday."

"Yes, they will," he answered. "Winston created his own gold mine. It's just called a lumber mill. He told me about it before he left to come West, how he was going to build a sawmill in the middle of nowhere and how people would flock to it. Lumber, he said, is what is going to build America. Businesses and homes and railroads. He was right."

Over the years, she'd stood here many times, and instinctively knew when someone was looking up the hill—from the window of Winston's office. She had that feeling now, and knew who was looking out that office window. Bugsley wasn't going to stop at anything when it came to Crofton and she felt caught in the middle, unsure which route to take. Winston would want her to support Crofton, but if she did, Bugsley may not help her with the mill. The men wouldn't respond to a woman boss. He'd told her that moments ago, too. Stepping away from the window, she asked, "What was the appointment you said we had?"

Crofton walked away from the window and took a seat in a chair near the front of the desk. "I'm assuming Winston had a lawyer here in town."

Even though it wasn't a question, she answered, "Yes, Ralph Wainwright."

"I think we should go see him."

She'd already figured on setting up an appointment, yet asked, "Why?"

"I'm sure Winston had a will."

"Yes, he did." Her knees trembled and she sat down in the chair behind the desk.

"I would like to see what it says."

She could understand that, and had no intention of trying to stop him, but couldn't help but wonder what all this meant for her. Elliott Cross's visit was once again weaving its way into her thoughts. He'd been right, she had no recourse when it came to admitting she wasn't Winston's daughter, but he'd been wrong, too. She didn't need assistance in fighting the will. There was nothing to fight about. "I can tell you where Mr. Wainwright's office is."

Crofton stood. "I'd prefer you visit him with me."

Glancing toward the window, he added, "As soon as possible."

Sara pulled open the desk drawer and lifted out the envelope she hadn't opened. "You may need this during our visit."

Chapter Seven

Winston had been adamant about maintaining the road, and because of the steep grade he'd built a switchback halfway up the hill. Crofton guided the horse around the curves with the ease of someone who'd done so many times. "Are there mountains where you live?" Sara asked, more in order to break the silence that had hovered between them since leaving the office than out of curiosity.

"No," he answered. "Not really. There's some high ground, but it's nothing like this. Why?"

"No reason." She pointed toward a road that intersected with the main one. "You'll turn left, and then another left on the next road. Mr. Wainwright's home is at the end of that road."

"He doesn't have an office in the business district?"

"No, I don't believe he ever has."

If Crofton thought that odd, he made no comment as he followed the directions she'd given. People stepped out of doorways to watch the buggy roll along the route and an odd sense overcame Sara. She'd always sat straight and tall while riding through town, but with Crofton sitting beside her, she didn't need to remind herself to do so. It was as if she felt pride in sitting next to him.

He drove them directly to the Wainwright home. Ralph had five children, therefore the house was large. The oldest, Ben, was ten, and his four sisters were six, five, four and two. Sara saw them regularly at church, and thought they were all adorable with their curly blond hair. They'd all been at the funeral yesterday, following along behind their father like baby ducks.

She waited until Crofton had climbed down and walked around to help her, but as soon as his hands touched her, she wished she'd already climbed down. The skin at her sides, where his hands grasped her, as well as her palms as she touched his shoulders, tingled as if she was too close to a fire. He released her as soon as her feet touched the ground and she had to tighten her muscles against an odd fluttering that rippled through her insides. Instincts, she suspected. A warning of some sort.

"Would you rather wait in the buggy?" he asked quietly.

"No." Putting one foot in front of the other, she focused on walking past him and up the walkway to the house.

Tall and thin with hair as blond and curly as his children's, Mr. Wainwright opened the door before she stepped onto the porch. "Good day, Sara." He held out a hand to Crofton. "Mr. Parks."

The lawyer's greeting didn't surprise her. One look and people could figure out who Crofton was, even without how word of his arrival had spread.

"I'm sorry to arrive unannounced," Crofton said. "But we would like a moment of your time."

"Of course. I'm glad to see you, both of you. Do come in." Ralph Wainwright waved a hand for them to enter before stating, "Mrs. Hughes was ailing this morning, but it will only take me a moment to put Ben in charge of the girls." With another wave of his hand, he added, "You can wait in my office, if you don't mind."

"We don't mind waiting," Sara said, "but if this is a bad time…" She wasn't sure when might be a good time. For any of them.

"No, this is fine." Ralph gestured toward a double set of open doors. "I won't be but a minute. Make yourselves comfortable."

Crofton followed as she walked into the office. Sara took a moment to admire how the collection of books sitting upon the shelves were dust-free before she removed her black cloak and sat in one of the leather chairs near a window that was framed with a white lace curtain. "Mr. Wainwright's wife died shortly after their youngest daughter was born. Deloris Hughes lives just up the road. We passed her place. It has a white picket fence around a flower garden. She takes care of the children when he needs help. I do hope she isn't seriously ill." She was babbling, but couldn't help it. A pit had formed in her stomach.

Crofton took her cloak and hung it on the coat rack before he sat in the chair beside her. "Was she at the funeral yesterday?"

"I believe so, but I can't say for sure. There were so many people I truly don't remember who I spoke with and who I didn't."

He nodded. "That's understandable."

"My apologies for keeping you waiting," Ralph Wainwright said as he entered the room. "And thank you for coming to see me. I'd told Mr. Morton I would need to see you as soon as possible, but didn't want to intrude upon you during this time."

The welling in her throat kept her from responding with more than a nod.

"I'm assuming my father had a will, Mr. Wainwright," Crofton said. "And I'm also assuming his holdings will now revert to Miss—Sara."

She wondered if he didn't say Miss Parks because he didn't want her to be called that, or because he didn't know her true last name. Few people did.

Busy with the dial on a safe in the far corner behind his desk, Ralph didn't answer right away. Once he had a large envelope in his hand, he left the safe door open and walked across the room. "Yes, Winston had a will. I have it right here, but first, I must have some sort of proof that you are indeed his son. It was my understanding that you had died as a young child. Perished in a fire if my memory is correct."

"That is correct, the story that is," Crofton said. "The one my mother told my father. In truth, I didn't die. She took me to England, where I resided until I was eighteen and learned that my father hadn't died. Around the same time my mother fabricated my death, she told me Winston had died while traveling to Colorado."

Sara was amazed he could recite the tale without any emotion reflecting upon his face. It may have all been a long time ago, but he had to hold hurt or anger, or at least frustration. She certainly would if someone had treated her so heinously.

Ralph sat in the chair opposite Crofton. "Why didn't you try contacting your father once you learned the truth?"

"That's a long story, Mr. Wainwright," Crofton answered.

Setting the large envelope on the short table between his chair and Crofton's, Ralph nodded. "I can believe it is, Mr. Parks, but, as your father's legal counsel, it is also one I need to hear."

Sara wanted to hear it, too. All of it.

Crofton leaned back in his chair. "I thought about sending him a letter, but decided I'd come to America and see him. It took a while, but eventually I hired on as a deckhand. Unfortunately for me, the captain of the ship wasn't as honest as he claimed. The merchandise we delivered to the Port of Baltimore had been acquired through unsavory ways and shortly upon docking, the cargo was seized. Through a line of misdeeds and lies, the captain led the authorities to believe the deckhands were responsible for specific items. I was arrested along with several others. All innocent, I should add."

Comparing every word to what he'd told her and Amelia earlier, Sara asked, "Is that when you sent Winston that telegram?"

"Yes," he said to her. "I'd thought, considering my grandfather had lived in Baltimore, and my father had at one time, the connection might assist me in proving my innocence." He pulled the worn telegraph from his pocket and handed it to the lawyer. "The judge overseeing the case had a wire sent to Winston, and received this reply, which led the judge to discovering my gravesite in Baltimore, complete with a large stone grave maker. Which also led to my deportation back to England."

"Deportation?" Sara repeated.

"Yes. For the most part, the truth came out. The judge believed the captain was behind the stolen merchandise, but ordered all of us to be removed from the country. I hadn't known that my mother had told Winston I was dead, and upon my return to England, I confronted her about it. She claimed it was for my benefit. That Winston had never wanted children, had only used me to make her move to uncivilized locations, and claimed she had to tell him that I was dead in order for him to agree to a divorce. She said she'd feared for both of our lives and believed we'd only be safe far away from him."

Sara's insides were quivering with anger at how a mother could do such things, what kind of wife she must have been. It was appalling and so very deceitful. Neither Ohio, from what she had heard from Amelia, nor Royalton were uncivilized. His mother should have seen the barren plains of Kansas. Not that she could remember much about it, but did recall the descriptions her mother and Winston used when talking about how they had met.

"That was when I had her provide this," Crofton said, handing Ralph the envelope Sara had never opened. "It is a legal affidavit, provided under oath, of her lies, and my true parentage."

"Why didn't you bring that to Winston?" she asked. "When you returned to America?"

"His response to the telegram was proof enough that at least part of her story was true. That he didn't want me to contact him."

"He thought you were dead," Sara argued.

He shrugged.

Not satisfied, she asked, "If you believed that, then why did you return to America?"

His eyes locked onto her, and she could almost feel how lost and alone he must have felt at one time. Or maybe still did. She had come to understand what that felt like in the past few days.

"Because I had no reason to stay in England," he said.

"Winston could not have sent this telegram," Ralph Wainwright said.

"What?"

"Why?"

Both she and Crofton had spoken at the same time. He furthered his question. "How do you know that?"

"Because of the date," Ralph answered. "Winston Parks was not in Royalton on the twelfth of April 1879. He was in Denver, meeting with me. Helen, my wife, and I, along with Ben, arrived in Denver on the tenth, on invitation from Winston. He had used the law firm that I worked for in Chicago during negotiations with the railroad, and invited me to move out here to become his private attorney. Your mother was with him, Sara, and we all remained in Denver until the eighteenth before beginning our journey to Royalton. The tracks were not completed all the way then, and the final part of our journey was by wagon. We didn't arrive here until the twenty-fifth. I remember that date because it is Ben's birthday, but all of the dates are very clear in my mind."

Sara remembered her parents returning home after that trip. Although Winston traveled fairly often during that time—the railroad wars were happening and he'd spent a lot of time in Denver—her mother had usually remained home. Mother had gone with Winston on that particular trip and it stuck in Sara's mind because even with Amelia and Hilton at home with her, she'd grown lonesome with both parents gone for so long. The implication of what Ralph's explanation meant churned her stomach. "Then who would have responded to the judge? Who would have sent that returning telegram?"

"I can't say," Ralph answered.

"Can you guess?" Crofton asked.

"I could, but that wouldn't be appropriate," Ralph responded.

"No, it wouldn't," Crofton answered. "Nor is it necessary. Nate was already dead in seventy-nine, therefore, any of Winston's correspondence would have gone to his right-hand man, Bugsley Morton."

"Bugsley wouldn't—" The way both men turned to

her had Sara clamping her lips closed. Crofton may have taken a dislike to Bugsley, but she couldn't believe he would have betrayed Winston in such a manner. Denied him of the opportunity to be reunited with his son.

"There was a lot going on at that time," Ralph said. "Men were vying for both railroad companies to win, along with plenty of deceit and trickery on both sides. Winston may have appointed someone to oversee his correspondence, and due to all that was happening, whoever that may have been might have thought this was a ploy to take Winston's focus off the railroad." Turning to her, Ralph's expression softened slightly, "Mr. Morton was rarely in Royalton during that time. He was usually with Winston, but I honestly don't remember if he had been in Denver with us or not."

She nodded, although she questioned his answer. A man who remembered the dates so clearly would have remembered who had traveled with them.

"Who responded, we may never know," Ralph then said to Crofton, "but I can accept this affidavit as the proof needed. May I keep this with your father's other legal papers?"

Crofton nodded. "I will never need it again."

"And this?" Ralph asked, holding up the telegram.

"Don't need that, either," Crofton replied.

Sara bit her bottom lip to keep from replying. The condition of the telegram, how it was so worn, said he'd looked at it often, and she couldn't help but empathize how he must have wished it had held different words. She balled her fingers into a fist because despite their differences, she had the greatest desire to just reach over and squeeze his hand.

"Then, if you're both willing, I shall open Winston's

will," Ralph said, reaching for the envelope he'd laid on the table.

Crofton turned to her. "Are you all right with this?"

After swallowing the lump that rose up in her throat for no apparent reason, she nodded. "Yes, of course, that is why we're here."

"I shall preface what I'm about to read," Ralph started while shuffling through several sheets of paper, "by saying I spoke to Winston about updating his will just a few weeks ago." Once again glancing her way, he added, "When he asked me to check into making your last name legally *Parks*. Unfortunately neither was accomplished prior to his death."

"Why had he waited so long for that?" Crofton asked.

"This will," Ralph answered, "was one of the first tasks I completed for Winston. He was worried that something might happen to him after Nate Long died."

"I meant having Sara's name legally changed," Crofton said.

Sara tried to read his face, to see why he was curious about that, but his expression hadn't changed. He hadn't glanced her way, either.

"Winston was worried about that for years, but he was also concerned about taking Sara's real father away from her." Ralph looked her way. "He said your father died while you were young, in a farming accident back in Kansas."

When she nodded, Ralph then included Crofton in his gaze, looking between the two of them as he continued, "Winston said he knew how he'd feel if Crofton hadn't died and someone else wanted to have him change his last name. How upset he'd be. He also said when you were just a little girl, you told him once that you couldn't call him father, because he wasn't your father."

Sara closed her eyes for a moment. She remembered that. She'd asked her mother if Winston was now her father, and her mother had said no. "That was a long time ago," she said quietly. "Before he married my mother. When we were traveling here." Shaking her head, she added, "I called him Father after that. Many times. Everyone referred to him as my father."

"I know," Ralph said, "but Winston insisted it not be pushed on you. However, when we last met, he said now that you were of age, you were old enough to decide what you wanted your name to be."

"He never asked me," she said. "I would have agreed. He's the only father I remember. The only one I ever knew."

Compassion filled Ralph's eyes. "He and your mother were on their way to see me when the accident happened. I had the paperwork complete for them to take back to you."

Sara pulled in air so fast her lungs rattled. She'd known they were on their way to town, but hadn't known exactly why. A tremble started at her toes and raced upward, stopping only when a weight landed on her shoulder. She glanced toward Crofton, and the hand he'd used to gently rub her shoulder.

"Are you all right?"

Whether she was or not didn't matter. Therefore, she nodded.

"The important thing, Sara," Ralph said, "is that Winston thought of himself as your father. From the day he married your mother, he became your father, and loved you as much as any father could."

She nodded again and blinked at the stinging in her eyes. Her nose was burning, too, and she sniffled slightly, wishing she'd brought along a handkerchief.

"Shall we continue?" Ralph asked.

"Yes, please," she said. Only once she returned home, would she let the tears fall. Right now, she needed to be the daughter Winston could be proud of.

"As I said, this will was written several years ago," Ralph said, and then, with a clearing of his throat he began to read, "I, Winston Parks, being of sound mind and body…"

Sara heard parts of what was read, but her mind wandered, recalling memories that were too poignant to ignore. How she'd greet Winston returning home after a trip, or simply a day at the lumber mill. She wondered how long it would be before she could no longer remember his laugh, or see his face when she closed her eyes. Her mother, too. She'd been so beautiful, and so caring and gentle. She never raised her voice or appeared mad or scared. Never appeared anything but happy. So very happy.

"Sara?"

Lifting her head slowly, it took a fuzzy moment for her to remember where she was, what had happened.

"Did you hear what I said?" Ralph asked.

Sara nodded as words filtered through her mind and came together with a single outcome. "Upon Winston's death, everything is to be divided amongst his children and my mother."

"That's correct," Ralph said. "Winston included provisions of how your mother was to select an overseer of the mill and other businesses, and continue to maintain proprietorship until one of Winston's children was of age and old enough Suzanne felt they were ready to succeed her."

"But mother is dead, too," Sara said needlessly.

"That too is correct," Ralph said with a gentle smile and once again shared glances between her and Crofton.

"I explained Winston had this will written up years ago. At the time the children he referred to were you, Sara, and your half brother Hilton, but Winston refused to use names. He said there may be more children and he didn't want any of them left out because he hadn't updated his will upon their birth. So, because of that, how this will is written and worded, all of Winston's holdings, except for the provisions he specifically stated were to go to Amelia, and myself, to continue to act as counsel on his behalf, are to be divided between the two of you."

Crofton's hand on her shoulder had gone completely still, and that sent a shiver down her spine. She turned his way, not knowing what to expect. The serene expression on his face increased her shiver.

He was looking at her, not at Ralph when Crofton said, "I have no need for a lumber mill. Sara gets it all."

"No," she said. "Winston would want you to have it. You were his first born."

"He thought I was dead." Crofton turned to Ralph. "Who, besides you, knows what's in that will?"

"No one. Besides myself, only Winston and Suzanne knew," Ralph answered. "But, I have to tell you, there is more than the lumber mill. There are other businesses, investments, land, cash. I have a list." As he held it out to Crofton, he added, "And the entire town assumes Sara will inherit everything."

"The entire town wants to marry her, too," Crofton said, taking the list.

It wasn't necessarily his tone that irritated her, or his statement, but something did. "No, they don't," she said. "They think you are here to claim the inheritance, and that scares them. The town will fail without the mill. Some people think I need to be married in order to fight you. That I'll need the help of a husband." The sense of righteousness rose inside her. "But I don't."

Crofton handed the list back to Ralph while the lawyer asked, "Who told you that, Sara?"

"Elliott Cross," she answered. "And that's what he'll tell others, too. If he hasn't already."

"Elliott Cross will say or print anything in order to sell a copy of his newspaper," Ralph answered.

"I know," she agreed, "but people believe what he writes."

"What does Sara need to do in order to claim her inheritance?" Crofton asked.

"I need to file a few papers, transferring holdings and such things, but since it's not being petitioned, we don't need to go before a judge," Ralph answered. "However, knowing you are Winston's son, I can't allow it all to go to her. It needs to be split equally." Ralph held up a hand at how Crofton shook his head. "It is my duty to carry out all activities in the best interest of my client, dead or alive, and Winston specifically stated his shares were to be divided equally amongst his children."

The way Crofton pulled his lips together, much like Winston used to do when annoyed, irritated Sara, but she kept her thoughts to herself. On one issue, but on the other, she said, "Start the paperwork. Equal shares." Then she looked at Crofton. "We have taken up enough of Mr. Wainwright's time for today."

Crofton nodded and stood. "I agree we have." Offering her a hand to assist her off the chair, he added, "I'd appreciate it, Mr. Wainwright, if none of this becomes public, at least for a while."

Ralph had stood as well. "For how long? People are curious, and as Sara stated, scared of the outcome. Telling them might settle the rumors down a bit."

"Just a few days." Crofton had collected her cloak and held it out for her. "It won't take longer than that."

Sara bit her lip to contain asking what he referred to as she slipped on her cloak. There would be time for discussion on the way home—where he wouldn't be able to avoid answering her questions.

They bid their farewells, and had barely stepped off the porch of the Wainwright house when her first question could no longer be held back. "Do you hate him that much?"

"Who?"

"Winston," she answered. "Do you hate him so much you won't take what he would have wanted you to have? What he dreamed about you having. You were his son. Are his son. The least you could do is honor him, honor his death, by publicly recognizing that."

"I've never denied he was my father."

"While acting like it was the most disgusting thing that could happen to a person," she argued, growing angrier.

Crofton knew it would be in his best interest not to argue with her. She was distraught. Pain had covered her face and filled her eyes while Wainwright had read the will. Her commitment to Winston was as apparent as the love she'd had for him and the community. In fact, Crofton didn't doubt she'd marry any one of those men who had come up the driveway if it meant the mill would continue to provide the jobs the town needed. He, however, knew the mill wouldn't continue without the railroad. That's what had happened back in Ohio. Once the major building stopped, the demand for lumber had dropped. It would happen here, too, sooner or later. Winston would have known that. It may not happen for a few years, but it would happen, and he had no desire to be a part of that. He had several thousand acres and almost as many cattle to oversee, and needed to get back there in order to do that. Once he found out who murdered Mel.

"And why must the will be kept secret?" she asked. "Letting it be known that it is split between the two of us is the best situation for everyone."

Crofton didn't want to argue that point, either, and walked around the buggy to assist her climb. She wouldn't be impressed to learn it was for her own safety. Men were already asking to marry her; once it got out she had indeed inherited Winston's holdings, they'd crawl out of the woodwork.

She spun to cast a cold glare. "You will answer my questions."

"You enjoy spouting orders, don't you?"

She glared harder.

He caught his grin, wondering if she'd ever spouted an order before he'd arrived. "Tell me, do people always obey you?" he whispered. The opportunity to tease her couldn't be wasted. She looked too adorable.

"Are you going to answer my question or not?"

"Not." He grasped her waist. "At least not here." Lifting her onto the seat, he added, "We'll discuss it at home." The word burned his tongue. Winston's house wasn't his home, hadn't been for many years, yet, he hadn't stuttered saying it. He turned and walked around the back of the buggy to the other side.

The report of a gun firing had him diving into the rig, shoving Sara onto the floor and covering her with his body all in one swift movement.

The whiz of a bullet made his scalp tingle, as did the sight of the hole it had made while ripping through the black leather canopy.

Startled, the horse tried to bolt, but the wheel lock

held, which had the horse stomping and snorting against the restraint and the buggy rocking.

"Stay down," he hissed as Sara tried to push off the floorboard.

"What happened?"

"Someone just shot at us."

"Are you sure?"

"There's a hole in the leather to prove it." Trying to tune in his hearing, he added, "Shh."

She obeyed and didn't budge an inch, not even when the silence grew so thick he eased off her to glance around the edge of the buggy. Whoever had fired the shot hadn't been too close. It had been a rifle, not a handgun, and he surveyed the buildings, checking the rooftops of the general direction the bullet had to have come from. There was no sign of anyone or anything out of the ordinary—other than the flutter of a curtain in a top-story window. He counted off the buildings, trying to recall what they'd driven past and guessed it to be a saloon. Not the one he'd visited the night before.

"Was that a gunshot I heard?"

Crofton maneuvered about until sitting on the seat, and while helping Sara onto the seat responded to Ralph. "Yes. Someone took a shot at us."

"Are you sure?"

He wanted to growl. *How sure does one need to be around here?* "Yes," he replied while climbing out of the buggy. "Wait here," he told Sara. Stopping near the horse, he rubbed its neck as Ralph joined him there. "What's that building?" he asked. "The third one on the left."

"The Day's End," Ralph replied. "It only has a set of bat wing doors on the front since it never closes. Not even on Sundays. Why?"

"That's where the shot came from," Crofton answered. "A window on the second floor."

"Maybe it was someone happy with the dove he'd just purchased," Ralph said with a flippant tone that didn't match the worry on his forehead.

Crofton followed the direction of the other man's gaze. Sara was leaning over the dashboard, clearly trying to hear their conversation. "I don't think so," he said under his breath.

Ralph leaned down as if checking the tug buckle connecting the girth beneath the horse's belly. "I don't, either, and I wasn't going to say anything," the man whispered. "But in light of what just happened, and between you and me, I don't think your father's death was an accident."

The hair on the back of Crofton's neck quivered. "Oh?"

"Winston traveled that road every day. Summer and winter. I don't believe his horse was simply spooked. Or if it was, I'd like to know by what."

"No one investigated it?"

"The sheriff's been out of town for two weeks," Ralph said.

The trace bar connecting the buggy to the harness shifted and both men stood, knowing Sara had climbed out. "Get back in the buggy," Crofton told her. "We need to head home."

"What about the gunfire?" she asked.

"It's probably just what Ralph said."

Crofton watched Sara climb back in the buggy while he lifted the wheel lock off the ground. "When's the sheriff due back?"

"Next week," Ralph answered.

"I'll be in touch soon," he told the lawyer and then carried the wooden block to the buggy, where he set it on the floorboard beneath his feet. He waited for Sara to arrange the long folds of her black cloak before he released the brake and turned the rig around. He kept an eye on that one window as the horse broke into a trot, as anxious to get out of the area as him.

"Do you really think that's all it was?" Sara asked. "An accident? That someone wasn't really shooting at us?"

"No one with a lick of sense would shoot at someone in the middle of the day, in town," he offered, although he wasn't convinced of that at all.

"I'd suspect not," she said. "But there are plenty of strangers in town with the railroad expansion. They know Sheriff Wingard is out of town. He helped the state marshal escort some prisoners to Kansas. Elliott wrote about it in the newspaper."

Crofton nodded as they turned the corner. The desire to go the opposite direction, past the front of the saloon was strong. Had he been alone he would have, and he would have entered the building, to see who had been in that room, but with Sara along, he had to think of safety first. Furthermore, in his mind, he had a pretty good idea of who he'd find in the saloon. Bugsley Morton was not going to get rid of him that easily. The man needed to know that, and he needed to know putting Sara in that kind of danger would not be tolerated.

The ride home was quiet. The shooting incident seemed to have eased her antagonism over the will and how he didn't want any of it. He didn't. Yet, he couldn't help but think of her. Men would be after her like hounds on a fox. He wanted to curse his father for putting her in such a predicament. Or himself for sending those suitors away two at a time. She was going to need a protector. Someone who would protect her with their very life.

He certainly didn't need another hitch in all that was happening. All he wanted was a southern line of the railroad. The track that had been promised. The one that would make his ranching enterprise as successful as his father's lumber mill.

At the house, he stopped the horse near the front door. "I'll put away the buggy."

The thoughtfulness of her gaze worried him for a moment, but then she nodded and climbed out.

Crofton drove the buggy to the barn and proceeded to unhitch the horse and let it loose in the corral before pushing the buggy into the stall he'd pulled it out of earlier. There was a second stall that sat empty, but the ruts in the hard-packed dirt said a second buggy had been stored there. The very one his father had driven to his death no doubt.

Things certainly would be different if that hadn't happened. It had though, and there wasn't a damn thing he could do about it.

He was in the process of hanging the harness on the hook for that purpose when someone entered the barn.

"I could have done that for you, sir."

Crofton recognized Alvin Thompson by the fact his left hand was cut off at the wrist.

"Lost it ten years ago at the mill," Alvin said, raising the arm Crofton had just pulled his gaze off. "I would have bled to death if not for your father."

Crofton gave a slight nod as the man stepped closer, with his right hand extended outward.

"Name's Alvin Thompson. I take care of the barn chores around here, and other things. Wood for the house and such." As they grasped hands, the man added, "But you already know that, don't you, Mr. Parks?"

There was a cleverness to the man's gaze, but no hostility. At least none that shone through. "Yes, I do," Crofton answered. "And I know you work at the mill and live in the old house."

Alvin nodded. "It was the first thing built out here. Your father and Nate Long put it up that first winter. After Nate died and Amelia moved into the big house, Winston asked me to move into the old place and take over the barn chores. Nate did most of them before that, and Amelia still sees to the chickens and garden and such. Winston just hired me to take care of the heavier chores. I agreed, but only if I could continue working at the mill, too. I can accomplish as much as anyone with two hands."

"I'm sure you can," Crofton answered, taking credit of the man's chip. He didn't begrudge him for that. He had his own chip. Furthermore, if he'd lost a hand, he couldn't rightly say how he'd react to it even fifteen years later.

The notion Ralph Wainwright had put in Crofton's head had been gathering credence, and he moved closer to the buggy in order to lay a hand on the wheel. "Do you service the rigs?"

"Sure do, regularly. Something up with this one?" Alvin asked.

It was a complete fabrication, but Crofton said, "I noticed a wobble on the left. The front axle might need some grease."

"Could be," Alvin answered. "Those rubber washers wear out. I'll have a look-see."

"I'd appreciate that," Crofton answered as he started for the door. Then, pretending the thought just came to him, he turned around. "I'm assuming you'll be the one to repair the other buggy."

"What other buggy?"

"The one from the accident," Crofton said.

Alvin huffed and shook his head. "There weren't nothing left to fix. When that horse got spooked, the buggy went over the side of the cliff."

He'd heard that, but also knew even the worst wrecks left salvageable parts. Especially out here, where everything had to be shipped in, which was expensive and time-consuming. "What about the horse?" he asked.

"Had to shoot it. It was as mangled as—" Alvin stopped and gave the wheel he now stood beside a hard shake. "It wouldn't have survived."

"That's too bad," Crofton said.

"It certainly was," Alvin said. "The entire accident was too bad." Shaking the wheel a second time, he asked, "How is Miss Sara doing?"

The way she'd shaken during the reading of the will had caused something to shift inside Crofton, as had her anger at him afterward. She'd loved Winston, and hated Crofton for not loving him as well. That wasn't his fault, but dang it, if it didn't make him feel a bit guilty. He'd get over it. And so would she. Someday. Probably long after he was gone. "Good, considering all," Crofton finally answered.

Hitching a pant leg, Alvin bent down. "I'll see to this here wagon, but you tell her if there's anything she needs, to just give me a shout."

Crofton gave a nod. "I will."

"That goes for you, too," Alvin said.

Not exactly sure how to respond, Crofton settled for, "Thank you."

"It's a good thing you showed up when you did," Alvin said. "She'll need some looking after."

Several questions came to mind, but Crofton chose to hold them for now. After another nod, he turned and left the barn. His intention had been to gather his horse and return to town. To the saloon, but, if whoever had shot at them had any wits, they'd have already left. He could go to the mill and find out if Bugsley had been there during that time or not, but it wouldn't prove anything.

Pondering that, and more, he walked up the hill toward the house. Winston had built the place on a set of natural terraces. The older home on the lowest, the barn on the next, then the house on the next, and the last, smaller terrace, was where the graves were. Near a natural grove of trees. The entire town of Royalton had been built on a large mesa, with the large mountains, their peaks covered in snow, surrounding the town on all sides.

Halfway up the hill, Crofton altered his path. Rather than following the road, he walked through the grass to the cliff ledge. The view was similar to the one from Winston's office. Crofton shifted slightly to scan the hillside, where the road started up the hill. It disappeared from view where it made the switchback and then reappeared for the second turn and the rest of the incline. The road would have taken some significant engineering and hard work to get it in the condition it was today. That didn't surprise him. His father had believed anything could be accomplished. What did surprise him was that there hadn't been an accident on this road until the fatal one that took Winston's life.

Accidents were called accidents because that's what they were. Mishaps. Events that caught you by surprise. It could have been that. The horse could have been spooked, which is what he'd been told and had believed. Until now. Who would have known Winston was going to see Wainwright that day and why did they stop it from happening?

He turned his gaze back to the lumber mill. All signs pointed to Bugsley Morton.

Glancing toward the road again, he scanned the hillside at the corner of the switchback. That was where the accident had happened. On impulse, he started down the hill. Within a few steps, he figured it would have been easier to take the road, but he was already committed. The brush and trees that somehow grew straight up out of the angled ground gave him aid as he made his way downward.

Chapter Eight

From her bedroom window, Sara watched Crofton disappear over the hill. She shouldn't care what he was doing, or why he was doing it, but she did. He'd said differently, but he didn't believe that shot had been fired by some happy customer at The Day's End. It was the rowdiest of places in town. Rumor had it they offered free meals just to keep the men drinking all hours of the day and night. Other rumors were about the girls who worked there. Mother had forbidden her to even look at those women. She'd agreed, but had stolen a peek every chance she'd gotten.

When Crofton didn't reappear, her curiosity took control and she tiptoed to the door and down the back set of stairs. Amelia had insisted it was time for a nap after hearing what had taken place, and would not be happy about being disobeyed.

Sara paused briefly on the bottom step when it creaked, and then peeked around the stairwell wall into the kitchen to assure Amelia wasn't nearby before quickly crossing the room. She opened the back door slowly, to keep the hinges from squeaking and shut it just as quietly.

She jutted around the chicken coop and hurried into

the trees that lined the edge of the cliff, then onto the small pathway that led to the clearing a short distance down the hillside. It was where they disposed of things no longer needed, empty cans, bottles and rags that couldn't be used for anything else. From there, she peered down the hill to where she'd seen Crofton disappear. Although some of the trees and bushes had lost their leaves, the fir trees were still too thick to see through.

Frustration grew, and she was about to believe he must have returned to the road when she caught sight of something moving. She set her gaze on an open area ahead of the movement and felt a sense of elation when she recognized him moving downhill.

He was walking sideways due to the incline, and using branches when the hill was overly steep. The direction he was headed would take him to the back side of the mill. As that thought occurred, so did a smile. Few knew about it, but there was a much faster way down the hill.

She spun around and ran across the clearing, jumping over cans and bottles and then ducked between the bows of two large pine trees. When the road was too snow-covered to travel upon, Winston would use this foot trail to go to and from the mill when absolutely necessary. He'd carried her through the snow on this path, when she'd been seven and had fallen and broken her arm. She'd used it a few times after that, but it had been years. Winston had told her it was an animal trail, one deer and elk used to go down the mountain to drink from the river, and that she shouldn't use it. Therefore she hadn't. Until today.

Pines, and a few aspen framed the sides of the trail, and the way the fallen leaves were crushed told her Winston was right. The trail was well used. She had to swallow against the lump that formed at the idea of coming upon a wild critter. Deer didn't worry her, but elk were common in the area and the unseasonably warm weather they'd been experiencing meant the bears might not have gone into hibernation yet, either. Neither bears nor elk were as docile as deer.

Her heart was racing and every sound made her jump by the time the trees gave way to the open area behind the mill. The big trees had long ago been cut down between here and the mill, but saplings had taken their place, leaving the ground uneven and difficult to walk through. The wind blew freely, too, making her wish she'd grabbed her winter cloak.

Between the wind and the relief of not encountering a wild animal, it was a moment before she recalled her mission and looked around for any sign of Crofton. Movement once again caught her attention. He seemed to be digging through the pile of old lumber.

Not worried if he saw her or not, she separated the saplings with both hands as she hurried toward him.

He spun around before she arrived, but didn't stand up. Just as she opened her mouth to ask what he was doing, a gunshot sounded. It was immediately followed by another, and another. Startled and unsure what was happening, it was the sight of Crofton rushing toward her that she reacted to. Hitching her skirt, she jumped to run, but tripped. Unable to catch herself, she fell backward, hitting the ground with such force the air left her lungs in a swoosh.

Fighting to breathe, and to sit up enough to see if Crofton was all right, she was pushed back down as soon as she lifted her head.

"Damn it, stay down."

He was covering her with his body like he had in the buggy and that had her heart pounding. Or maybe it pounded so hard because she still fought to breathe; then again it could be the searing pain shooting up her side. She twisted slightly, and hissed as the pain sharpened.

Most of the weight shifted off her, but he was still atop her, with eyes blazing. "Damn it, chasing off rustlers is safer than bringing you to town."

Irritated by his glare and attitude, she replied, "You didn't bring me to town." She'd have liked to say more, but her side hurt too much.

"You, there! Get up. With your hands in the air. No sudden movements!"

The pain in her side dulled as she recognized Walter Porter's voice. "It's me, Mr. Porter. Sara."

"Miss Sara? What on earth are you doing out here?" Mr. Porter asked. "Who's that with you?"

"Crofton Parks is with me," she said as loudly as possible while flinching as the pain renewed.

"What's wrong?" Crofton asked. "Were you hit?"

She opened her mouth, but the pain turned so sharp she couldn't speak.

Crofton instantly jumped off her and crouched beside her, running his hands over her sides and down her legs. "Where? What hurts?"

"My back, no my side," she managed between the shooting pains. Nothing had hurt like this before, not even her broken arm.

"Lie still," he said, which was in complete contradiction to how he slid his hands beneath her back and rolled her toward one side.

She hissed at the pain, and again at the shock on Walter Porter's face as the man slid to a stop beside her.

"Oh, dear Lord," Walter said. "A bullet couldn't have hit her, could it?"

Fear raced through her and she twisted about to look

at Crofton, and the hand he had used to touch her side. The one covered with blood.

"No," Walter said. "No. I fired in the air. I swear I did."

Sara was torn between assuring the man she'd be fine and wondering if she was dying. The pain was still there, but not as sharp. Maybe that's what happened right before one dies. They become numb.

"She hasn't been shot," Crofton said.

Relief washed over her.

"But we need a wagon and a doctor," he said.

"Why?" she asked.

"I'll be right back," Walter said. "Don't move. I'll be right back."

One part of her didn't want to know, the other part needed to know. "What's wrong with me?" she asked. "Why do I need a doctor?"

Crofton sat down and shifted her until she leaned against him while still lying on the ground. He pushed the hair off her face. "You'll be fine," he said. "Just fine."

She tried to twist enough to see her back, but his hold wouldn't allow it.

"Just hold still," he said, wrapping his arm around her tightly.

Her heart started racing again. "What aren't you telling me? What's wrong? Let me see."

He closed his eyes for a moment and bit his lips together before he leaned down and his lips touched her forehead, which was more startling than the gunshots had been.

"I'm sorry, Sara, so sorry," he whispered.

His breath was warm on her forehead, and his lips touched the skin again. Tears formed and she couldn't say exactly why. Blinking at the sting in her eyes, she asked, "For what?"

"When I shoved you to the ground…" He took a breath and blew it out slowly. "You landed on a stick."

"You didn't shove me. I tripped. I fell." Relief at not being shot didn't help the pain. "I fell on a stick?"

"Yes," he said quietly. "A sharp stick. It's embedded in your side. A surgeon will need to remove it."

Fright returned, as did newfound pain. Probably because she thought it should hurt. Or maybe because it truly did. New tears formed, too. "It's stuck in me?"

His smile was weak, meant for assurance, and he once again pushed her hair back. "Yes, but you'll live."

"You're sure?"

He nodded.

Having never been in such a situation, she wasn't sure how to react. The concern filling his eyes helped her choose. "I bet that's a disappointment to you."

He frowned, but then a sparkle flashed in his eyes and he smiled. As crazy as it was, that made her feel better.

"Just lie still," he said.

The pain was such she had no intention of moving, however, she jolted slightly when he moved. "Where are you going?"

"Nowhere," he answered, giving her shoulder a squeeze. "I'm just going to take off my shirt."

"Why?" Frightened again, she asked, "For a bandage? Am I bleeding that badly?"

He kept her from twisting far enough to see more than blood staining the side of her dress.

"Hold still," he said, while leaning over her and pulling his arm out of his jacket and shirt at the same time. "I'm just going to cover the wound."

"You'll freeze. It's cold."

"It's not that cold."

The rattle of a wagon and shouts arrived before the crowd did. A large one. Led by Bugsley.

"What happened here?" Glaring at Crofton, Bugsley continued, "What did you do to her?"

Unsure why, Sara said, "He didn't do anything. I fell and landed on a stick."

"Where's the doctor?" Crofton asked.

He was tucking part of his shirt beneath her and though he was being gentle, the pain had her holding her breath.

"Here, I'm here." Dr. Dunlop knelt down beside her. "I'm gonna take a look-see, Sara, so I know what needs to be done."

She nodded. The shouts around them continued, but she closed them out and squeezed the hand that took a hold of hers as the doctor shifted her more onto her side.

After what felt like a tremendous amount of poking and prodding, Doc Dunlop sat back on his knees.

"I'll need to do surgery, Sara," he said. "I can either do that at your home, or mine. Before you decide, I must tell you, the ride to your house will be very painful, and a touch dangerous."

"You'll do it at your place," Bugsley said. "Boys, get her loaded up."

"No," Crofton said. "It'll be at the house, and I'll put her in the wagon myself."

"Now see here," Bugsley said.

"Doc," Crofton said, "help me get this stick secured so it doesn't move when I pick her up."

Sara squeezed her eyes shut, but knew the instant Crofton stood. "Where are you going?"

"Just to your other side," he said. "I don't want to bump the stick by picking you up on this side." He'd stepped over her while talking.

After a bit of maneuvering, Crofton's shirt was tied around her waist and the pressure seemed to ease some of the pain.

"I'm going to pick you up now and carry you to the wagon, Sara," he said. "All right?"

Bugsley had knelt down above her head. "Sara, listen to me, the ride will be too painful. You can have the surgery at doc's house and I'll take you home afterward."

She held a sense of loyalty to Bugsley, for she'd counted on him greatly the past few days and Winston had trusted him for many years, but she was scared, and hurt, and wanted to go home. Just go home. Actually, she wished she was still there. That she'd never followed Crofton down the hill. Turning her gaze to him, her throat burned as she whispered, "I want to go home."

"I know," he said softly. "That's where I'm taking you—don't worry. But I have to lift you up. Ready?"

Squeezing her eyes shut, and holding her breath, she nodded. "Yes."

Crofton lifted her off the ground and she hooked one arm around his neck. Moving the other arm hurt too much. He walked slowly, carefully, but pain had infused her side as he lifted her off the ground and continued to grow with each step he took.

"Not much farther," he said.

Still holding her breath and letting out only little bits of air at a time, she nodded. "I know." Not wanting him to believe she was a complete coward, she released a bit more air and added, "The stick's not in my eye."

Crofton couldn't remember the last time he felt admiration for anyone, but he did for Sara. She was courageous and strong and so stubborn. He, on the other hand was nothing shy of stupid. He should have known she'd follow him. Dang it, he'd been so focused on the accident, especially after viewing the crash site and noticing how the buggy debris had been dragged to a pile of unusable scrap lumber behind the mill, he hadn't considered she might be watching him. Might follow.

The fact someone was watching the area had crossed his mind, which is why he'd stayed low while sneaking across the open areas. Sara hadn't. She'd been parting those saplings with as much pomp and circumstance as Moses had the Red Sea. He'd almost laughed at the sight of her. Until the gunfire started.

He hadn't thought, just leaped to cover her like he had back at the lawyer's house. Her injury was his fault. Completely his fault. As would be her death.

Mentally, he reprimanded himself. The injury wasn't life threatening—as long as infection didn't set in.

At the wagon, he used a rock as a step to climb into the bed and then slowly eased down until sitting. The doc climbed in next and Crofton instantly said, "Give her something to ease the pain." Tears were trickling down her cheeks, her brows were knit together and her bottom lip was white from how hard she'd been biting it.

"I can't yet," the doc said while covering her shoulders with the coat Crofton had discarded. "I'll give her some chloroform before I remove the stick."

"Give her some now," Crofton ordered.

"I can't," the doc said again. "If I give her some now, I won't be able to give her more later. That may be too much for her."

Feeling helpless was something Crofton had never experienced, and he sincerely did not like it. Nor did he like the fact Bugsley Morton had climbed into the wagon as well and was flapping his lips.

"I told you the ride would be too much for her," the man said. "Driver, take us to the doctor's house."

Sara's head was against his shoulder. "No," she whispered. "Please take me home."

"Don't worry," Crofton assured. "We are taking you home." He spoke loudly enough the driver heard, and the glare he gave the other man sitting on the seat of the buckboard was so hard he had no doubt they'd go in the right direction. That man was Walter Porter, and his expression said he was full of guilt, too.

"Mr. Morton," the doctor said, "Sara has told us she wants to be operated on at home, so that's where it will be." Shifting his gaze to Crofton, the doc included, "I'll need help, and Amelia's one of the best assistants in town."

The ride wasn't smooth, nor was it short, and Crofton was burying his teeth in his bottom lip by the time they got to the house. He'd told the driver to take it easy so many times, Sara had told him to shut up. She'd said it with a weak grin, but it had been the paleness of her skin that had made him bite his lip. The wound wasn't bleeding profusely, but she was tiny, and most likely didn't have much blood to lose.

Hurrying, fearing she might bleed to death at any moment, but cautious his movements didn't jostle Sara too much, he scurried out of the wagon, and rushed for the house, shouting for Amelia.

She met him on the front porch, full of questions.

"Gather what the doc needs and meet us in Sara's room," he ordered, rushing through the open doorway and up the stairs.

Sara didn't say a word, until he pushed the door of her room open. "I don't want to get blood on the quilt," she said. "My mother made it for me."

He started to say a quilt didn't matter, but stopped at the pleading in her eyes.

"I'll get the quilt," Amelia said.

"Get some towels, too," the doctor said, entering the room behind her. "So we don't ruin the rest of the bedding."

Panic instantly appeared in Sara's eyes, and Crofton held her closer to his chest as she began to tremble. "You'll be fine," he whispered. The guilt eating at his stomach was more ferocious than anything he'd experienced. He'd never knowingly hurt a woman, and although this had been an accident, there was no denying her suffering was because of him.

Oddly enough, at that moment, Alvin's missing hand came to mind, and so did his father. Winston had taken responsibility for the man losing his hand by making sure he had a job, a home, and he would expect no less from his son.

Therefore, Sara's recovery was his responsibility.

He turned to the doctor. "What else are you going to need? Water? Bandages?"

"Yes, and yes," the doctor answered. "Amelia knows. You can set Sara down if she's getting too heavy."

"No, I'll wait for the towels," Crofton replied.

After throwing back the quilt, Amelia had left the room, but her hurried footsteps could be heard already returning. Besides, holding Sara assured him she was still alive. He still didn't believe the stick was life threatening, but it was a lingering thought, along with worry of infection setting in after surgery.

"It'll just be another minute, Crofton," Amelia said, entering the room with a stack of towels. With quick movements, she splayed them out over the center of the bed and then added another sheet. All of them were white and he could almost see blood already staining them. His hand holding Sara's back was wet and the shirt wrapped around her waist was fully saturated with blood.

"There, lay her down now," Amelia said.

Crofton looked at the doctor. "Do you want to untie the shirt?"

"No, I'll cut it off, along with her dress," the man answered. "That will be the easiest."

The doctor appeared quite confident and capable, yet Crofton wasn't fully prepared to turn Sara over to his complete care. "Get on the other side of the bed," he instructed. "Make sure the stick doesn't get bumped while I'm setting her down."

As the doctor hurried around the foot of the bed, Crofton turned toward Amelia. "Roll up a couple more of those towels to keep her propped on one side."

"You're as good at giving orders as Winston was," Sara said weakly.

Crofton was relieved to hear her voice. She hadn't opened her eyes since asking to have the quilt removed. "It's a trait all of us Parks have."

She shook her head, barely, but enough. "My last name isn't Parks. It never will be."

He didn't expect her statement to affect him, but it did. There was a longing in her tone, a sadness. Never having expected to wish he had siblings, he bit his lips together at the idea of cursing Winston for never adopting her, giving her the last name she obviously had wanted.

"Ready," Amelia said. "Be careful now."

Crofton nodded, and gently eased Sara onto the bed. The doctor instantly went to work cutting apart the shirt and the dress beneath it. The stick had entered her side just above the waistband of her pantaloons, and the tip of it could be made out poking out of her skin just below her ribcage. It was at an upward angle, from back to front, and he hoped it hadn't snared any of her organs.

"You can leave now, Mr. Parks," the doctor said. "Mrs. Long and I can handle it from here."

Not ready to go anywhere, Crofton stepped around Amelia who was cutting away the material covering Sara's stomach, and proceeded to position a pillow more evenly under Sara's head. He'd admitted she was a beautiful woman before, but right now, looking down on her, he suspected not even angels were lovelier than her.

"Thank you," she whispered.

He bit his lips at how her simple gesture of gratitude stung. "Shh," he said, brushing the hair away from her face. He wanted to bend down and kiss her forehead like he had earlier, to offer a bit of condolence for her pain. His pulse started pounding, and he lifted away his hand.

"Excuse me, Mr. Parks," the doctor said. "I have to give her something for the pain now."

Amelia took his arm at the same time the doctor elbowed him aside. "Come along, Crofton. I'll be with her the entire time."

As Amelia tugged him toward the doorway, Crofton planted his heels. "I'll stay in case—"

"You need to go make sure all those men downstairs aren't muddying up my floors," Amelia said while giving him a solid shove toward the door.

Crofton had forgotten about everyone else other than the angel who had been in his arms. Including Bugsley Morton. By the time he deduced he really didn't care what Morton, or anyone else was doing downstairs, the door to Sara's room had been firmly shut—with him standing in the hallway. He grasped the knob, but before turning it, a lick of common sense washed over him. He wasn't a surgeon, or a nurse, and would probably be more of a hindrance than a help.

Accepting how that churned his guts sent a fiery shot of anger up his spine. He spun around and headed for his room down the hall, where he grabbed the dirty shirt he'd collected from the stable. He hadn't been cold while holding Sara, but he was now.

Shaking aside a shiver, he put on the shirt and made his way to the stairway. Voices, several of them, hushed but harsh, quickened his footsteps. The group of men grew silent and still as he stepped off the bottom step.

Crofton chose his words with purpose. "You can return to the mill, Mr. Porter. I'll send word of Sara's recovery."

He'd recognized Walter Porter as the same bug-eyed man who'd been behind the counter when he'd visited the mill yesterday, and took note of how Walter glanced at Bugsley as if awaiting further orders. Crofton wasn't in the mood to be ignored. "That goes for the rest of you, too. I appreciate the swift assistance you provided, but it may be hours before the surgery is complete." Having just thought of that, he had half a mind to run back upstairs to ask the doc how long it would take.

"I was just telling Mr. Morton that I'd prefer to wait here," Walter said, squaring his shoulders and tipping up his chin. "Sara is as close to a daughter as I'll ever have, and my concern for her greatly overrides all else."

Walter shuffled his feet slightly, as if second-guessing his sternness as Crofton eyed him squarely.

"No insult intended, Mr. Parks. Your father hired me to be the mill clerk shortly after he started this place. I barely knew how to add two and two, but that didn't stop him from giving me the job, or from making sure I learned everything I needed to know." Walter waved a hand at the few others standing behind him. "Same with most of them, and we've all watched Sara grow up. We know how much Winston loved her, and we do, too. If you don't mind, we'd just as soon hang around right here, 'til we get word from Doc she's all right."

Crofton didn't need to know any of that. He also didn't doubt it was true. "She's going to be fine," he said, needing to believe that as much as anyone else. He also noted the anger in Bugsley's eyes and the tightness of the man's lips. Bugsley had already ordered these men to return to work, and they'd refused.

Crofton took a moment to ponder that, before he nodded. "All right, you're all welcome to wait." Eyeing Alvin in the crowd, he nodded toward him. "Care to see if Amelia left a pot of coffee on the stove?"

"Right away, sir," Alvin answered. "If not, I'll make a pot."

It was a small crowd, four others beside himself, Morton, Walter and Alvin. "There's room for everyone to sit in the front parlor."

The men offered their thanks, shaking his hand and introducing themselves as they made their way across the front hall. He didn't bother noting their names. Some he'd already learned, but for the most part, his mind didn't have room to collect information right now. As Walter followed the others, Crofton turned to walk toward the office. He didn't want coffee. A stiff shot of whiskey is what he was after.

A growl rolled about in the back of his throat as Morton grasped his arm. He let his glare voice his demand, and when the man let loose, Crofton once again started for the office.

"What were you doing digging through the rubbish pile?" Morton asked.

Crofton considered not answering, but then decided now might be the perfect time to get a few answers. "Just satisfying my curiosity," he said while walking toward the office.

Just as he suspected, Morton followed.

"By digging through trash?" Morton asked as he entered the room. "What did you expect to find?"

Crofton crossed the room to a small table near the fireplace and proceeded to fill a glass with amber liquid from the half-full decanter. He'd bet no one had touched the bottle since Winston died, and that made his hand tingle slightly. After replacing the glass stopper, he lifted the glass and gave a silent salute to his father before he downed the drink in one swallow. As the mellow, rich flavor flowed over his tongue and down his throat, he wished he'd taken the time to savor it.

"Half the town throws stuff back there," Bugsley said.

Setting the glass down, Crofton turned about. "I don't think so. There were a few empty bottles, but for the most part, it was just scrap lumber from the mill."

"We pile it there," Morton said, glancing toward the liquor table. "Lumber that's no good except for burning. People are free to collect it as needed for firewood. They tend to throw out whatever else they don't want back there, too."

He'd been at the rubbish pile long enough to learn plenty, but mayhap not long enough to know exactly what Morton was referring to. Another trip might be in order. Letting that settle in his mind, Crofton changed the subject. "You're aware that Sara and I visited my—our father's lawyer today."

"I heard as much."

Or saw. Crofton withheld that thought. "Nice man," he said, "Ralph Wainwright, and thorough. Nothing got

by him. Then again, my father only hired the best." He
grinned while walking toward the desk. "If they weren't
the best when he hired them, he cultivated them into
being exactly what he wanted. He knew one man couldn't
do it alone. That he needed followers. Those with the
same drive and passion." Making sure his words were
hitting home, he paused before continuing, "The unique
thing about Winston Parks was that he knew how to lead.
Give a man an inch and he'll take a mile, but reward him
for earning that inch, and he'll give you a mile."

"What the hell does that mean?"

Crofton smiled. It meant a lot to him. His father had
told him that years ago, and it had stuck with him. He
may not have put it into practice as well as his father
had, maybe because he hadn't understood it as well as
he did this minute. Even the best employee could become
greedy. Want more.

"Just that my father paid his employees well." He sat
down and leaned back in the chair, placing his hands behind his head. "You worked for Winston, what, twelve,
thirteen years?"

Morton opened his mouth, but then closed it as a devil-
may-care-but-I-don't glint filled his eyes. "You're wor-
rying about the wrong man." He took a chair and rested
an ankle over the opposite knee.

A tiny part of Crofton had to admire the man's au-
dacity. Then again, Winston would never have hired a
full-blown idiot. But, he might have accidentally hired
a schemer, if the man kept himself hidden well enough,
and Morton had plenty of hidden secrets. Crofton pon-
dered that for a moment. Winston would have known that,
too. So why had he hired Morton? "Oh?" Crofton asked.
"And whom should I be worried about?"

"Your own hide," Morton said. "Winston's son or not,

this entire town will soon be out for you. Your father was the king of Royalton, and Sara's the princess. Think about that. The men in the parlor will see you lynched before the week's end if she's permanently injured."

Chapter Nine

Crofton squeezed the wood of the balcony rail beneath his hands. The evidence—if he could call it that—was gone. The entire rubbish pile had been set afire. Morton must have seen to it as soon as he left the house right after the doctor proclaimed Sara would be up and about in no time.

That had been hours ago. The time had barely ticked by while waiting for the doctor to come down the steps. Right after Bugsley had threatened a lynching, Crofton had escorted him from the office. Leaving Morton in the hall, he'd entered the parlor and started playing host to the men sitting there. Not because he was afraid of what Morton had said, but because he knew it to be true. True royalty or not, Winston had been the king of Royalton, and much like England had Queen Victoria, the town would expect much from Sara. He hadn't attempted to make friends with the waiting men—if that had been his intention, he'd have offered them some of Winston's whiskey—nor had he cared if any of them left the house liking him more than when they'd arrived. He'd simply needed something to do.

Overall, his waiting companions had turned out to be

a good bunch of men. Especially Walter Porter. The man sincerely cared about Sara, and was mourning both Winston and Sara's mother's deaths as if they'd been family. Walter took pride in the lumber mill, too, lots of it. So did the others. And they were concerned about how Sara would cope with the duties that had fallen upon her slim shoulders.

Crofton turned toward the door he'd left slightly open when he'd wandered onto her balcony. He was worried. That was a heavy burden for one as small as Sara. She was so unprepared.

The night air had chilled him, so he reentered her room. A lamp burned beside her bed, the light flickering softly inside the glass chimney. Amelia had left it lit when she'd finally gone to bed an hour or more ago, with specific instructions he was to wake her if Sara so much as whimpered.

She hadn't. Not yet anyway, but the doctor had said she would. Said she'd have a whopper of a headache when she awoke the first time from the chloroform he'd used to keep her asleep while he stitched up her side. Thankfully the stick hadn't damaged anything vital, just some flesh, the doc had said. Crofton was happy to hear that. Carrying her had told him she didn't have an abundance of extra flesh on any part of her body.

Her bedroom, like the rest of the house, was large, and the furniture grand. The bed had pillar posts at all four corners, and was situated in the center of the room with tables on both sides. A tall dresser and matching armoire were in one far corner, separated by a dressing screen. A bench with several pillows sat beneath a set of wide windows on the wall overlooking the front of the house, along with a short bookcase. The door to the hallway was on the opposite wall, and in that corner was a round table covered with a tablecloth that matched the two upholstered chairs sitting beside it. The thick quilt that had been covering the bed was now folded neatly over the foot of the bed.

He frowned slightly, remembering how she'd worried about getting blood on that quilt. It was pale yellow with tiny white stripes. Her mother must have been quite a seamstress, for everything in the room, including the curtains had been sewn from the same material.

A rustle of the sheet covering Sara made him take a step toward the bed, but the creak of a board beneath his feet had him stop and wait to see if it had been his imagination or not. Hearing a tiny moan, he carefully crossed the room and knelt down beside her bed. His heart hammered inside his chest, and for a moment, he wondered if he'd started to think of her as his sister. There was no other reason for him to care as much about her as he did. More than he'd cared about anyone else in a very long time. He'd had plenty of friends through the years, and had seen them ill and injured, but they'd never pulled at his heart like she did. He'd give all he had to take her place right now. To be the one lying in that bed instead of her.

She opened one eye and licked her lips before hoarsely whispering, "Do I smell smoke?"

He'd also come to know her better than he'd known others in a very short amount of time. If he told her no or not to worry, she'd try to sit up and proclaim him wrong, so he went with the truth. "Yes."

"What's burning?"

Her voice sounded so full of gravel it pained him to hear it. He took the glass of water off the table beside the bed, and holding it near her chin, slid his other hand beneath her head. "Here, take a sip of water."

After she did so, and while he set the glass aside she asked, "What's on fire?"

Though her voice was stronger, it was far from normal. "Don't worry," he answered. "It's just some brush."

"It's too dry. There hasn't been any snow yet and it could get away—"

"It was well guarded and now nothing more than ashes." Removing his hand from beneath her head, he asked, "How are you feeling?"

"Awful." Still lying on her side, she lifted one hand and pressed the heel of her palm against her temple. "It feels like someone is squeezing my head with both hands."

"The doctor said that would happen and that you have to sleep it off." He felt her cheek. She was warm, and he had no idea if that was normal, or if it meant she was feverish—which was what the doc said to watch for. Figuring he'd go fetch Amelia, he first pulled the covers over her shoulder and tucked them near her neck.

She wrapped her fingers around his. "Thank you."

Both of her eyes were open, staring directly into his and he couldn't have broken the gaze if he'd wanted to. It seemed to pull him right in. "You're welcome," he said, his voice almost as gravelly as hers had been.

"I shouldn't have followed you today."

The flip inside his chest had to have been his heart tumbling. "I shouldn't have knocked you to the ground."

The hint of a smile turned up the corners of her lips. "You didn't. I fell."

She'd been saying that all along. He knew differently. He may not have touched her, but running at her had startled her to the point she'd tripped and fallen. Unable to stop himself, he leaned forward and kissed her forehead. "If you say so."

This time when she closed her eyes a tear slipped out

from beneath her lashes. "You remind me so much of Winston when you do that." She sniffled. "You've reminded me of him all day. When I was seven, we'd had a terrible ice storm, and I slipped going to the privy and broke my arm. The road was too icy for the horses, or to walk, so Winston carried me down the hill on the trail, and then back up after Dr. Dunlop put a splint on it. The doctor said we should stay at his place, but I wanted to come home."

"Of course you did," Crofton whispered. "Every child wants to be at their home." He knew that so well. For years he'd dreamed of returning to Ohio, to his home. To his family. Fighting those ghostly memories, he said, "I'll go get Amelia—maybe she has something that will help you go back to sleep."

Her hold on his hand tightened. "No, please don't leav—bother her. I'll go back to sleep." After a deep breath, she let go of his hand. "You should go to bed, too. It must be late."

"I'm used to not sleeping." He had no idea why he'd chosen to tell her that. Not being able to sleep more than an hour or so at a time had been something he'd long ago gotten over. It had started at the first school his mother had sent him to in England, where the headmaster would roam amongst the beds at night. The one time the man had pulled him from his bed, Crofton had broken loose in the hallway and run. Hadn't stopped until he'd run all the way home. His mother had been very angry, and that had been the first time Thomas Bennett had stood up for him. The compromise had been a new school. There the headmaster hadn't roamed the rooms at night, but Crofton still hadn't been able to sleep. Short catnaps had already become a norm.

"Why?"

"No reason in particular." Reaching behind him, he grabbed a leg of the chair Amelia had sat upon most of the evening and pulled it closer to the bed. "You go to sleep now. I'm going to sit right here until you do, or I'll get Amelia, it's your choice."

Another faint smile briefly tugged at her lips as Sara watched him sit down. "Don't wake Amelia," she said. "I'll go to sleep."

"Then close your eyes," he said, with false sternness.

She complied, but her smile grew.

He grinned, too, and then leaned over and blew out the lamp. The moon shining through the windows provided enough light to see if she moved. He briefly considered cracking the door, just enough for the fresh air to cool the room. Despite the lateness of the year, the weather had barely dropped enough to send bugs into hibernation. It wasn't that way down on his ranch. The bugs lived year-round there, and grew as big as the cattle and bit harder than some snakes. He hadn't minded. Just took the bugs in stride with all the other things that went along with ranching.

That—his ranch and life there—almost seemed like a distant past. He'd only been in Royalton a few days, but he should miss his home, shouldn't he? The people there. It had been his life the past few years. The one thing that he'd taken an interest in.

Disgust tightened his jaw. Evidently not that much of an interest. He'd completely forgotten to send June a wire to let her know what was happening. Not willing to take those thoughts any deeper, he concluded it was just as well. June would expect more news than he had to share. Morton could very well be the one behind Mel's death, and if that was true, Sara was in considerable danger.

That's where his mind was. Not on his ranch, Mel or the railroad. The chip on his shoulder had become an anvil.

This could all have been avoided if he'd been the one to come to Royalton instead of Mel, but he'd been too cowardly.

Cowardly was right. That's exactly what he'd been. He hadn't wanted to face being rejected by his father one more time. Not even for the sake of his ranch, of the ranchers around him. Things would be very different right now if he'd ridden up here months ago, or years. He'd been down in New Mexico two years before moving to Arizona. Two years. But he'd been too stubborn to ride north. He'd even told Mel to let it play out, that eventually the railroad would lay tracks into Arizona. Mel, though, along with June, Gray Hawk and others, had wanted it now, as promised.

Now. He huffed out a breath. Now his father and Mel were dead, Sara had her side stitched up like a cloth doll, and he'd made a fair few enemies. Namely Bugsley Morton. That issue didn't bother him. His father's and Mel's deaths and Sara's injury did. As did the fact that he'd changed Sara's life drastically. If he'd never shown up, she'd have inherited everything. Bugsley would have stepped in and run the mill while she continued to live happily in the home she so sincerely loved. Maybe married one of those poor fools who'd run up the hill asking for her hand.

He didn't like that idea. Of her marrying one of those men. That was practically laughable. Those men thought she was some docile little princess they'd be able to control. He knew better. That was what she portrayed with her serene little smile and meek nods, but he saw behind all that. Had on their first encounter, and again when he'd explained Winston's mathematical notations.

She was brave, too. Lord knows what kind of wild critters she could have encountered on her hike down that mountainside.

Blood daughter or not, she'd inherited some of Winston's grit. Now that he'd taken time to think about all this, whatever wool Morton had already been trying to pull over her eyes, she'd been onto him. That's why she was studying those books so hard.

A smile tugged at his lips and he leaned his head against the back of the chair and closed his eyes. With a bit more knowledge, she'd be a force to be reckoned with—one who might just be more of a match than Morton bargained on. That would be fun to see. Princess Sara turning into Queen Sara overseeing her kingdom.

When Crofton snapped his eyes open, he was surprised to see sunlight filling the room and Amelia standing over him. Sara was awake, too, and fluttered the fingers of one hand at him. He blinked away the lingering film of sleep and fading thoughts of kings and queens, before taking a second look at her. Her cheeks were pink and her eyes shining. How the hell could she look so adorable? So healthy? A few hours ago she'd had a foot-long stick poking out of her side.

Half wondering if he'd dreamt the entire episode, he turned to look at Amelia.

She tossed a shirt at him. Examining the pristine whiteness, he asked, "How'd you get it…" Stopping, he glanced up. There were no mending stitches on the shirt. His had been cut off Sara.

"I didn't," Amelia said, knowing his thoughts. "It was your father's. There's a closet full of his clothes. No sense giving them to someone else when you can wear them. There's a razor in the water closet you might consider using, and coffee downstairs on the stove."

Her tone wasn't harsh, just serious, as if she wasn't in the mood for any disputes. That wasn't new. She'd never been in the mood for disputes.

"I gotta check Sara's stitches," Amelia continued. "If Doc Dunlop shows up before I get downstairs, send him up."

In spite of a lingering headache and an extremely sore side, Sara couldn't stop a smile from forming. Disheveled and sleepy-eyed, Crofton looked even more handsome than when he'd been wearing his ready-made suit. She wasn't sure why that tickled her fancy, but it did. Could be because she knew he'd finally gotten some sleep. For the longest time, every time she'd opened an eye, he'd been sitting in the chair, staring at the door leading to the balcony. The sorrow on his face had made her insides ache more than her injury—at least in a different way. Her side didn't ache. It hurt. There most definitely was a difference.

"How are you feeling this morning?" he asked while rising from the chair.

"Fine," she answered. "You?"

"Me? I'm fine," he answered. "But I always am."

She laughed when he winked one eye, and again as Amelia rolled her eyes toward the ceiling. Placing a hand over her side, Sara told him, "Go get cleaned up and eat. You're making my side worse."

"Can't have that," he said, heading toward the door.

A sense of dread washed over her. What if he took her seriously and never returned?

As if reading her mind, he spun around and winked again. "I'll be back. Don't you two be talking about me while I'm gone. I know it'll be hard, but contain yourselves."

"Shoo," Amelia said. "We got better things to talk about than you."

He left the room, but shouted in his wake, "No, you don't."

"That boy," Amelia said, shaking her head as she closed the door. "Always was just like Winston. Full of himself."

"He certainly reminds me of Winston," Sara said, feeling a bit wistful. "More and more."

"He's the spitting image of his father, that's for sure. Inside and out." Amelia arrived at the side of the bed and carefully folded back the covers. "How are you feeling this morning?"

Sara pulled her eyes off the door and let out a sigh that came from nowhere. "Fine."

"Don't be getting all distressed now," Amelia said. "Nothing got hurt that won't heal. Doc says you'll be fine in no time. Of course, I already knew that, and I'm sure it hurts, that's why I brought up some laudanum. It ain't as bad as it could have been, you know. That stick could have—"

"I don't want any," Sara interrupted, not wanting to think of could haves. "I had a headache all night from what Dr. Dunlop already gave me." Her head had done more than ache all night. She'd had odd thoughts and dreams. All had been centered on Crofton. He'd been sitting beside her bed all night. Still, that shouldn't have made her think so much about the kisses he'd placed on her forehead. They'd been simple touches. Just acts of kindness. Yet, they'd filled her with something far more. A warm tenderness she'd never experienced before. One that made her want to smile.

"That wasn't laudanum Doc gave you. But we'll worry

about that once I've seen your side," Amelia said. "Can you sit up? It'll make taking this wrap off easier."

"I'm sure I can," Sara said.

In the end, sitting up turned out to be one of those things that was far easier said than done. Every muscle she moved seemed to be attached to her side. She was breathing through her nose to keep from groaning aloud by the time she was sitting up, and she found herself wishing Crofton was there to help her. His strength had a gentleness that was as therapeutic as it was accommodating. The pain eased considerably when Amelia stacked the pillows behind her back. The addition of the rolled-up blanket that had been pressed upon her back all night to keep her from rolling onto her side helped, too.

"How's that?"

"Better," Sara admitted. "Much better."

"You're gonna be sore for a while," Amelia said. "You'll want to take it easy."

"I believe you," Sara admitted. "A few minutes ago, I might not have. I felt much better before moving."

"I'm sorry, but I have to get this bandage off. The blood is starting to dry and I don't want it sticking."

"I know," Sara answered. "Go ahead. I'm fine now."

Amelia's smile was soft and gentle, and tenderness filled her eyes. "You've always been such a good girl, Sara. Always putting the concerns of others before your own."

"That's how it should be," Sara answered, glad to think about something besides the tugging happening at her wound while Amelia unwound the strips of bandages around her waist.

"Not always," Amelia said. "It's a good trait, the ability to think of others, but sometimes it's important to think about ourselves. Our own needs and wants."

"I don't have any needs or wants," Sara said automatically.

"Sure you do," Amelia said. "You just don't recognize them. Now, don't take me wrong. Your momma was an amazing person. A beautiful and wonderful lady who loved you dearly. So dearly, she was overly thankful to Winston for bringing you and her here."

Confused and with a sense of concern, Sara asked, "Overly thankful?"

Amelia dipped a cloth in water and then held it against the wound. "Yes, overly thankful. If that man had asked her to fly to the moon and back, she would have found a way to do it."

Even more confused, Sara asked, "What?"

"I was just trying to think of something extraordinary," Amelia said. "Not that I needed to. Winston would never have asked Suzanne to do anything. He never did. He loved her completely, but she, well, I think she thought she wasn't worthy of his love. Because of where and how you and she lived when Winston stumbled across your path. He already owned all this, and I think that scared her. I told her and Winston told her, that he hadn't always had all this. When Nate and Winston met, long before the war and the first mill Winston built, he barely had two coins to rub together. I knew them both back then, Winston and Nate. Winston had a dream, a vision he could see as clearly as you see your hand in front of your face, and he'd stop at nothing to make it come true."

"And Nate?" Sara asked as Amelia lifted the cloth and began removing the last of the bandage.

Amelia sighed. "I loved Nate with all my heart and soul, but without Winston, Nate and I would still be back in Ohio, trying to grow a crop that would never amount to much."

Trying to grasp what Amelia was getting at, Sara asked, "But still alive?"

"No. The Good Lord knows when he puts us on this earth when our time will be up. We don't. Nor do we know how it'll happen. He likes to keep us guessing. And for that matter, trying. Nate was a good man, a wonderful husband, and I would have followed him around the world." She wound the bloody bandage into a roll and set it on the floor. "I was just smart enough to make sure Nate followed Winston. He was my anchor. I knew as long as we were tethered to Winston, Nate and I would have a house over our heads and food on the table."

"Are you saying my mother did the same thing? Tethered herself to Winston so she and I would have a house and food?"

Amelia smiled and shook her head. "No, your mother loved Winston as much as he loved her. Suzanne just…" After rinsing the rag in water and wringing it out, she once again placed it against the wound. "Was afraid. Afraid she might do something to hamper that love. She was afraid you might, too. That's why she imposed upon you to always be on your best behavior. To never make waves. Never upset anyone. To think of others first."

As that thought swirled inside her mind, Sara said, "To never upset Winston." Shaking her head while trying to make sense of it all, she added, "But they were happy together. Always. They never argued."

"No, they didn't," Amelia said. "Yet your mother, the poor dear, never truly understood that neither of you could have ever upset Winston to the point his love for either of you would have faltered."

Sara's thoughts had deepened, and with the consideration flowing along with memories, she saw things in a different light than she had before. Amelia could very well be right. Her mother had been adamant that Winston not be upset, and, as a child, with a child's way of thinking, she'd always wondered why. He'd never done anything that caused her to fear him in any way.

"This looks really good," Amelia said. "Really good."

Lost somewhere in her mind, Sara asked, "What? What looks good?"

"The stitches," Amelia said. "I'll get your mirror."

Curious to see the wound, Sara twisted, but the sting forced her to wait for the mirror.

Arriving back at the bed, Amelia held the mirror so the reflection showed a line of dark criss-cross stitches. The skin was red and in places, purple, and swollen, but a hint of disbelief also entered Sara's mind. It didn't seem bad enough to hurt like it had. Like it did.

"I'm leaving it open until Dr. Dunlop checks it. No sense wrapping it up, just to unwrap it again. I'll get you a clean shift and blouse. Do you need to use the chamber pot?"

"No," Sara answered, still gazing in the mirror. When Amelia took it away, she said, "I'll wear that light blue dress with the yellow flowers. The waist is very loose."

"No, you won't," Amelia said. "You'll have on a blouse, but nothing but your bloomers below the waist."

Thinking of Crofton being in the house, Sara said, "I can't walk around in my bloomers."

"That's right, you can't, and won't." Amelia had moved to the dresser and was lifting out a shift. "It's bed for you all day, young lady."

"I can't lie in bed all day."

"Yes, you can, and will." With a broad grin, Amelia approached the bed again, carrying both the shift and a white blouse, along with a hairbrush. "I'll assign Crofton to sit in that chair all day if that's what it takes to keep you in bed. I know he'll agree, both with insisting you stay in bed and standing guard." Then as if there was no further argument needed, she said, "I'll brush the snarls out of your hair before we get you dressed."

The idea of Crofton sitting in the chair all day, as he'd done all night, sent a tiny quiver up Sara's spine. "I'm sure Crofton has far more important things to do today."

"That won't matter," Amelia said as she continued brushing.

It mattered to Sara. He'd already spent all night in her room, and she didn't want him thinking she needed someone to take care of her all the time. He'd start believing she couldn't do anything on her own. What he thought mattered to her. More and more.

Amelia set the brush on the table beside the bed and lifted up a pair of scissors. "I'm gonna cut the rest of this shift off. Nothing left to save of it after I took the scissors to it yesterday and no sense causing you more pain."

Sara agreed with the no pain part, and held her hair out of the way. Once the shift was cut in two, she pulled her arms out. Her mind was still on Crofton, and the idea of him sitting in her room all day.

One arm at a time, Amelia helped her put on a clean shift and then a blouse, all the while holding the bottoms of both garments to keep them from touching her side. Sara was still buttoning the blouse when a knock sounded on the door followed by Crofton announcing Dr. Dunlop had arrived.

She gave Amelia a nod when the woman's eyes questioned if she was ready, and watched as Amelia walked around the bed and then crossed the room to open the door.

Dr. Dunlop entered, closely followed by Crofton. Her heart skipped a beat. He had shaved, and looked even more handsome. Winston had been handsome, so of course his son was, but no one had ever made her heart skip before.

"How are you feeling this morning, Sara?" Dr. Dunlop asked, rolling up his sleeves as he walked toward the bed.

Pulling her eyes off Crofton, she answered, "Fine. How are you today?"

"Much better now that I see you sitting up and looking as beautiful as ever." Patting the quilt covering her legs, he continued, "Crofton told me you slept most of the night, but did have a headache. How is that now?"

Dr. Dunlop had lived in Royalton for as long as she had. Maybe longer, and over the years, she'd noticed his once black hair turning snow white. It was still as curly as a child's, just fuzzier. She was now taller than him, too. That had happened a few years ago.

Feeling eyes on her—Crofton's as well as the doctor's—she smiled. "The headache is gone."

"Completely?"

On impulse, she touched a temple, testing for the pounding that had been there last night. "Yes." The thought of Crofton once again sitting next to her bed made her feel flushed. "Will I be able to get out of bed today? I fear I'll get sore lying around."

"No, not today," the doctor answered. "I don't want these stitches disturbed, and that will happen if you are up and about." He started removing the pillows behind her. "I'll need you to lie down and rest on your side so I can examine my handiwork."

Sara gingerly turned onto her side, and tried not to flinch at the pain moving caused. Crofton still stood near the door, and she kept her eyes on his boots, somehow thinking that might help. Amelia had walked around to the other side of the bed, and was conversing with the doctor, explaining how she'd soaked the bandage off.

"I'll just cover it lightly this time, so it can dry out a bit," Dr. Dunlop said. "Right after I put some ointment on—I don't want the stitches drying too quickly or the skin will pucker."

"I have that same ointment," Amelia said. "It's good for burns. I get it from Rosalie Winters."

"So do I," Dr. Dunlop answered. "It's good for just about everything. It's all I use."

"She makes it from cottonwood buds," Amelia said.

As hard as she tried, Sara couldn't keep her attention on the doctor and Amelia's conversation. She didn't care what the ointment was made from or who had made it. Crofton had moved. He now stood closer. Right beside the bed, and heat rushed into her cheeks at the idea of him looking at her bare side. Injury or not.

When he took her hand, a case of the jitters ripped through her.

"Tired of all the poking and prodding?" he asked.

"Yes," she answered. "And the stares. I'm not some sideshow on display."

"You aren't?" he asked.

She had to bite back a smile at the humor shimmering on his face, and keeping a straight face was hard as she replied, "No, I'm not."

"I'm almost done, Sara. Just a bit longer," Dr. Dunlop said. "Has this young woman had breakfast yet?"

"No," Amelia answered.

"Hard to heal on an empty stomach," the doctor said. "Work, too."

"Are you hinting that you haven't had breakfast, either?" Amelia asked.

"Didn't have time," the doctor answered. "I was too worried about Sara. Barely slept a wink."

Crofton was grinning at her, and Sara had to smile in return. "I think the least we can do is feed Dr. Dunlop, Amelia," she said. "We can't have the town's only doctor emaciated."

"I agree," Crofton said. "I'll help him finish up if you want to go get breakfast started."

"For your information," Amelia replied, "I just have to fry the eggs."

"To go with the biscuits in the warming oven and the gravy on the stove," Crofton said.

"Yes," Amelia replied, "and—"

"Done," Dr. Dunlop interrupted.

Sara smothered a giggle at the way he winked at her. Dr. Dunlop had always been able to make her laugh. Even that day she'd broken her arm.

After both he and Amelia promised to return shortly, they left the room. Crofton didn't follow. Instead he sat in one of the chairs she and her mother had upholstered to match the rest of the room. They'd spent hours picking out the material and then transforming the room from the little girl's room it had been for years to a young lady's bedroom. Winston had always supported their ideas about decorating the house.

Shifting her attention, she asked, "Aren't you hungry?"

Crofton pressed a finger to his lips and glanced toward the open doorway before whispering, "I ate while I was downstairs."

She shifted slightly, just her head in order to see him better. "Oh? And shaved and got dressed?"

He shrugged. "I'm quick."

Closing her eyes for a lingering moment, she questioned how her pain seemed to go away when he was near. It made no sense, but plenty of things weren't making sense right now. Effects from the awful medicine Dr. Dunlop had given her, no doubt.

"Do you want to sit up?"

Sara opened her eyes, and a bit of fear emerged. Sitting up had hurt earlier, and she wasn't certain she wanted him helping her. Lying on her side all day wasn't a nice thought, either. Weighing her options, she said, "Yes, but could you open the door to the balcony first? I'd like a breath of fresh air. It's rather warm up here. Amelia must have all the fires lit."

"Sure." He stood, but walked to the bed. "I think I'll help you sit up first. Don't want you trying it on your own. You could pull out the stitches."

Certainly not appreciating how he'd read her mind, Sara tried to cover it up. "I wasn't—"

"Yes, you were." He was already removing the blanket roll that kept her from turning onto her injured side. Once it was out of the way, he said, "Now just relax. I'll lift you up so you don't have to work those muscles."

She tried to relax, but when he pulled back the quilt, every muscle in her body quivered. The sheet still covered her, but she felt exposed. He slid is hands beneath her, one under her knees, the other her back, and the tingling inside her increased. Slow and easy, he lifted her off her side and set her back down on her bottom.

"Did that hurt?"

Sara was unable to decipher if there had been any pain or not because the tingles were too great. She hadn't recalled feeling anything like them before. He'd carried her yesterday, and now that she thought about it, that had seemed to take her pain away. As had the way he'd held her hand. Did he remind her so much of Winston that something inside her thought he was her stepfather? That seemed highly unlikely, but there wasn't another explanation.

"No," she answered. "It didn't."

"Good."

After propping the pillows behind her, he pulled the quilt back up, and while folding the top edge over her lap, the back of one of his hands bumped one of her breasts. The connection was brief, but sent a fiery sensation through her so fast she gasped.

He stepped away from the bed. "Now I'll open the door to the balcony."

Heat burned her cheeks, and she was more than thankful that he pretended nothing had happened. His touch had been accidental, but her heart was racing nonetheless.

While he opened the door and stepped onto the balcony, she drew a deep breath and held it for several seconds, trying to gain control of her body and thoughts.

"What's the bowl and the glass for?" he asked.

She let the air out slowly, feeling far more relaxed, mainly because of his change of subject. "The hummingbirds. That's how I feed them."

From where he stood near the railing, he turned around to cast a quizzical gaze her way.

"I put sugar water in the glass and turn it upside down in the bowl. I like watching them while I'm—" Heat once again filled her cheeks at the idea of saying getting dressed. "Making my bed." She brushed her fingers over both sides of her face while adding, "They sit on the side of the bowl and drink the water that seeps out from beneath the glass."

"Hummingbirds?"

"Yes, hummingbirds. You do know what they are, don't you?"

"Yes, I've seen hummingbirds," he said. "I've just never heard of someone feeding them before."

"Well, now you have. They won't come while you're standing out there, though. They're a bit skittish."

"It's winter," he said. "Don't they fly south?"

"Yes. They are usually gone by this time of the year, but not this year. One pair hasn't left yet." She did enjoy those tiny little birds, and didn't mind telling him about them. "I'm hoping one of them isn't injured and can't fly as far as they need to. They will come and eat while I'm out there, but not when anyone else is."

He frowned slightly as he returned to the room, closing the door behind him. "Do you have other friends? Besides hummingbirds?"

Stung, she replied, "I have lots of friends."

He gave one of those nods people use when they really don't believe what has been said.

Sara wasn't sure why the need to defend herself became so strong. "I do. Amelia's my friend, so is Bugsley and Dr. Dunlop. And Walter and Alvin."

"Those are people who work for you, or worked for Winston, I should say. I'm asking personally. Don't you have friends your age?"

"Of course I do. Why?"

He shrugged. "Just curious."

"Why?"

"No reason."

He had a reason—she just didn't know what it was. That was irritating. Her friends were no concern of his, either. She had friends. Lots of them. It was just most of the girls her age had already married and were busy with their husbands and new babies. A few had moved away. Janis Wellstone had. She'd joined a traveling theatre troop that had performed in Royalton last year. Crofton would have thought Janis was pretty. All the boys in school had thought so. Janis had been pretty. Thinking of Janis's long blond hair, Sara ran a smoothing hand over her mass of brown hair. It had a tendency to look a mess—that's why her mother insisted on braiding it all the time as she got older, making sure it was secured in a tight bun. Her mind shifted to how Crofton had pushed stray hairs away from her face yesterday, and again last night.

"What did I smell burning last night?" she asked.

He lifted a brow, most likely at her complete change of topic.

"I smelled smoke, and you said it was just some brush, but it's not the right conditions to burn right now. What was burning?"

"The rubbish pile."

That made no sense. "Why? People gather the scrap wood to burn."

He sat in the chair and crossed his arms while gazing out the window. "I believe it was burned so I wouldn't be able to inspect it any further."

"Inspect what?"

The length of his silence made her think he wasn't going to answer, but then he turned and met her gaze. The contemplation in his eyes made her stomach gurgle.

"The carriage Winston and your mother were in." He sighed heavily. "It had been dragged to the rubbish pile from the accident site. I followed the trail that had been left."

Her heart thudded and her throat grew dry. "I didn't know where it had been taken," she said, as much to herself as him. "I was told the horse had to be put down on the spot, and never questioned where anything had been taken."

"There was no reason for you to," he answered.

There was a hint of condolence in his tone, and that made her nose sting and her eyes burn. A part of her wanted to pull the sheet over her head and let the tears flow. She couldn't imagine a day would come when she didn't feel the loss of her mother and Winston so strongly, even when she told herself that time would eventually come. "But I should have," she said. "I'm the one responsible for everything now, and I should have at least questioned…"

"You didn't need to be concerned with the details."

Sara blinked away the tears before shifting her gaze back to him. "But you did. Why? What didn't someone want you to see?" Her thoughts altered briefly. "Who burned the pile?"

He shrugged.

Thinking aloud, she said, "Bugsley is the only one who could have ordered that, or burned it without…"

The way he nodded caused her to let the rest of her thought remain unspoken. Bugsley would have stopped anyone else from burning it. If only Winston was here—

In an attempt to avoid another rush of loss, she said, "What did you find? And don't lie to me. I don't need any more of that." Along with everything else, a sense of frustration welled inside her. "I don't need any more of anything."

"No, you don't," he said, pushing to his feet. "Except sleep. That you do need."

"No, I don't." She had no idea what had transpired inside her, but all of a sudden she was mad. "Sit down."

He looked at her cautiously while lowering back onto the chair.

"I've just lost my parents, my entire family, and I'm in bed with my side stitched up, and you, Crofton Parks, are going to start answering my questions. I want to know what you found in that rubbish pile. I want to know why you never came to see your father, why you hate him so badly, a man who loved you so much, and…" Her eyes were stinging again and she had to stop long enough to sniffle, before finishing, "I want to know what happened to that big black dog of yours."

Pity filled his eyes as he shook his head. "Sara—"

"Don't," she snapped. "Don't Sara me. I've been told to keep quiet my entire life, and I'm tired of it. I want answers. I want to know what's going on around me. I want…" She truly didn't know what she wanted, but there was a powerful force inside saying it was something, and that he had the answers. "I deserve that much, Crofton," she said. "Don't you think I deserve to know?"

Tears blurred her vision, and continued to trickle from her eyes as fast as she wiped them off her cheeks. Blinking past the blurriness, she was surprised to see him nodding.

"Yes, Sara," he said quietly. "I believe you deserve to know."

The quick clip of footsteps made her wipe away the tears and look the other way when Amelia walked through the open doorway.

"Did I hear shouting? Oh, goodness," Amelia continued without pausing for an answer. "Are you crying, Sara? Why? Are you hurting? What's wrong, honey?"

Sara couldn't do more than shake her head.

"It's my fault," Crofton answered.

"What did you do to her?" Amelia asked while plopping a tray on the bed.

The tray wasn't heavy, but the force with which it was set down, and due to already being skittish toward pain, Sara bit her lips against the idea of more pain. She'd been about to say it wasn't his fault. That he needed to quit taking the blame for everything, but was glad the words hadn't been spoken. Letting him take the blame was easier. Letting him have everything would be easier.

"I told her about the rubbish pile being burnt." Crofton arrived at the side of the bed and removed the tray from her lap.

Always the sensible one, Amelia said, "That's nothing to cry over."

Crofton set the tray on the table between the two upholstered chairs all the while drawing a deep breath to calm the commotion inside him—his head and chest. "She's just lost her parents and is stitched up from her hip bone to her ribs." He hadn't realized he'd used almost the same words Sara had until they echoed in his head. "She's hurting and in pain. Just about any news could make her cry, and rightfully so." Taking Amelia's arm, he turned her toward the door. A part of him said he was the one who should leave, but the other part of him said he had to stay and protect Sara from any additional pain. "Go see to Dr. Dunlop. I'll make sure Sara eats her breakfast."

As good as she was at giving orders, Amelia was not good at taking them, and dug in her heels. "I—"

"Go," he insisted, while tugging on her arm harder. Lowering his voice, he whispered, "Your fussing will only make her feel bad."

With a *humph*, Amelia pulled out of his hold.

He followed her into the hallway.

"Don't go saying anything else to make her cry, or you'll answer to me," Amelia hissed.

"I won't."

"I mean it."

"I know," he said.

"I brought you up a plate, too," she said, glancing

back into the room. "The two biscuits you took out of the warming oven won't be enough to tide you over until lunch."

"Thank you."

She shot him a glare that only held a small portion of anger, and then marched down the hall.

He rocked on his heels for a moment, not quite ready to return to the bedroom. That meek little hummingbird lying in the bed had the fortitude of a hawk when she wanted to. She'd just never been allowed to show it, and he couldn't help but wonder why. Winston had never held anyone back. Walter had proved that when he admitted to barely knowing how to add when Winston hired him. Intrigued, Crofton turned and entered the room.

Her eyes were red-rimmed, but dry as she looked up at him. "Thank you."

"You're welcome." He transferred one plate, cup and silverware from the tray to the table and then carried the tray to the bed. "But you do have to eat." Nodding at the plate, he added, "All of it."

Chapter Ten

Crofton upheld his threat, watching until Sara had swallowed the last bits of her food. He'd eaten his plate clean, too, and stacked her empty one atop his before setting everything on the tray. Leaving it on the table, he moved a chair closer to her bed.

"Feel better?"

She nodded. "Yes, thank you. Amazing how food does that, isn't it?"

"I suspect that's because it takes our mind off other things for a time," he answered.

Her grin was small and fleeting. "I'm sorry I yelled at you."

"Don't be," he said, meaning it. She'd probably never lost her temper on anyone and he didn't mind being the first. "I can't say how I'd behave if I was in your position."

"But you are in my position. Well, you're not in bed with stitches, but your father died, leaving you responsible for..." Her sigh echoed across the room.

"Half of everything he owned," he finished for her.

She squirmed a bit as if uncomfortable, on the inside. Where her soul lived. He recognized it because his was giving him a bit of trouble. There wasn't time for him to worry about this girl. He'd been in town five days and wasn't any closer to discovering who'd killed Mel, and wouldn't learn much today. If the four men who'd trekked up the hill asking about Sara were any indication, going even as far as town was out of the question.

"I've been thinking about that," she said, glancing toward the balcony door, to where the bowl and glass sat on the rail.

Through the glass panes he saw the bowl and glass and had to grin. Leave it to her to figure out a way to feed hummingbirds. In December no less.

"I don't deserve to inherit any of Winston's holdings. You're his son. His blood relative and I'm—"

"Not up to the challenge?" he asked.

Her expression turned harsh, and for a minute he wondered if she'd snap again. He wouldn't mind battling with her, but considering her condition, would rather not. He barely knew her, yet the desire to help her was overriding just about all of his other thoughts. He could understand why so many had trekked up the hill asking for her hand. She was easy to like, and any man would be proud to have her on his arm.

After a thoughtful gaze that ended with a slight shake of her head, she said, "There is no challenge, and I don't want anything. I'll sign whatever I need to sign."

"There's nothing to sign." He rested an elbow on the arm of the chair and set his chin on his fist. "I don't want anything, not half, not all, but, considering what the lawyer said, neither one of us has a choice."

"But Winston would have wanted you to have it," she said with an exuberant amount of passion. "I know he would have."

Crofton ran both hands over his thighs. When she got all emotional he wanted to wrap his arms around her, but couldn't. If he did that, he might kiss her. Not a peck on the cheek, but really kiss her. Where the hell had these yearnings come from? He'd never been known for his chivalry, and had kissed more than his fair share of maidens, but this was out of the ordinary even for him. As was the misery it provided. She was a young innocent girl with more on her plate than she could handle, and all he could think of was her. Kissing her. Holding her. Protecting her.

"You know it, too," she whispered. "Deep down, you know Winston did. Why can't you admit that?"

Crofton stood and walked to the door leading to the balcony, where to his surprise, a hummingbird darted around the bowl. "Maybe he did, and maybe I do." The bird sped away. "But it doesn't matter, does it? He's gone, and I have a ranch that I need to return to. I don't have time for a lumber mill or railroad contracts." Turning about, he added, "And, just as you pointed out to me, let me point out that Winston would have wanted you to inherit his holdings. Perhaps not the mill, or at least the work and responsibilities that go along with it, but he would have wanted you to have the money. To be financially set. Don't try to deny that."

Along with a heavy sigh, she nodded. "You're right." Meeting his gaze, she said, "I guess we're both stuck with it all, whether we want it or not."

Bracing a hand on the door, he nodded in agreement. "Looks that way." The irony of it all had him running his other hand through his hair. "I came here to find who murdered my friend, and he had come here to find out why the railroad pulled the route they'd promised. One that would go down into New Mexico and then west to the coast. It would give all the ranchers down there a way to get their cattle to markets." This wasn't the topic he'd planned on mentioning, but it just shot out, and as long as he'd started, he saw no reason to end. "That had been the plan, but suddenly, that plan changed. With no explanation. Mel had ridden up here, knowing Winston had won the bid to provide the lumber, and hoped there would still be time for some additional negotiations. Rumor had it that the plans had changed due to the lack of lumber in our region. Which didn't make a lot of sense. Winston's bid included shipping the lumber no matter where the tracks led."

She'd been listening closely, and he saw the moment she latched on to the same thing he had. "You thought he changed the route because it would benefit you. Benefit your ranch. Didn't you?"

"Seems as likely as any other reason."

"He didn't know you were alive," she said. "Ralph said there was no way Winston could have responded to that telegram. As far as he knew, you had died in Ohio."

"We don't know that for sure."

"I do," she insisted. "I lived with Winston. If you had been alive, he would have told us. Me, Mother, Amelia. There's no way he would have kept that a secret. I know that with all my heart and soul. And you do, too, if you'd get over your anger at him."

"I hold no anger toward him."

"Yes, you do." Compassion filled her eyes. "He didn't desert you. Deep down, you know that. He was as much a victim as you were. Winston didn't know about that telegram, I'm convinced of that, and he had no idea you were alive."

"Well, someone knew," he said. "Someone knew I was Winston's son, and…" His thoughts faltered briefly, in a direction he hadn't gone down before, yet had to.

"And what?" she asked.

It was just a hunch, but a solid one. "And that same someone wanted to make sure Winston didn't discover it." Conviction rolled inside him like a boulder let loose atop a hill. "Someone didn't want him to know I was alive."

"What do you mean?"

He held up a hand, giving his mind a chance to play out. Things were falling into place and he needed a moment to let them settle. It made too much sense. Way too much sense. Crossing the room, he sat in the chair and scratched at his tingling scalp. This was something he hadn't considered until now.

"When I returned to America after being deported, after confronting my mother and learning the whole truth, or as much of it as I could believe, I considered coming straight to Royalton, but I didn't want to show up with no money, no future. I wanted..." Frustrated, he stood. "I wanted to be someone my father could be proud of."

"Winston wouldn't have cared about that. He would have been proud of you just for being you."

She was so innocent, so naive. He, on the other hand had been hardened by life, and that was hard to explain, especially when a part of him felt extremely vulnerable. What was it about her that brought up things inside him he barely recognized? For whatever reason, she did, and she made him want to tell her things he normally wouldn't have shared with anyone. Tell her how his mother had convinced him, alive or dead, Winston wanted nothing to do with him. How that had driven him to prove he didn't need a father, didn't need Winston Parks. That's what had been behind his ranch. The drive to be successful despite all the stumbling blocks life had shoved in his path.

"That may be true," he said, "but there was no reason for me to believe it. So, I started working my way West. I got a job with the railroad, but there wasn't a future in that for me. I wanted more. Something of my own. Cattle are what I chose. I ended up at a ranch in Texas and that's where I met Mel. We worked for the same outfit. When we heard about the promised railroad tracks heading down into Arizona, we gathered up the few head of cattle we'd both managed to acquire and headed West. After claiming neighboring plots in Arizona, we focused on building our herds."

"Winston certainly would have been proud of all you've accomplished."

He stood and crossed the room again to look out the balcony door. Another hummingbird—or maybe the same one—fluttered near the bowl. He sighed. "We'll never know if Winston would have been or not." Turning about, a truth he'd never let known—had barely admitted to himself—came forth. "I never shied away from using my name."

"You hoped Winston would hear about you."

Not certain he wanted to believe that was true, he instead chose to admit, "Someone heard about me." Frustrated, he didn't let the thought stop there. "And I'd bet a week's wages it was Bugsley Morton, and now he's burned the rubbish pile so I can't prove that someone had tampered with that buggy."

"T-tampered? Fath— Winston's buggy? No."

Her stuttering hit him like a bullet. He hadn't meant to tell her that. What was it about her that turned him into a blubbering idiot? Arriving at the bedside, he eased the pillows away from her back. "You've been up too long. A nap is in order."

"Don't do this to me, Crofton," she said. "Don't treat

me like—like I'm a child or...a china doll with no brain. Don't treat me like everyone else does."

The sadness and frustration on her face struck yet another chord inside him. She'd lived most of her life as Winston's daughter. Someone to admire, but not touch, not talk to. That couldn't have been easy, and wouldn't have been if she'd been a male.

"Why do you say the buggy was tampered with? What did you see?"

He rubbed his head, but couldn't stop his lips from moving. "The right reach brace had been sawed, not in two, but enough that when the buggy took the first turn, the weight snapped it."

"How—"

"A saw blade leaves marks."

She shook her head. "You can't believe Bugsley—"

"Yes, I can," he said. "Think about it? Who else would gain from Winston's death? Who else would want to make sure Winston never learned I was alive? You may think he's your friend, but I—"

A knock on the door stopped his rant, which was just was well. She wouldn't believe his thoughts about Bugsley.

The door opened and Dr. Dunlop walked in. "How are you feeling? Better after eating?"

Sara glanced toward Crofton—what he'd said was swirling inside her head, but manners had her pulling up a smile for the doctor. "Yes, thank you."

"That's good to hear," he said. "I'm heading back down the hill now, but I'll return this evening to check on you."

"Supper is served at six," she told him.

He grinned. "I know. I already obtained an invitation."

"That he did," Amelia said from the doorway. "Now tell her about company."

"What about company?" Crofton asked before she could open her mouth. "What company?"

"She's had several people asking about her condition," the doctor answered. "But Amelia sent them away. It's best for Sara to remain in bed and rest today."

"It certainly is," Crofton replied. "Who was here?"

"Just a few callers," Amelia said.

"Who?"

Crofton sounded overly harsh. She understood his frustration, and in part, why he thought what he did, but it couldn't be true. Bugsley would never have purposefully kept Winston from knowing Crofton was alive, and he certainly wouldn't have tampered with the buggy. Crofton must be mistaken.

"It doesn't matter," Amelia said. "I sent them away."

"Damn good thing you did," Crofton answered. "Fools. Did they think we'd let them come up here? Into her bedroom to ask for her hand in marriage? Is every man in the town a harebrained idiot?"

"No," Sara answered sternly. "They are not. And neither am I."

The room went completely silent and the air grew uncomfortable, but she never pulled her gaze off Crofton. He didn't pull his off her, either. The connection didn't scare her. It actually gave her insight, a strength she'd never acknowledged before. She'd prove him wrong. Wrong about Winston, wrong about Bugsley and the community and wrong about her.

Amelia cleared her throat. "I think it's time for Sara to take a nap. Crofton, will you walk the doctor out?"

He didn't answer verbally. Just gave a nod and started

for the door. Dr. Dunlap bade them goodbye before following Crofton out the door.

Sara waited until the door was closed and then told Amelia, "I am going to take a nap. You can leave, too."

"What's wrong? What did Crofton say now?"

"Nothing. I'm tired and going to take a nap. Rest. Just as the doctor suggested."

Amelia frowned but said no more as she removed the pillows. Sara didn't wait for help. She eased herself down on the bed, noting the pain wasn't nearly as bad as she expected. Maybe that was because she wasn't thinking about her injury.

She waited a few minutes after Amelia left before flipping back the covers and gingerly climbing off the bed. Her side was sore. More than sore. It hurt. But there was something she needed to do. Two somethings. A trip to the outhouse was the first. The second was to visit Winston's office. He'd made notes about the railroad going south, and she had to find them again. She'd scanned through so many packets she wasn't sure where she'd read it, or exactly what Winston had written, but when Crofton mentioned it, her mind recalled seeing a note about that southern route somewhere.

Moving slowly and cautiously, she crossed the room and took a dressing gown off the hook on the inside of the armoire door. Getting fully dressed was out of the question. Both because of the amount of pain it might cause, and in the time restraints. Kitchen duties would only keep Amelia busy for so long.

Upon entering the hall, she heard voices coming from the front foyer. Crofton's and Amelia's. Hoping they'd remain there for a time, she went in the opposite direction, taking the back staircase. By the time she exited the house, the stiffness was wearing off, and she'd adjusted her stride to compensate for the soreness of her side.

The kitchen was still empty when she returned from the outhouse, and a quick surveillance of the front parlor revealed Crofton and Amelia were now on the front porch. He was walking down the steps with Amelia following. Thanking her lucky stars—at least she hoped they were her lucky stars—for if either Crofton or Amelia saw her she'd be shooed back up to bed, Sara made her way into the office.

There she closed the door and took a moment to listen to the silence before making her way to the desk. She pushed aside the leather-bound ledgers before opening the bottom drawer. The one that held correspondence with the railroad. Letters and telegrams, and several sheets of paper containing Winston's handwriting.

This had to be where she'd seen his notes on the southern track. Thinking it had nothing to do with his current contract, she hadn't spent much time reading them before.

She'd prove to Crofton that Winston hadn't had anything to do with preventing the rails from going south. Perhaps then he'd be able to remember his father as the kind and loving man he had been. That's how she would always remember Winston. He was as much a victim in what his first wife had done as Crofton. How someone could have done that to people they loved was inconceivable. His mother had though, and that explained why he'd think the worst of Winston. Trusting or believing the best of anyone must be difficult for him. Realizing that made her heart hurt. Hurt for Crofton.

Settling into convincing him not all people were like his mother, Sara started reading.

Her breath caught in her lungs several times, not because of what she was reading, but at the sound of someone knocking. A sigh of relief exhaled each time she realized it was on the front door and not the office door. Soon she didn't even notice if the knocking had stopped or not. What she was reading wasn't what she'd expected.

"What do you think you are doing?"

Sara snapped her head up so fast a sharp sting ripped down her side. Pressing a hand against a burning sensation that let her know where each stitch was located, she grimaced at Amelia storming across the room.

Crofton wasn't far behind.

"I—"

"You're supposed to be in bed," Amelia interrupted. "I couldn't believe it when Crofton said you weren't up in your room."

He hadn't spoken yet. Didn't need to. His eyes said it all. He was as mad as Amelia.

Her thoughts instantly turned back to what she'd read and she quickly gathered the letters and telegrams. "I—I had to go to the outhouse and determined sitting up felt better than lying down, but I'm tired now." Dumping everything into the still open drawer, she added, "I'll go lie down."

"You better believe you will," Amelia said. "And you won't be getting out of your bed for the rest of the day."

Pushing the drawer closed, Sara gingerly stood. "I'll just lie down on the sofa."

"No, you won't," Amelia insisted. "If you can't manage the stairs, Crofton will carry you."

"I can manage the stairs just fine," Sara stated. "I just don't want to. I'll need to go outside again shortly."

"We have chamber pots for such things," Amelia said, taking Sara's arm in a firm hold.

Sara refused to take a step. "Which would be more uncomfortable than walking to the outhouse." She hadn't used a chamber pot for years, and had no desire to change that. Although her cheeks were burning at speaking about such things in mixed company, she wasn't about to leave the office. Not when anyone could pull out the letters she'd just read. Namely Crofton.

He was still staring at her, but his expression had changed, which made her swallow hard. There was no way he could know what she'd read, and she had to make sure he didn't discover those letters until after she had talked with Bugsley. A letter to Winston suggested one of his men had accompanied the railroad on a survey of the southern route and ultimately it sounded as if that was why the track was canceled. Bugsley would know who had gone on the survey expedition, and why the route had been determined unfeasible.

"Tell her, Crofton," Amelia said. "Tell her she has to go up to her room."

After a lengthy and silent pause, he shrugged. "The sofa's large enough. She can take a nap on it."

As relief flooded her, Sara nodded. "Thank you." Hoping they would both leave her alone, she skirted around the desk and walked toward the sofa.

"That sofa isn't large—"

"Will you go get Sara a pillow and blanket?" Crofton interrupted Amelia. "I'm sure that will make her more comfortable."

Sara lowered onto the sofa carefully because her side was throbbing, but watched the exchange between the other two. Amelia wasn't happy, and Crofton, well, he was acting a bit strange. Secretive. It had been a few hours since she'd entered the office, and began to wonder what he'd been doing during that time.

"Do you need anything else?" he asked. "A drink of water or something to eat?"

"No," Sara answered, growing uncomfortable in her own skin. "I'm fine."

He crossed the room and stopped near the sofa. "Need help lying down?"

"No, I'll manage," she answered, folding the edges of her dressing gown tighter across her stomach.

"Then swing around." Without warning, he bent down and lifted her legs.

"I can manage," she repeated, but it was too late. He guided her legs onto the sofa and by default her body followed.

After setting her legs on the sofa, he removed the leather-soled slippers she'd received for Christmas last year. Pale green and made of silk, they matched her dressing gown. Heat infused her skin from where he held first one and then the other ankle. She wasn't only speechless; she was thoughtless due to the sensations rippling up her legs.

"Aw, here comes your pillow and blanket." His smile was far from genuine.

Hesitant, Sara dragged her gaze toward the doorway to watch Amelia enter and walk to the sofa. Soon there was a pillow behind her head and a blanket covering her from chest to toes.

"There now," he said. "Are you comfortable?"

Nodding was about all she could muster. There was something going on with him, but she had no idea what.

"Good, then just take a nap," he said. "Amelia and I will make sure you aren't disturbed."

They were almost to the door before her sanity kicked in. "Wait. If Bugsley comes to visit, please wake me. I need to talk with him."

Far more compliant than she expected, Crofton said, "Of course." He then pulled the door shut.

The tingles now encompassed her head. Sleep was the last thing she could do.

Chapter Eleven

Amelia, still grumbling about how Sara needed to be upstairs, walked across the foyer and into the dining room. With his hand still on the doorknob, Crofton counted to thirty before he twisted the knob and pushed open the door.

Just as he suspected, Sara was on her way across the room. She stopped and stared at him with guilt written across her face more boldly than a newspaper's headline.

"Suddenly not tired?" he asked.

"I…"

She clearly couldn't come up with an excuse, so he gave her the truth. "Wanted to make sure no one discovers what you were reading?" It would be far easier to be mad at her if she wasn't so adorable. She'd been caught red-handed and didn't know what to do about it.

He did.

Taking her arm, he led her back to the sofa. "You can sit right here and tell me all about it."

She sat, but said, "I have nothing to tell."

Taking a seat in one of the chairs, he scooted it a bit closer to the sofa, making it difficult for her to escape. "You don't?"

She shook her head. There wasn't as much fear in her eyes as worry, and that struck him. Made him wonder who she was so worried about. He had a good inkling. And that irritated him to the core. "Your friend Bugsley won't be stopping by today."

That got a reaction. Her eyes narrowed. "What did you say to him?"

"I didn't say anything to him." He sat back and took a moment to contemplate why she had such commitment to Bugsley when it was clear the other man wasn't on her side. At least not for her benefit. "I would have said plenty to him," Crofton replied. "If I'd found him. It appears he's gone into hiding."

"Into hiding? What's that supposed to mean?"

"It means he knows I'm onto him."

"There's nothing to be onto," she insisted. "Bugsley—"

"Set the rubbish pile on fire last night," he interrupted, in no mood to listen to her stand up for the man. "While you were digging into Winston's desk drawers, I went to town. No one has seen Bugsley since last night, when he lit the pile on fire according to Walter, who by the way sends his utmost apologies for firing those shots yesterday. He hopes you forgive him." The clerk was sincerely sorry for what had happened. There had been tears in his eyes when he spoke about it this morning.

"Of course I forgive him," she said. "It was an accident."

"Partially an accident."

"What does that mean?"

"You falling on that stick was an accident," he explained. "Walter firing off those shots wasn't. Bugsley had been upstairs, in Winston's office, and shouted down that someone was snooping around the rubbish pile and ordered Walter to chase them off. Walter thought it odd, since people were always picking up the scrap lumber for kindling, but followed orders." Crofton's jaw tensed as he chose not to tell her more about that. He'd been in Winston's office at the mill. Visited it again just today, and anyone looking out that window would clearly have seen her crossing that clearing. Bugsley may have been too busy watching him examine the buggy, but his gut told him that hadn't been the case. Bugsley clearly hadn't wanted her to get any closer to that pile. It may be because he didn't want her to see the wreckage, but, if that was the issue, ordering Walter to scare her off with gunfire seemed a bit extreme.

"Maybe he thought whoever it was might fall and get hurt."

Fueled by his own thoughts and fury, Crofton shot to his feet. "What is it about Morton that you can't see beyond?"

Bounding off the sofa, she asked, "What is it about Winston that you can't see beyond?"

"This is no longer about Winston," he shot back. "It's about Bugsley Morton."

"A man Winston hired. A man he trusted. No one knows more about Winston's business than Bugsley. If we want to know why Winston decided against the southern route, we need to ask Bugsley."

Prepared to argue Bugsley had the most to gain by Winston's death, Crofton's mind stalled momentarily at her words. Although he suspected it, a part of him hadn't wanted to believe it. "How do you know Winston decided against the southern route?"

Slowly, as if exhausted, she lowered onto the sofa. "Because I read the correspondence he had with the railroad. It appears he sent a man with the surveyors, and afterward said he wouldn't have anything to do with a southern line."

"What correspondence?"

She pressed her hands onto the sofa as if to stand again.

Remembering her injury, he grasped her wrists. "Stay there. I'll get them. They're in the desk drawer, aren't they?"

"Yes, the lower left."

Her sorrowful expression aroused something deep inside him. Leaning forward, he kissed her forehead. "We aren't enemies, Sara. We're in this together. My arrival has opened a can of worms, a dangerous can, and that danger won't end until I—we discover who is behind all this."

She frowned. "You truly believe you—we are in danger?"

"Yes, I do, and I don't believe Winston's death was an accident."

"But that was before you arrived."

"Someone knew I was on my way." Having said more than he should have, for she was injured and didn't need more to worry about, he took a hold of her shoulders. "Lie down. You do need to rest."

"No—"

"Yes," he insisted. "Amelia will have my scalp if she comes in and you aren't resting. Lying down, resting."

She gave in with a heavy sigh, reclining against the pillow.

He covered her with the blanket before telling her, "I'm going to get those letters out of the desk, but I'll bring them over here so you can look through them, too."

It may have been a peace offering, or just a way to make sure she did rest for a bit, he wasn't exactly sure.

Either way, that's what he did, and together they spent the afternoon reading through Winston's stack of correspondence with the railroad.

Amelia had delivered lunch to them in the office. Shortly after eating and receiving a reprimand from Amelia—who gave him one, too—Sara dozed off.

Crofton rose and walked to the window to stretch his legs. The letters hadn't provided much information. Just that one of Winston's men had surveyed a proposed route for the southern tracks and, as she'd said, Winston then said he wouldn't be a part of it. There wasn't an explanation of any sort. The ranchers hadn't been given one, either. Just told that the railroad had changed its mind.

Placing both palms on the windowsill, his gaze landed on the lumber mill. Could it just be a coincidence? That the railroad pulling out of the southern line really had nothing to do with him? That his father hadn't known about his ranch? That no one knew he was Winston's son?

If that was the case, why was Mel killed?

He closed his eyes for a moment, trying to gather all the bits and pieces that didn't seem to fit together correctly. His gut told him he'd have to find Morton to solve the puzzle.

As he opened his eyes and his gaze once again fell upon the mill, he squinted to pinpoint on what he'd thought was a cloud of steam. It was growing rather than dissipating and turning blacker by the second.

Cursing beneath his breath, he spun and ran from the room.

"What's wrong?" Amelia asked as he darted around her in the foyer.

"The mill's on fire."

"Oh, dear!" She grabbed his arm just as he opened the front door. "There's a trail behind the chicken coop.

The one Sara used yesterday. It'll get you there faster than a horse."

He rushed out the door, down the steps and around the house. He easily found the trail. It was wide enough he didn't need to worry about tree limbs smacking him, but thoughts of Sara using this trail yesterday filtered in and out. It was steep in places, with downed trees and ruts. She could have been injured—worse than she had been.

The farther downhill he ran, the stronger the smoke smell grew. Small critters, squirrels, raccoons and several families of rabbits scampered up the trail, dodging into the woods when they encountered him on their pathway. Crofton ran faster, fearing the entire mill was already engulfed in flames.

Shouts filled the air as he entered the clearing and through the growing smoke he could make out a water brigade forming. Arriving at the mill, he shouted at several men too stunned to move. "Get shovels, axes, anything you can find to break up the dirt and throw it on the flames! The office is already on fire! The mill itself will be within minutes if we don't hold it back!"

As those men scrambled, he yelled at others near the stables, "Get those horses out of here!"

Black smoke rolled through the air like an ocean wave, burning his eyes and throat, and the heat was enough to scald the hair off a hog. The clanging of a bell had him squinting through the smoke and then rushing toward the horse-drawn fire wagon rolling into the yard. "Over there! Next to the water wheel! Water down the mill first!"

Crofton continued shouting commands, putting order to the chaos of men not sure where to start, and soon they were all working together, like a colony of ants. They fought the fire with dirt, water, shovels and axes.

During his time sailing, he'd learned men didn't become as fatigued if they rotated duties, therefore, he shouted for the water brigade to switch with those using shovels and axes, and for those manning the pump atop the fire wagon to swap with those holding the hose.

He took turns at each job, until his back, arms, legs or hands began to cramp and then ordered another rotate. Each swap became smoother, and not a single man slowed down—everyone continued pushing themselves to the limit.

His muscles burned, his eyes stung and watered so profusely he could barely see, but he pushed harder, even though it seemed they weren't making any progress, that the flames would win. It felt as if hours had passed, when, almost as if someone had turned the page in a picture book, the flames began to subside.

"She's dying!" he shouted. "She's dying!"

Renewed by the sight, and the idea victory was close at hand, Crofton had the energy to pump the hand pump atop the fire wagon faster and harder. Others were rejuvenated as well. Their shouts of triumph filled the air until the very last flicker was snuffed.

Crofton's eyes still stung, but the air that had been black a short time ago was once again clear, full of sunshine. He hopped off the top of the wagon and once on the ground, took a long moment to survey the damage.

He twisted about when someone slapped his back. Other than the whites of his eyes and teeth, the man's face was black with soot. It wasn't until the man spoke that he recognized Walter's voice. "The office is gone, but we saved the mill."

"That's nothing shy of a miracle."

Crofton had no idea who the man was that had said that. Like Walter, and him, everyone was soot covered.

"What happened?" he asked. "Where'd the fire start? How'd it start?"

Walter shook his head. "I don't know. One minute all was fine, the next flames were shooting in the window above my desk."

"From the back side of the building?" Crofton clarified.

Walter nodded. "Think it was an ember from the rubbish pile? There was nothing else back there."

"No," Crofton answered. "I checked that over this morning. There wasn't even a warm ash."

Covered in soot, sweat, and in some cases, dripping wet from the water they'd pumped and bailed out of the river, others gathered around, assessing the damage and asking how it had started.

"Good job, gentlemen," Crofton said, praising their efforts. It had taken all of them to salvage what they had, and he appreciated each and every one of them. "The entire mill would be gone if not for all of you. I can't thank you enough."

"What caused the fire?"

Turning to see who asked the question, Crofton scanned the crowd of townspeople gathered near the entrance of the mill. One walked forward with a pad of paper in one hand and a pen ready to start writing in the other. Not so much as a speck of dust darkened Elliott Cross's suit.

Crofton walked toward the newspaper man. "We haven't had time to discover that yet, Mr. Cross, but I'm sure you'll learn what it was as soon as we do."

"Where's Bugsley Morton?" Cross asked, scanning the group of men. "He wasn't in the office building, was he? Trapped inside the blaze?"

"No," Walter answered. "No one was trapped inside the building."

"Then where is he?" Cross asked.

Crofton couldn't think of one reason why that would be Cross's top concern, and as mutterings from the others surrounding them started to grow, he said, "Bugsley's whereabouts are the least of our worries right now, Mr. Cross." Speaking loud enough for all to hear he continued, "Unless you're willing to get dirty, I suggest you take your pen and paper back to your office." Turning about, he then gestured toward several men. "Start rummaging through the debris. Make sure there aren't any hot spots." Pointing out several others, he said, "Inspect every inch of the mill, top to bottom. Make sure there aren't any embers smoldering."

Just like when he'd arrived, no one questioned his authority, and scattered, other than the newspaper man.

Lifting his chin, Cross said, "I'll need an interview as soon as you know anything. The citizens of Royalton will expect a full report."

"And you'll give it to them," Crofton answered. He had no reason to dislike the man, but he did. Cross was one of several who'd offered their hand in marriage to Sara. The desire to turn about and glance up the hill hit Crofton, but he kept his gaze on Cross.

"Of course I'll give it to them. That's my job. Your father appreciated both me and my newspaper."

"I'm sure he did," Crofton lied. A businessman rarely appreciated a newspaper man like Cross. One who wrote to sell papers, not to tell the truth.

Tucking his pad of paper and pen in his pocket, Cross nodded. "I'll be at the newspaper office when you're ready for that interview."

Crofton didn't bother with a response. He spun around,

found Walter among the men shoveling aside burnt boards and made his way in that direction. There was nothing left of the office other than a heap of charred remains. He began kicking into the rubble, looking for any signs of embers, but stopped when a wire caught on the toe of his boot.

The wire was still connected to a frame that had been burned to nothing more than a single corner. It had to have been one of the pictures that had hung in Winston's office.

A gut-wrenching fireball landed in the very base of Crofton's spine and spun there, tearing up more emotions than he'd experienced in years. Not since he'd been a child. Not since he'd said goodbye to his father that fateful morning years ago.

Blinking against the sting in his eyes, he glanced up the hill. The brick mansion stood there, as pristine and audacious as ever, but for the first time since arriving in Royalton, a profound loss filled him. His father was dead. Gone. It wasn't a lie this time. It was the cold, hard truth.

He glanced back down at the wire still caught on his boot. If he could be thankful for one thing, it was that Winston hadn't lived to see this. Didn't know someone was out to sabotage all he'd worked so hard to build.

Chapter Twelve

Sara wasn't sure what annoyed her more—the fact she'd slept through the burning of the mill office, not being able to go assess the damage for herself, or how Crofton had barely been home the past two days.

Her side was doing much better, but Dr. Dunlop still refused to allow her to travel even as far as town. He claimed the bouncing of a wagon could rip out her stitches, as could walking that far. And of course, whatever the doctor said, Amelia enforced.

"I think we'll wait supper a few minutes tonight, until Crofton arrives. He's had cold meals the past couple of days."

Turning and giving Amelia a glare, Sara said, "No, we won't. The evening meal has always been served at six o'clock in this house and will continue to be. Crofton knows that. It's his choice to miss meals."

Puckering her lips, Amelia hissed and shook the wooden spoon in her hand. "You sure have become snippety the past couple of days. It would do you a bit of good to remember if not for Crofton, you wouldn't have a mill right now. The entire town realizes that. Why don't you?"

Holding in a sigh, Sara said, "He didn't put the fire out by himself."

"Practically," Amelia insisted. "Ask anyone. Walter told you how Crofton ran down that hill and started shouting orders. So did Dr. Dunlop."

"I know what people told me," she said. "And I know how someone let me sleep through it."

Turning about to stir the pot of stew, Amelia said, "There wasn't anything you could do about it, and you needed the rest. It was only a day after you'd been stitched up."

"I remember exactly when it happened, and whether I could do anything or not isn't the point."

"Then what is? That Crofton saved the day? You should be glad you have a brother like that."

"He's not my brother!" she snapped. Walter had called Crofton her brother when visiting her and it goaded her like nothing ever had. "And he didn't save the day."

"Think what you want." Amelia set the spoon down and grabbed a potholder to open the oven door. "Your mother certainly wouldn't approve of the attitude you've had lately."

Sara ignored the flash of guilt that bubbled inside her stomach, and finished loading the tray with plates and bowls.

"Don't think about lifting that," Amelia said, pulling a pan of yeast rolls from the oven.

The idea of doing just that, if for no other reason than she was tired of being told what not to do, crossed her mind. So did the idea of Dr. Dunlop lecturing her once he heard about it. "I wasn't going to lift it," she said. "Lord knows I don't want to be held hostage in this house any longer than necessary."

Amelia huffed as she picked up the tray.

Grabbing the butter dish and napkins, Sara followed Amelia into the dining room. The guilt in her stomach had grown. It wasn't like her to be so aggravated or rude, and her mother certainly wouldn't approve of it. "I'm sorry to be so grumpy," she said. "It's just frustrating. Not knowing what's happening."

"You know what's happening," Amelia said. "How they've already cleaned up the debris and have started building the new office building. You can see it from the window."

She could, and had. She'd watched both the clearing away of burned boards and the framework of the new one going up from the window in the office and from her balcony. It didn't satisfy her, though.

"It's not like you could do anything down there," Amelia said.

"I know."

"If you want to know more, ask Crofton."

"When am I supposed to do that?" she snapped. "He comes home after I'm asleep and leaves before I'm awake."

"So that's what's bothering you."

"Yes. No." Confused, she shook her head. "I'm responsible for carrying out Winston's dream. How can I do that if I don't know what's going on?"

Amelia shook her head.

"What?" Sara asked.

"Winston would not have expected you to carry out his dream," Amelia said. "He'd already done that. That mill was his dream."

"His first dream," Sara said. "Building the railroad all the way to the border and beyond was his new dream. That's the one I'm talking about."

"Honey, that mill wasn't Winston's first dream. He had many, and fulfilled them. One of which was to see you and your mother happy. That's what he would still want. For you to find your own dream and make it come true."

"Maybe that's my dream then, to see his final one come to fruition."

Amelia shook her head again. "You're too much like your mother."

"You say that like it's a bad thing," Sara said, following Amelia back into the kitchen.

"Because in this instance, it is," Amelia answered. "Don't live your life making someone else happy. Make yourself happy."

"Who says I'm not happy?"

After lifting down a platter for the yeast rolls, Amelia turned around, but just as she opened her mouth, the sound of the front door opening made her close it. With a smile, she said, "Crofton's home. Go tell him supper will be on the table in a few minutes."

"I'm sure he knows that," Sara said, mainly because she was trying to tell her insides to calm down. A part of her wanted to run and greet him much like she used to Winston, which was utterly ridiculous.

"Then go see if he wants a drink or something before we eat," Amelia said. "A man returning home after a long day at work deserves to be greeted upon his arrival."

A jarring memory flashed inside Sara's mind, of how her mother always hurried to meet Winston as soon as he walked through the door. She'd kiss his cheek and ask him how his day was.

"Go on," Amelia said. "Remember your upbringing. Who you are."

Sara remembered who she was, and what she needed to do. She just wasn't overly happy about any of it right now.

Crofton wasn't in the foyer when she arrived, but in

Winston's office. The clank of the glass stopper said he was helping himself to a drink.

It was as if she had two people battling inside her when it came to Crofton. One who wanted to dislike everything about him, and one who understood he had more right to be in this home, to claim everything of Winston's far more than she did. That part of her was also drawn to him. Admired how much he was like his father. How strong and admirable, and kind and caring.

She didn't know what to do about either person inside her.

"Feeling better today?"

Her breath caught at the sound of his voice, and the sight of him standing in the office doorway made her heart tumble. The effect he had on her, inside and out, was as hard to understand as the two invisible people inside her.

"You certainly have more color," he said before lifting the glass in his hand to his lips.

Finding the ability to speak, or at least the manners her mother had instilled upon her, she said, "Thank you. I am feeling much better. Dr. Dunlop says the stitches can come out in a day or two."

"He told me that."

"When?"

"Today. He stopped at the mill after seeing you this morning. He's very impressed with his handiwork. Says you'll hardly have a scar."

Her face heated up at the idea of Dr. Dunlop discussing her body with Crofton.

"But only if you continue to follow his orders."

He would have to include that, even though he knew she'd followed the doctor's orders on all accounts. Amelia tattled to him constantly. Changing the subject to something she did want to talk about, Sara said, "It appears the rebuilding of the mill office is going well."

His sleeves were rolled up to his elbows and his dark hair was brushed back from his face, indicating he'd washed before entering the house, but the sawdust clinging to the bottom of his pants said he'd been working all day.

"It is." He nodded toward the dining room before taking a step toward her. "And I'm starving. Whatever Amelia has cooked smells delicious."

"Beef stew." Sara's insides were acting up again, fluttering about as he walked closer. "A-and buns, and candied apples."

"Yum." He took a hold of her elbow. "Shall we?"

She nodded, unable to do much more.

"Is your side hurting?"

"No," she answered honestly, while also trying to make her feet cooperate.

"Aw, so you're that stiff because you're still mad at me."

Sara bit on her bottom lip to keep from replying as they arrived in the dining room. She certainly was still angry, but couldn't say it was at him. Everything seemed to upset her. And confuse her.

Not having done anything that would have built up an appetite, she pushed her food around on her plate and listened with only one ear as Amelia and Crofton talked about the food, the weather that was still unseasonable and old memories. That bothered her, too. She was tired of this. Tired of not having any idea of what to do, how to do it or how to feel about it.

"You've barely touched your food," Amelia said. "You'll never heal if you don't eat."

Would it matter if she did heal? Not really. Crofton had

taken over the mill. Amelia had the house as clean and neat as ever, meals on the table, even had started putting up Christmas decorations. Alvin took care of the outside chores and hauling in wood. There was truly nothing here that needed her. Then again, nothing ever really had.

"Sara, do you not like the stew?"

Glancing at Amelia, Sara set her fork down. "It's delicious. I'm just not hungry."

With a thoughtful expression, Crofton set his napkin on the table. "In that case, would you mind joining me in the office? I need to talk to you."

Not sure she wanted to talk to him, or anyone, she asked, "About what?"

"The lumber mill," he said.

Of course that's what it was about. What had she expected him to say? She did want to know what was going on, or at least should, but if being completely honest, she didn't. Yet, this wasn't about what she wanted. Nodding, she pushed away from the table.

"Why don't you two talk on the porch instead?" Amelia asked. "We won't have weather like this much longer. The fresh air would be good for Sara. I'll bring you out some tea."

Crofton looked at her, and Sara shrugged, not really caring.

He once again took her arm, causing her insides to quiver and her knees to quake. Tired of that, too, she wondered if she needed to talk to Dr. Dunlop. Maybe something else had happened to her when that stick poked her.

The sun was dropping behind the mountaintops in the western skyline, giving off a breathtaking view. She used to like that, sitting out here after the evening meal, watching the sun set. Mother and Winston would sit at the table and she'd sit on the settee, usually stitching on one of the embroidery pieces mother insisted she restitch until getting it perfect.

"You know what I've been thinking about today?" Crofton asked.

"No," Sara answered. "I've been here all day."

He grinned, but then his expression grew solemn. "I've been thinking about my first trip to England."

"When you were little?"

"Yes, I don't remember much about it, not just because I was only eight—I remember plenty of other things from back then, before then. I don't remember much about that trip because I didn't care. I didn't care where we were going, what I ate, if I ate, who talked to me, who didn't. Things that used to matter didn't. My entire life had changed, and I didn't like anything about it."

Sara wasn't totally sure why he was telling her this, but considering how she felt, was inclined to know more. "When did things change—I mean when did things become normal again?"

A small table was between them and he reached across and laid his hand on top of hers resting on the arm of the chair. His touch was warm and made her skin tingle, but there was also comfort in it.

"What's normal? Life is always changing, and in many ways, it's what we want."

More confused than ever, Sara asked, "It is?"

"Yes," he answered. "Take Winston for instance, he didn't want things to stay the same. He wanted to build the biggest lumber mill in Colorado, so he worked toward that. Made changes, did things, so it happened."

She hadn't thought of things in that way, and it made sense, but she shook her head as another realization formed. In this, too, he was an awful lot like his father. Unlike her mother, Winston never told her what to do or how to do it. He always gave her things to think about. "You're saying all this to make me feel better, aren't you?"

He shrugged.

"It's not the same, Crofton. Winston didn't want to die. My mother didn't want to die."

"I'm sure they didn't," he answered. "And there isn't a lot we can do about it."

Growing even more heavyhearted, she said, "There's nothing we can do about it."

"That's where you're wrong, Sara." He rolled her hand over so their palms touched. "When I first arrived, you were ready to take over the lumber mill, make Winston's dream come true. I know a lot has happened since then, and I'm not making light of your injury, but the woman I came home to tonight would never have followed me down the hill, and I want to know where she is."

"I don't know what you are talking about. I'm right here."

"Then why aren't you demanding to know what's happening at the mill? Who started the fire? Why aren't you still searching through Winston's office, trying to figure out how much lumber they'll need to fulfill the contracts?"

She'd thought about doing those things today, but the desire wasn't there. Not like it had been. "I don't know."

"Yes, you do."

"No, I don't."

"Yes, you do," he repeated louder this time.

Goaded, she said yet again, "No, I don't."

He pulled her hand onto the table, and forcefully held it there. "Yes, you do, and I want to know what it is. Have you seen Morton? Do you know where he is?"

She tried to pull her hand away, but he was too strong.

"No, I haven't seen Bugsley." Her heart was beating fast, and she told herself it was because Crofton was making her angry. Pretending to care about her, how alone and confused she felt, when in fact he only cared about finding Bugsley. "Even if I did see him, it wouldn't matter. He wouldn't tell me any more than you do. That's why I haven't continued to search through Winston's office, because it won't matter. There's nothing I can do that will matter."

"So instead of trying, you're just going to sit around and let everyone else do whatever they want?"

"Dr. Dunlop ordered me to sit around—"

"That didn't stop you that first day," he said. "Why now? If you haven't spoken to Bugsley, then what's changed?"

Fury made her heart race, but her mind had shifted slightly, as if trying to figure out what had changed. When something clicked, she spoke without thought. "You. The mill was on fire and you didn't even wake me, or come back to tell me about it. Instead you took control of it all, without asking or telling me anything."

"I did what had to be done."

Telling him he'd been the one to say they were in this together was on the tip of her tongue, but suddenly she was hearing herself in her mind. How foolish she sounded. To hear Amelia say that if not for him the entire mill would have burned to the ground. "Why did you do that?" she asked. "Do what had to be done? You keep saying you didn't want anything of Winston's, but you not only fought the fire, you're working as hard as he ever did rebuilding the mill. Why?"

He let go of her hand and ran his fingers through his hair before saying, "For you."

Warmth flooded her. "Me?"

"Yes, and for the town, and maybe for Winston." Leaning back in his chair, he waved a hand toward the barn and surrounding property. "You were right when you said this entire town depends on the mill. It does. And it depends on that railroad track being built. Without it, the town will dry up and blow away. Everything Winston created will be for naught. I don't want to see that happen. Not for me. I have my ranch that I will return to, therefore, it has to be for you. For my father's legacy." Resting an elbow on the arm of his chair, he placed a thumb under his chin and turned to look at her. "The entire town of Royalton is worried, Sara, and you have to show them they don't need to be."

Disappointed, and confused, she asked, "Me?"

"Yes, you. You are Winston's daughter. They've always looked upon you as, well, somewhat of a princess, and they're worried about whether you can take over where Winston left off."

A shiver tickled her spine. She had told herself that shortly after Winston had died, but hearing him say it made it real. "What if I can't?" she asked. "I don't know what would have happened if you hadn't arrived when you did."

He nodded slightly. "Things would have been different. You might have married one of those men who'd come knocking."

"No, I wouldn't have." That much she knew for certain.

"We'll never know for sure," he said. "Because I did arrive. What we have to do now is focus on what we do know."

Not exactly sure what that even was, she asked, "Such as?"

"That someone shot at us when we were leaving the

lawyer's office, that Winston's buggy had been tampered with and that someone set fire to the mill."

Having those things pointed out to her sent a shiver up her spine. "Set fire? I thought embers from the rubbish pile started the fire."

"Who told you that? Morton?"

Flustered, she said, "I haven't seen or spoken to Bugsley since my accident, and considering no one told me how the fire started, I just assumed it was from the rubbish pile."

"It wasn't. I checked that pile hours before the fire started. There were no embers."

While his answer was still settling in, Amelia arrived with a tray of tea and sugar-glazed cookies.

"Oh, it's a beautiful evening," she said. "The fresh air is already doing you good, Sara. The shine is back in your eyes."

Heat flushed into Sara's cheeks, and she diverted her gaze to the barn, and beyond. Something unfamiliar caught her attention, and she turned back to Crofton. "What's in the middle of the road down by Alvin's house?"

He waited until Amelia had reentered the house before saying, "A guard."

"A guard."

He nodded.

"What for?"

"I don't want men traipsing up the hill when I'm not home."

"What? Why?"

"You might say yes to one of their proposals. Where would that leave me?"

"Leave you?" Fury returned. Prior to the accident no one had wanted to marry her, and they still didn't. They just wanted the mill. "I have no intention of marrying anyone. And I have lived here almost my entire life, and never once have there been guards on the road."

"You'd never been shot at before, either," Crofton answered. A smile itched his lips. He withheld it, but allowed a keen sense of delight to ripple his insides. He was getting what he wanted. The past couple of days had been busy. He'd left early and arrived home late, and hoped Sara was simply getting the rest she needed. However, Amelia had voiced other concerns. How Sara moped around all day. He understood all she'd been through, and didn't begrudge her for being under the weather, but, considering all that was happening, it couldn't last any longer. There was too much at stake. Furthermore, he liked seeing the fire in her eyes.

"No, I hadn't," she said, "and we don't know for certain that we were shot at."

"I do," he said. "And Morton still hasn't shown up. I want to know when he does, and I believe the first person he'll want to see is you."

"So you're setting a trap for Bugsley?"

How she still had compassion for Morton irritated him. Keeping her angry, so angry she felt a fire in her belly that would offset all her other emotions, he said, "Yes." Before she could open her mouth, he continued, "He's behind all this. The one with the most to gain, and I'll prove it."

"What if he's not? What if the real culprit gets away while you're focusing on Bugsley?"

"They won't."

"You don't know that."

"Yes, I do."

"How?"

He had no proof, but from the day he'd seen Morton

escort her away from the mortuary, dislike for the man had settled deep in his gut. A feeling that strong, that deep, couldn't be wrong. "I just do."

"Well, you're wrong," she said, rising to her feet. "And I'll prove that."

He waited until she'd stomped past him before grinning.

Chapter Thirteen

The rebuilding of the office was completed and the entire operation was up and running within a few days. The continuation of lumber being milled for the railroad hadn't been interrupted. Crofton had made sure of that. The other thing he made sure of was that Sara wasn't pulled back down into a slump. After the fire he'd had the safe from the mill hauled up the hill and put in Winston's office, and had gladly provided her with the combination. He kept his fingers crossed that as she scoured through every sheet of paper, she'd find the evidence that would finally make her see Morton was behind it all.

Even though many maps and other records had been lost in the fire, they'd been able to piece together what was needed between the safe and what Winston had kept at home. However, Sara hadn't discovered what Crofton had hoped she would. He could question that she might hide any information she'd discovered about Morton, but inside knew that wasn't Sara's way. If she'd found something, she'd have told him. If for no other reason than to prove she was right and he was wrong.

He wasn't. There hadn't been any other events since

the fire. No one shooting at him, no additional accidents or fires. Because Morton was still in hiding.

Her searching had provided the contracts with the railroad, and she'd deciphered Winston's notes and recorded them into a new ledger that specified exactly how much lumber was to be harvested, the proportions of each cutting and delivery dates, taking into account the progression the railroad made each day. She had enlisted Walter's assistance with some of it. The clerk made regular treks up and down the mountain each day.

Crofton was proud of all her hard work, and of her, but couldn't tell her that. She was driven again, and needed to remain so to keep vigilant. Just because nothing had happened recently, didn't mean it wouldn't at any moment.

Returning from one of his daily trips to the house, Walter entered the mill office and set a basket on the newly varnished counter. "Your lunch," he said. "Amelia asked that I remind you to bring the basket home with you tonight."

"What is it?" Crofton asked, not really needing to know. Whatever Amelia cooked was delicious, just as it had been when he was a child. He could still remember waiting for lunch break back at school in Ohio. It had been his favorite time of the day and his lunch pail had always contained the best meals of any of the other children.

He was remembering more than lunches lately. Especially with Christmas growing nearer each day. Amelia had always decorated long before the actual day, and was doing so again. Each evening, entering a house filled with the scent of pine and cinnamon made him remember how much his father had enjoyed the season. The one thing he couldn't remember was if he'd received a Christmas gift since his father had died. He'd remained at school over the holidays. At first because his mother hadn't wanted him underfoot, later by choice.

"Boiled eggs, already peeled, ham slices, cheese and apple pie." Walter grinned. "There's enough for two."

"As there has been all week," Crofton said, shoving memories aside while pulling the cloth off the top of the basket.

"I could get used to this," Walter said. "Already am." Rolling up his sleeves, he added, "I'm getting used to the idea of Sara as a boss, too. It was a concern for all of us—we worried about what would happen with Winston gone. Then you showed up and we worried about that." Taking a moment to examine the egg he was about to put in his mouth, Walter added, "Funny thing what folks worry about, isn't it?"

"It is," he answered, just because it was expected. Although it was odd the things he was worried about lately. There were mill-related issues, but they were mostly due to how people would relate to Sara running things, and how she would handle that. In the long scheme of things, that's what he was working toward. She would have to take over things 100 percent. He would make the trip up this way now and again to check on her, but she'd be on her own most of the time and that's what he'd focused his attention on lately. Making sure the mill could practically run itself. Namely due to the railroad contracts. Once those ran out, he might have to commit a portion of time to help her get other endeavors in place to keep the number of people working that were employed by the mill.

He wouldn't mind that. Coming up here to help her. The mill had grown on him. He liked the challenge it held. Working with lumber was far more enjoyable than cows. It shouldn't be, he'd invested a lot of time in building up his ranch, but had to admit, he hadn't enjoyed it as much as he did the lumber business. That could have a lot to do with following in his father's footsteps, or it could have a lot to do with Sara.

He worried about her in general. Without help, the mill might become too much for her. Eventually she would take a husband, and that didn't settle well with him. He wasn't overly sure he wanted an outsider running Winston's enterprise.

Walter was speaking again and something he'd said caught Crofton's attention.

"What?"

"I said it's commendable, stepping in to help your sister like you have," Walter explained.

"Sara's not my sister." Crofton couldn't pinpoint what bothered him about people saying that, but it did. He had no trouble accepting Winston had loved her as a daughter, or her inheriting the mill and everything else, but he could not, would not, accept she was his sister.

Walter nodded slightly and ate another egg before saying, "She plans on coming down to the mill tomorrow to pass out the payroll like Winston used to. I said she didn't need to, but she insisted."

"I'll discuss that with her," Crofton said, not liking that idea, either.

"I figured you'd want to," Walter said, "that's why I brought it up, even though she told me not to."

"Smart man," Crofton said.

"Another smart man would make sure she doesn't discover I told him."

Crofton chuckled. He liked Walter, and his way of thinking. "Agreed."

They spoke of a few mill issues as they ate their meal,

and then Crofton gathered his hat and jacket while Walter put the used plates back inside the empty basket.

"I'm heading to the train station," Crofton said. "I'm catching a ride out to the bridge site. Won't be back until around five, so I'll see you tomorrow."

"Good enough," Walter said. "I'll leave the basket on the counter for you to pick up. Don't want Amelia getting upset by you not following orders."

"More like you want to make sure she has the basket for tomorrow."

"That, too," the other man agreed with good humor.

Crofton headed for the train station, and though his mind should be on the tasks at hand, they'd once again reverted back to Sara. Her stitches had been removed and the doctor had given her permission to assume normal activities, which included going to town, either walking or in a buggy. Keeping her at home wouldn't be as easy as it had been the past few days. That in part was why he was heading to the bridge site ten miles west of town. The tracks needed to cross the river, and span the wide-open space from delta to delta high above the water. The building of the bridge would continue for several months. It was also where Josiah Westerlund was stationed. Time had come to assure the man that Winston's untimely death would not interrupt the mill's ability to complete the contracts as promised.

The station was a hive of activity, both because a west-bound train full of passengers from Denver and farther east had arrived and, on an alternate track, a train pulling carloads of needed supplies was being prepared to depart. Crofton jumped onto one of the boxed-in cars that held nothing but rows of benches for the workers who traveled back and forth at intervals throughout the day. Immersing himself in all aspects of his father's business had provided him with far more knowledge than he'd had when he arrived in Royalton, and his respect for all his father had accomplished continued to grow. A part of him had latched on to the excitement of the railroad expansion that fed the town, and he found himself wanting to see this project to fruition probably as much as his father had. Or as much as Sara did. That was really where his loyalty lay. He wanted her to be a success more so than he'd ever wanted it for himself.

He'd ridden on trains before, but now held a new appreciation for being able to travel ten miles in less than an hour, complete his business and return to town in time for supper. Sara continued to insist supper was served at six, and he refused to disappoint her on that matter, either.

Josiah Westerlund met him as soon as he stepped off the train. A big man, with a handshake that said he not only oversaw the workforce, he worked alongside them.

"It's good to meet ya," the man greeted him with a thick northern accent. "There's been some rumbling about the mill, with the fire and all."

"I'm sure there has been," Crofton answered. "That's why I wanted to come and personally let you know all is well. Nothing to worry about."

"Ya, Mr. Morton said the same," Josiah answered, gesturing for them to move toward a canvas village of sorts. Several dozen tents and other structures housed and were used by the workers and those who lived here rather than taking the train back and forth to Royalton regularly. Once the bridge was complete, the entire village would follow, setting up on the other side, and then farther down the tracks. "And I read the paper."

Yesterday's edition of the weekly paper held the headline Prodigal Son Returns and had surprised him. The article had been rather flattering and focused on how he and Sara were working together and how the Parks Lumber Company had continued to operate at full capacity throughout the recent disasters. If it hadn't stated he and Sara were brother and sister several times, he might have appreciated Elliott Cross's writing abilities. Letting that subject go, Crofton asked, "When was Morton out here?"

"Not since the day afore the funeral," Josiah said. "Can't lay tracks on frozen ground, so we couldn't stop working to attend, but we did take a break and blow the whistle at noon, in honor of your father. He was a good man. He made the trip out here every Monday."

"I understand that, and thank you, he was a good man." Following the man inside one of the larger tents, Crofton asked, "Has Bugsley been out here since?"

"No." Lifting a pot off a crudely built iron stove, Josiah asked, "Coffee?"

"Sure." Crofton stopped near the huge table where several large sheets of paper had rocks holding down each corner to keep them from rolling up.

"I laid out the plans so you could see the progress," Josiah said. "We are right on schedule. This weather has held out, just as Winston said it would. Giving us time to get her set before the ground freezes and the snow flies. We'll be able to build the trestles through the winter months and come spring, start laying tracks on the other side."

The man took the time to show him every aspect of the bridge building, and though he would never allow her to trek over some of the trails he took to see the bridge base, Crofton did consider bringing Sara out to the site on his next visit. Seeing the actual progress would be good for her. Josiah answered all his questions, and asked several of his own, and by the time he was ready to board the train now headed back toward town, Crofton considered

Josiah an ally. The man had readily agreed to send word immediately if Morton showed up at the site.

The trip back was quick and convenient, and after picking up the basket from the mill office, Crofton took the pathway up the mountain rather than the road. Just like on the road, he'd ordered men to guard the path, making sure no one had access to the house in his absence. With Walter's help, the guards had been handpicked and each day he took the time to stop and chat with each one.

Bill Mix was on the trail this evening, and stepped out of the woods as Crofton made his way up the hill.

"See anything today, Bill?"

"A bull elk that's gonna be on my supper table one of these days," Bill answered.

Crofton nodded. "He's all yours, but not until we know no one's sneaking around out here."

"I hear you on that one, Boss," Bill said. "See you tomorrow."

Crofton continued on his way, scanning the area as he walked. Other than the path, the foliage made the hillside almost impassable, and he appreciated that. At the house, he entered through the back door, delivered the basket to Amelia and took the back stairway to the second floor to change his shirt. The train was convenient, but the soot and the dirt trekking down to the bridge base had left on his clothes would be frowned upon at the dinner table.

At first he'd questioned wearing Winston's clothing; now he was glad to have a clean supply at hand. Amelia had been right. They might as well be used.

As he took the corner at the top, his reflexes acted faster than his mind as he grabbed Sara with both hands to keep her from barreling into him. "Hey, there, slow down. Where you off to in such a hurry?"

Her face was flushed, her hair shimmering in the low

evening sun shining through the windows, and her eyes sparkling. The smile on her face was as bright as the rest of her. All in all, she dang near took his breath away.

"I saw you come up the hill," she said. "I was just going down to say hello."

"Well, in that case…" He stepped back and bowed at the waist before taking her hand and kissing the back of it. "Hello."

Her lifting laugh filled the hallway as she curtsied. "Hello." She popped back up and asked, "Walter said you were going out to the bridge site, did you?"

He stepped around her and removed his coat while walking toward his bedroom, where Amelia had filled the freestanding closet with clothes. "Yes, I did."

Her skirt and slips rustled as she twirled about and followed him. "And?"

Unbuttoning his cuffs, and then the front of his shirt, he pulled it off as he entered his room. "And what?"

"How's the bridge look?"

Tossing the shirt and coat on a chair, he crossed the room. "Not much like a bridge." Selecting a shirt much like the one he'd removed, he added, "Actually, I was thinking that next time I go out there, I'd let you tag along."

He expected an excited reply, so when silence lingered, he turned about. She stood in the open doorway, and it took a moment before he realized what she was staring at.

Never in his life had he blushed, but at that moment, he may have. Her gaze was glued to his bare chest and that sent a swirl of heat from his shoulders downward. He stopped the thought of where that heat pooled. She'd lived a sheltered life, and obviously had never seen a man without a shirt on before.

Her gaze shot upward, to his face and her cheeks turned as pink as her dress. He considered commenting, but figured she was embarrassed enough. Or maybe, just like when he'd accidently bumped her breast the day after her accident—an event that still made his hand burn—he wasn't willing to go down that route.

"Would you like that?" He sounded like a frog croaking.

"What?"

Clearing his throat, he said, "See the bridge?"

Her eyes sparked before dimming. "That wouldn't be proper."

Several other improper things were popping around in his head. He put on the shirt while walking toward her. "I think it would be proper for the mill owner to see what her lumber is building."

The expressions on her face showed her entire thought process, and he loved the smile that was the end result. "You're right."

Because of the blood racing through his veins, he didn't attempt to stop himself. Bending slightly, he kissed her forehead. "I'm always right," he whispered against her skin.

The shiver that rippled his skin may have started within him or it may have come from her. Either way, he was certain it encompassed both of them before he stepped away.

"I won't go so far as to say always."

Her smile was so adorable he laughed at the delight it filled him with. "I would."

She stretched on her toes and kissed his cheek before spinning about. "Hurry up. I'm hungry."

Stunned, it was a moment before he realized he was holding two fingers against his cheek, right where her lips had touched, and a moment longer before his feet remembered what they were made for. Catching up with her in the hallway, he buttoned his shirt as they walked side by side, and then gave her his elbow to hold on to as they descended the front staircase together.

Floundering a bit inside, he managed a bit of small talk as they walked. Asking about her day, but not truly hearing what she said. His mind was fathoming if she had kissed him. A simple peck on the cheek couldn't be considered a kiss any more than the ones he'd bestowed upon her forehead, but the touch of her lips had affected him.

Probably for the first time in his life, he had no idea if Amelia's cooking was as good as he claimed or not. With Sara sitting across from him it was hard to think of anything else. She'd not only healed the last few days, she'd blossomed. Like a wild rosebush come spring, her petals had furled back to reveal a delicate splendor one couldn't help but admire.

After the meal, they retired to the front porch, as they'd done the past few evenings. She had on a knitted white shawl, and pulled it tighter.

"We won't be able to do this much longer," she said. "The weather is growing colder."

"It is December," he pointed out, mainly because he didn't want to think about how much he enjoyed sitting out here with her.

"I know. It feels strange setting out Christmas decorations while it's so warm outside."

He watched her expression, looking for sadness, before saying, "They look nice, though."

"Thank you. Amelia likes having them out all month. So did mother." She smiled and shook her head. "Did you know the government commissioned surveys of four railroad routes through the West after the war?"

He leaned back in his chair. "Yes." His father had acquired the entire series of bound books containing those reports years ago. They covered everything from the geographical elements, vegetation, minerals and climates, to the animals and people residing in each region. In the evenings, while studying those volumes, his father had told him about such things and how he felt Colorado would be the best place for them to build their next lumber mill. He'd been excited about the adventure and overly discouraged upon learning he and his mother wouldn't accompany his father on the first trip West.

"One proposed route was through Arizona and New Mexico, but the desert between there and California made that route impractical, if not impossible."

"That's why the route that was proposed headed north after Arizona rather than straight west. To connect with the already established route heading west. The one that is currently being built," he explained.

Her sky blue eyes held a twinkle. "Perhaps, then, that route hasn't been completely canceled, simply delayed until the rest of the route is completed."

He didn't like shooting down her hopefulness, but the truth was the truth. "No. They completely canceled it. They'd already started acquiring land, and the mineral rights, twenty miles on both sides of the proposed track, but right before making those agreed-upon payments to the property owners, they pulled out." Turning to fully engage her as he spoke, he continued, "It didn't make any sense because they hadn't met any opposition. People were willing to wait the years they said it would take. Even an extension of that timeline wouldn't have been opposed, but they completely withdrew the deal off the table."

The way she nibbled on her bottom lip said she was contemplating what he'd said.

Continuing, Crofton said, "Railroad expansion is very profitable. Offshoot branches are being built across the nation and there is a lot of money to be made on the smaller lines. There is no regulation of what they can charge to transport goods, but people are willing to pay high prices in order to ship their grain and cattle to larger markets because they make more of a profit than what they would locally. Congress has yet to figure out a way to regulate the rates, which is why railroad expansion is still happening, and why pulling out that southern line doesn't make a lot of sense. None really, unless someone had the money to buy off the line."

"Buy off the line? Are you now suggesting Winston—?"

That had been his thought at one time, but it had altered over the past week. "No, I don't believe Winston bought off the railroad, but something happened."

"And that something caused your friend's death."

His thoughts hadn't been on Mel recently, on finding his murderer and that gouged at his conscience. He hadn't thought of his ranch much, either, of the work others were doing for him while he was up here.

"Is that Elliott Cross coming up the driveway?"

Crofton glanced toward the road. "Looks like it. He probably wants our praise for the article he wrote."

"It was a nice article," she said. "Hardly contained a bad word or insult."

"Which is out of the ordinary for Cross from what I've heard."

Her smile said she agreed but considering the other man would soon be within hearing distance she chose not to say it aloud.

Crofton stood as the man approached the porch. Living in the company of Sara and Amelia had made him more aware of the good manners that had been instilled in him as a child, but it didn't mean he used them on every occasion. "Cross."

"Mr. Parks, Miss Parks," Elliott answered, tipping his head in Sara's direction. "I do hope I'm not interrupting anything this evening, but it was brought to my attention, Mr. Parks, that you visited the bridge site today and I was wondering if you'd care to make a remark on the progress you witnessed for next week's edition."

Crofton believed the newspaper man was interested in the bridge progress, but couldn't get past his dislike of the man. "You can travel out there at any time, free of charge. Josiah will give you a complete report."

"I intend to," Elliott answered. "An additional quote from you will simply add weight to my article. You are quickly being accepted as the new most influential man in Royalton."

Crofton took the man's words for what they were meant to be. A poke in the eye rather than a compliment.

With a grin as sly as a weasel's Cross said, "The town was concerned about the future. That is until Sara's big brother arrived to save the day."

Instantly angered, Crofton growled, "Insulting Sara will get you nowhere, except kicked off this property."

"Insulting Sara? I wouldn't dream of doing such a thing," Cross insisted. "No one would. Everyone is very happy the two of you are getting along so well. A dispute between siblings would certainly be a disruption." Turning to Sara, he said, "Perhaps if your dear brother doesn't have a comment, you do, Sara?"

The man's continued reference to them being brother and sister was making Crofton's jaw burn.

"If you have something to add, I'd be honored to include it. I've attempted to come see you several times, but your guards wouldn't let me pass until this evening. I'm assuming that is because your brother is at home. It appears he wants to keep you all to himself."

Crofton had plenty to say, especially about the man's implications, but Sara spoke first. "He was simply assuring I got the rest I needed, Mr. Cross. I also must point out that like when Winston was alive, we do not attend to business in the evenings. Both Crofton and I will be at the mill tomorrow and will provide you with statements then." She rounded the table. "Now, if you will excuse us."

She'd hooked her arm through his elbow, and pride welled inside Crofton. He lifted a brow at Cross before turning to escort Sara into the house.

As he closed the door behind them, she shivered from head to toe.

"What's that about?" Crofton asked.

"He makes my skin crawl," she said.

Her nose was wrinkled up and her face puckered. Without thought, Crofton wrapped both arms around her and pulled her close. "He's just set on selling his newspapers."

She wrapped her arms around his waist and laid her head on his chest. "I know."

He hadn't been hugged in a long time, nor hugged someone, and it felt so good that Crofton tightened his hold, keeping her within his arms. Her sigh filled him with contentment, and he had no desire to let her loose.

She was the first to move, shifting slightly and lifting her face upward. The shine of her eyes, of her face, filled him with the same sense of awe as watching the sun rise over the mountain peaks. When he bent forward, he wasn't aiming for her forehead.

Warm and moist, her lips met his in an unhurried rush that was as sweet and tender as it was stirring. The connection held a secret, a promise that made him want more. He pulled her closer, tasting and seeking something that seemed elusive. As if he was starving and she the nourishment he needed but couldn't quite get.

A sound or outside awareness tugged at his mind and pulled him out of the kiss. As his eyes opened, over Sara's head his focus landed on Amelia standing in the dining room doorway, glaring at him as if he'd just splattered her freshly laundered clothes with mud.

Chapter Fourteen

Sara didn't want to open her eyes. She wanted Crofton's lips to be pressed against hers again. She'd never experienced anything so wonderful. So powerful. It had been as if she'd entered a real-life dream world, beyond the curtains of reality where angels sang and all was tranquil and elegant and perfect. Oh, so perfect.

As she came to understand it wasn't a chorus of angels singing in her ears, but rather her own heart thudding so fast it echoed inside her head, she lifted her lids. Crofton was looking over the top of her head, and she twisted to see what held his attention so completely.

Spying the empty dining room, she turned back to him. He smiled softly and pressed a finger to her lips, an action which kept her heart racing.

"I need to make sure Cross left," he whispered. "You should run on up to bed."

"Of course Elliott left," she said. "And it's barely even dark yet."

"I know, but you're still healing, and need the rest."

He was more like his father than even he could know. Always needing to protect those he loved. Her own thought made a tiny shiver tickle her spine. Crofton

couldn't love her. As the shiver turned into a chill, she
nodded, and without looking back, headed for the staircase.

Once in her room, she leaned against the closed door
and pressed both hands to her lips. What was happening?
She'd kissed Crofton. Sincerely kissed him. Twice. Once
on the cheek, an impulse that had come out of nowhere,
but the second one had been more than an impulse. A lot
more. It had come from a place deep inside her. A want.

Yes, she had wanted to kiss him more strongly than
she'd ever wanted something before. Anything.

She hadn't been frightened, or worried or afraid it
wouldn't happen. She'd known it would and had accepted
that without even thinking about it.

Pushing off the door, she crossed the room and opened
the door to the balcony. Two hummingbirds fluttered
around the feeder she filled each morning for them, and
she watched them dart around the glass, pausing briefly
to drink the nectar through their long beaks. It was a
pair, a dull-colored female and a bright green male with
a red band around its neck. Two males would chase each
other away, as would two females, but this couple didn't.
Instead they flew about in unison, moving around the
glass so the other could take a turn.

Months ago, when the pair hadn't flown south like all
the others, she'd cut a hole in the side of an old basket,
put an old fur hand muff inside and attached the basket to
the side of the balcony rail near the corner of the house,
hoping the birds would find enough warmth inside it to
live through the winter.

Used to her, the birds continued to feed as she moved
to the balcony rail. Although the office was closed, steam
still rose above the mill. Crews would continue cutting
logs into lumber until night fell. Elliott Cross's article

had claimed that the mill hadn't slowed since Winston's death, not even after the fire, because of the team managing it. Her and Crofton. Crofton did deserve the praise, but the past few days, ever since he'd jolted her out of that low place she'd managed to slip into, she had been helping. Tomorrow she would go to town and oversee the monthly payout of wages to the workers. It would be a new experience. Winston had never allowed her or her mother to partake in such things. He might have allowed it, but her mother would never have agreed to it. Amelia was right. Mother was a wonderful person, but had long-ago embedded herself into a very small role. She was so thankful to Winston for marrying her, for saving their lives, that she had never dared venture any further.

Sara had to wonder, if only briefly, if that had been all Mother had ever wanted. Being Winston's wife had provided things she'd never dreamed of—her mother had said as much, but could it have provided more if she'd wanted more?

As her thoughts twisted and collided, loud and clear, as if she stood right beside her, Mother's voice echoed in her ears.

"You were born in a dirt dugout in the middle of Kansas, didn't own a pair of shoes until you were five years old and Winston bought them for you. You haven't wanted for a thing since. Don't you ever forget that, Sara. Ever."

She could hear herself answering, "I won't, Momma, I won't."

They'd had that conversation more than once, even though she had never forgotten where she'd come from and why she was here.

Had she forgotten it recently? Working with Crofton the past few days, learning about the mill, the railroad, and searching for answers had filled her with a unique sense of being. Like she didn't need to pretend she belonged here because she truly did belong here. She had never been unhappy in her life, but maybe she'd never been truly happy, either.

Still gazing at the mill, she rested her hands on the rail. She did want to see the railroad built. But was she doing it for Winston? Or herself. Or Crofton?

Brought right back to where it had started, her mind once again settled on the kiss downstairs. The memory made her smile, but before the well of happiness had time to consume her, a knock sounded on her door. She had only made it as far as the balcony door when Amelia walked in the room.

"Going to bed already?" she asked.

Sara shrugged, not overly sure.

"Confused?"

"Yes," Sara admitted. "About several things."

"I expect you are," Amelia said. "Throw two people together long enough and they come out either hating each other, or loving each other."

Sara didn't respond. She certainly didn't hate Crofton, but did she love him? And if she did, what did that mean? Not of a mind to contemplate the great wonders of that, she moved to the door. "I have some papers I need to go over in the office."

"Crofton went to town," Amelia said, following her down the hallway. "But I'm here if you want to talk."

Sara nodded, but had no intention of talking. She didn't intend to read through more of Winston's paperwork, either. The answers she sought needed to come from within. And they had very little to do with the mill or the railroad.

Crofton hadn't returned home when she left the office

hours later, and he was absent from the breakfast table. She'd tossed and turned half the night thinking and wondering. This morning, while getting dressed, she'd concluded it was all for naught. She didn't have time for love. Crofton didn't, either. Not with all that needed to be done. Which was best. Thinking about love meant thinking about marriage. She'd told several people she wasn't interested in that, and going back on her word would make them question everything she said. There was more to it than that. She couldn't marry her stepbrother.

"Crofton says you're going to town today," Amelia said from where she stood near the stove.

"Yes, would you like to join me?"

"Already told Crofton I'll drive you down the hill. Gotta pick up a few things at Wellington's."

Despite her sleepless night, and her confusion, Sara was looking forward to the day. "We'll leave around eleven. The payout is at noon."

Amelia handed her a plate with two peeled boiled eggs. "I know—Crofton took the cash box from the safe with him so you won't have to worry about carrying it."

"I plan on inviting people to our Christmas party while in town. I'm going to do that while delivering thank-you notes to people who assisted with the service. I haven't had a chance to do that yet."

Sara waited for Amelia's response. They hadn't discussed the annual Christmas party that Winston always hosted, but this morning, she'd concluded it needed to happen. Not on Christmas day, Winston always insisted that be just family. "We'll have the party next Sunday. That's more than a week before Christmas—do you think people will be able to come?"

Amelia smiled. "I think that's a fine idea. Sunday will work perfectly. Oh, and I pressed that blue dress of your mother's for you. The one with the jacket you always admired," Amelia said.

Sara glanced down at the green-and-white-striped dress she'd chosen to wear this morning.

"That has too much lace. It's a girl's dress," Amelia said. "You're a businesswoman now, and need to dress like one."

"I hadn't thought of that."

"I'm sure there are a lot of things you haven't thought about, but in time you will. Besides, it's cold out today. You'll need a jacket."

A queasiness filled her stomach. "I'm sure I will, but I'm not—"

"Comfortable wearing your mother's clothes?" Amelia asked. "I'll tell you what I told Crofton—no sense in good clothes going to waste. I'll carry it upstairs while you're eating."

Sara did wear the dress, and was glad. Putting it on was like receiving a hug from her mother, and the image in the mirror looking back at her did look like a grown woman. She was glad of that, too.

The temperature had dropped considerably, hinting that snow may not be far away, and Sara was glad to be wearing the warm suit. As Amelia parked the buggy in front of the dry goods store, Mable Hollister waved from the post office across the street.

"I'll go see what she has for us," Amelia said, "and meet you inside Wellington's in a minute."

"Actually," Sara said, but had to wait until the train whistle died to continue. "Considering you haven't seen Mable for a while, and she'll want to chat, why don't I take the thank-you note over to Reverend and Mrs. Borman? Their place is just around the corner and will probably take me less time than it'll take you to get the mail."

"All right," Amelia agreed. "I'll be as quick as I can."

Sara climbed out of the wagon, and waved to Mable Hollister before stepping onto the boardwalk. The train whistle was sounding again, urging passengers to hurry. At precisely eleven fifteen it would leave for Denver. She contemplated that as she turned the corner, where she stumbled slightly. "Bugsley? Where have you been?"

Crofton had watched the buggy coming down the hill from the house until it had gone out of view, then he'd turned from the window and sat at the stool behind the counter in the mill office. He hadn't gotten much work done today. His mind was too busy wandering. After kissing Sara last night, he'd come down to town with the intent of visiting one of the many saloons, but instead had come here, to the mill. He'd forged a connection to the place, and had hoped that would help him sort out a few things.

Whether he liked it or not, Sara needed to be here for the payout today. There wasn't a lot of time to teach her everything she'd need to know when it came to managing the mill. He couldn't risk staying longer than necessary. Not after that kiss last night. He'd become comfortable lately. Too comfortable. His mind wasn't on the things it should be. He'd forgotten the reason he'd come to Royalton, and that had opened him up to other things. Things he didn't have time for.

Someday when his life was settled, the ranch profitable and his oats sowed, he'd think about finding a woman and getting married. For years, he hadn't wanted those things. Hadn't wanted or needed anyone. But lately, living with Sara and Amelia, he concluded he did want a family again. Someday. Not yet. If he'd learned one thing from his mother, it was that women needed attention. Constant attention. He didn't have time for that right now. Wouldn't for several years.

That was all easier to admit than the idea he'd fallen in love with Sara. There were so many things wrong with that thought, he had to shake his head in an attempt to scatter them.

Forcing his attention on the ledger before him, he double-checked each employee's name and the total amount they would soon be paid.

He'd just completed the last page when Amelia arrived, waving one arm.

"I wasn't going to say a word about what I saw last night, but now I am," she shouted. "How dare you? How dare you?"

He knew what she'd seen last night, but didn't know what had set her off. "How dare I what?"

She slapped a letter on the counter top. "That is a woman's handwriting."

"Yes, it is," he answered, picking up the letter. "Her name is June."

"And who is June?"

"She is my friend Mel's sister," he said. "I'm sure she's wondering why I haven't contacted her yet."

"Or gone back," Amelia snapped. "To her. Your wife!" Her eyes, dark with anger, glared as she leaned closer. "Why didn't you tell us you were married, and why—"

"Married? I'm not married to June or anyone else."

"You're not?"

"No," he said, rounding the counter to walk to the door. Probably as mad as Amelia, Sara must still be in the buggy. As foolish as it was, the idea that she was upset over him being married thrilled him. "June has been married to Gray Hawk for ten years and…"

His thoughts left him and the tickle in his stomach turned rock hard at the sight of the empty buggy. "Where's Sara?" he asked while rushing out the doorway to glance around.

Amelia shook her head. "Why would Mable tell me—?"

There was no hint of Sara anywhere. "Where's Sara?" he repeated, not caring who Mable was or what she'd said.

"She's delivering thank-you notes," Amelia said. "And inviting people to the Christmas party."

Fury along with a sense of panic he'd never experienced exploded inside him. "You left her alone? Where?" Without waiting for answer, he shouted for Walter.

"She's at the parsonage," Amelia said.

"She'd better be." Crofton ran for the buggy as Walter walked out of the office. "If I'm not back in five minutes, shut down the mill and send every man out searching for Sara." The knot in his stomach changed his mind. "Don't wait! Shut down the mill now!"

Slapping the reins over the horse's backside, he spun the buggy around and headed toward town at a full gallop. Wagons, horses and people careened out of his way, and he didn't slow the horse down until the buggy took the final corner. He jumped sideways on the seat in order for his weight to keep the little rig from flipping, and bounced erratically as it landed back on all four wheels moments before he pulled on the reins and slammed on the brake.

The buggy and horse were still rolling forward when he leaped out and ran up the walkway leading to the parsonage.

Reverend Borman opened the door before Crofton arrived at the steps. "What's the hurry?"

"Is Sara here?" Crofton asked.

"No. Why? What's happened?"

"Have you seen her?" The urgency welling inside Crofton grew and he spun around to scan the buildings and yards nearby. "I have to find her immediately."

"Hold on a minute," Reverend Borman said. "I just arrived home. Let me ask Martha if she's seen her."

"Yes, I have."

The woman's voice had Crofton spinning back to the house.

"A short time ago, while hanging clothes on the line I saw her and Mr. Morton from the backyard. I was just going to mention to the reverend that the man must have been found."

Crofton was biting his tongue to keep the curse words from flowing. "Where did you see them? What direction were they going?"

"Toward the train station," Mrs. Borman said.

Without offering his thanks, Crofton spun and started to run. He started cursing aloud, too, at how, after all that'd happened, Sara could still hold trust in Bugsley. She knew Crofton had been looking for Morton—everyone knew.

"Damn it," he muttered while darting into a narrow passageway between two buildings as a shortcut to the train station. "How can she still trust that man?"

Crofton shot out from between the buildings and headed toward the depot at a full run. Not slowing until the ticket booth was within a few feet, he grabbed the ledge while skidding to a stop. "Did Sara Parks get on the last train? The one that left a few minutes ago. Was she on it?"

The ticket taker turned about, but it was the person behind the clerk that caught and held Crofton's attention. The woman was clearly a working girl, and she'd been working.

Darting around the caged front, he shoved open the side door. "How much were you offered to distract him?" Crofton asked, pointing toward the clerk but speaking to the woman. "While Bugsley Morton snuck Sara Parks on the train?"

"Distract?" The clerk shook his head. "I wasn't distracted."

"Weren't you?" Crofton demanded. "Then you saw whether Sara Parks boarded the train or not."

The man bowed his head.

Crofton almost exploded as he turned to the woman. "Where is Morton taking her?"

She pulled the short sleeves of her dress onto her shoulders. "I have not seen Mr. Morton. I was merely—"

"You will be on the next train out of town if you don't tell me what you know right now," Crofton roared. "There won't be jobs for anyone in this town if something happens to Sara Parks," he continued, including the ticket taker in his glare. "I'll burn the mill down myself and laugh as this town dries up and blows away."

"That's what you came here to do," she said. "But Bugsley isn't going to let that happen. He knows you aren't really Winston's son, and will prove it."

With confirmation his instincts were right, Crofton turned to the ticket taker. "Is that train scheduled to stop between here and Denver?"

"No, sir, but—"

"Wire every depot between here and Denver," he ordered. "If that train stops, I want Morton arrested."

"Morton didn't get on the Denver train," the clerk hollered as Crofton ran out the door.

Spinning about, he asked, "Where is he then?"

"They hitched Mr. Lincoln's private cars to the workers' train and headed to the railhead."

"Damn it!" He'd heard the worker train rattle past the mill and hadn't even glanced out the window. Leaping off the platform, he commandeered a horse and rode to the mill. The place had been shut down, and he steered the horse toward the train engine that had hauled down a load of logs this morning.

"Did you find her?" Amelia shouted, running to meet him.

"No," Crofton said, dropping to the ground.

"Oh, dear, maybe she's—"

"She's on her way to the railhead," Crofton supplied. Several of the men had gathered around and he gestured toward the train. "Unhook that log car and find the engineer!"

Among the men, Walter asked, "What for? Did you find her?"

"Morton has her," Crofton answered, "and that engine's going to take me to the railhead right behind them."

"That engine's made for short routes," Walter said.

Crofton had already weighed his options. He had no idea what Morton was planning, but his gut knew what the man was capable of, and that included murder. "A horse will take too long to get there."

Chapter Fifteen

The pounding in her temples was as strong as the sting in her eyes and the rumbling of the train car rolling on the tracks. Sara glanced between Bugsley and Levi Lincoln. "Married?"

Both men nodded. She willed the tears not to form, not to flow as she glanced around the elegant car. Settling her gaze back on the men, she asked, "And why do I need to tell the workers that—" she rubbed her burning nose "—that Crofton is married?"

"Because they have to know there is at least one Parks they can trust," Bugsley said.

Both he and Levi Lincoln were sitting across from her, in chairs covered in red velvet with elaborately carved arms and legs. She'd ridden in one of the railroad's private cars before, but wasn't enjoying it this time. When Bugsley had asked her to accompany him to Mr. Lincoln's private car, she'd suggested the men meet both her and Crofton at the mill. He'd agreed, but once they'd arrived at the train car, he'd literally forced her aboard, something she would not forget. Ever.

Lips pinched, she glared at him. "Married or not, they can trust Crofton."

"I don't understand where you acquired so much admiration for him," Bugsley said. "So much trust."

She stopped before saying Crofton said the same about him.

"He's been lying to you since he arrived."

"No, he hasn't."

"So, he told you he was married?"

Her stomach didn't drop this time, but her heart ached a bit harder.

"I didn't think so."

The pain spread throughout her body. "Crofton—"

"Will do what Crofton wants. That's what he's always done. He could have visited Winston years ago, but instead chose to wait until after his death, so he could step in and take over everything, knowing his father wouldn't have allowed that if he was still alive."

"That's not true. Winston would have welcomed him," she insisted, even as her mind tried to comprehend Crofton being married.

"You only saw the Winston you wanted to. I knew the businessman. That's truly what he was. His business meant more to him than family ever did. He would never have left them in Ohio if that wasn't true."

"The apple doesn't fall far from the tree, my dear," Mr. Lincoln said. "Crofton is a lot like Winston in that aspect. He left his family behind in order to seek his fortune, too.

"I found many of the things Mr. Morton told me suspicious, but when he said Crofton claimed someone deliberately sabotaged Winston's buggy, I knew I had to come out here and take care of things myself."

"That's where you've been?" she asked Bugsley. "In Denver, tattling on Crofton."

He leaned forward and touched her hand, which she promptly pulled away.

"I promised Winston I'd take care of things for you, and that's what I've been doing." With a wave towards Mr. Lincoln, he said, "The railroad's not happy about Crofton's arrival, and may pull their contracts if he takes over. That would be the end of Parks Lumber and Royalton."

Her spine stiffened. "They can't do that." Turning her gaze toward Mr. Lincoln, she asked, "Where would you get the lumber you need?"

"Parks Lumber isn't the only lumber company in these mountains," Mr. Lincoln said. "Others are already vying for the chance to put in bids. To take over."

A wave of frustration washed over her so fully her heart sank. She'd heard Winston discuss rival companies more than once. Anger at Crofton built inside her. He'd never mentioned a wife. Then again, most everything he'd said were lies. Claiming he didn't want any of the inheritance, but as soon as they'd met with Ralph Wainwright he'd jumped right in to do just that.

"We have to stop him, Sara," Bugsley said. "The railroad's a powerful force to contend with, and they'll stop at nothing to get what they want."

She wished the curtains were open, so she could see outside, and not feel so trapped. There were a lot of other wishes rolling around inside her, too, but wishes rarely came true. This time they couldn't. Winston couldn't return from the dead.

"Did you hear me, Sara?"

"I heard you," she said. "But I still don't see how me telling the workers Crofton is married will help anyone."

"Well, dear, that is something we need to discuss in detail," Mr. Lincoln said.

"What details?"

"The workers at the railhead need their jobs. Especially as winter is setting in. If they believe someone is jeopardizing that, I may not be able to stop them."

"Stop them from what?"

The men looked at each other and then back at her. Her legs shook as their implication became clear. Swallowing, she asked, "Are you suggesting—"

Both men nodded.

"I'm sorry, Sara, but yes," Bugsley said. "The death of his friend should have told Crofton that no one meddles in the railroad's business, but he was too stubborn to listen. There again he's a lot like Winston."

Tears stung her eyes as she whispered, "What can—"

"You can tell the workers that Crofton is married and will be returning to his ranch," Mr. Lincoln said, "and that Mr. Morton will be in charge."

She shook her head. "Crofton inherited half of everything."

"That may be true, my dear, but once you are married to Bugsley the railroad will back you in challenging the will."

Crofton had never cursed so much in his life. He actually ran out of words to shout at the engine that barely chugged along the rail line.

"She's built for pulling power," Chris Bolton said. "Not speed. I told you that before we left."

"I know what you told me," Crofton shouted over the noise of the locomotive. "I can run faster than this."

The engineer shook his head. "We'll be at the railhead shortly. I just hope we don't encounter the worker train returning. This girl isn't fond of backing up—"

"We won't be backing up," Crofton declared. He'd never felt so useless, and the image of Sara hurt and scared intensified with each minute that ticked by.

"Well, it won't be long," the engineer replied.

But it was long enough to drive Crofton to the edge of sanity. By the time the engine rolled into the canvas town, he'd practically worn out the soles of his boots from pacing the small area. Before the wheels came to a complete stop, he bolted down the metal steps and headed for the private car that was parked on the switchback.

Snow had started to fall and was already piling up on the ground. He glanced toward the billowing canvas tents. Dozens upon dozens of them. Sara could be anywhere. It would be like looking for the proverbial needle in a haystack.

"Damn it," he growled as he turned his attention back on the private car. She better be inside it.

Through the snow, he clearly made out Woody Wilson leaning against the side of the train car. Recalling the gunslinger sitting with Morton in the saloon the day of Winston's funeral sent Crofton's anger to a new level.

"Where is she?" he asked upon stopping directly in front of Wilson.

Dressed in black from head to toe, the man tipped back the brim of his hat. "Who?"

"You know."

With a nod and a quick glance around, Wilson said, "That information will depend on how much it's worth to you."

Not in the mood for any games, Crofton grabbed Woody's throat with one hand and pulled the gun from the man's holster with the other. Pressing the barrel into Wilson's gut, he growled, "No, it depends on how much your life is worth to you."

"I ain't the one who put the fly in your buttermilk," Wilson said.

Crofton pulled back the hammer. "Where is she?"

"Don't go doing anything rash, now," Wilson said. "Your sister's fine."

A sister was not how he thought of Sara, but Crofton wasn't about to tell the gunslinger that. Grabbing one of Woody's arms, Crofton used the gun to motion the man toward the rear of the car, "Tell them to open the door."

Questions filled his mind, and although Wilson might have some of the answers, Crofton chose to stay silent. He also paid close attention to his surroundings. Woody Wilson had been waiting for him. That meant others were, too.

"Who says she's in the car?"

Crofton wouldn't put it past Wilson to lead him on a goose chase. "Tell them to open the door."

As he neared the back of the car, Wilson shouted, "Got company out here."

The door opened and Wilson stepped aside, gesturing for Crofton to enter first.

Not about to have someone on his back, Crofton waved the gun, telling Wilson to enter first. Scanning behind and in front of him, Crofton followed up the steps and into the car. He recognized the bearded man seated at the table. Levi Lincoln had been promoted into a ranking officer of the Santa Fe railroad last year. The car, full of plush furnishing and framed maps, said the railroad believed in providing their officers with the best of everything.

"Thank you, Mr. Wilson," Levi said.

Woody nodded and then turned, hand out.

At the moment the gun in his hand was the only bargaining tool Crofton had. He smiled, but shook his head before sticking the gun into the waistband of his britches. In the rush of things, he'd left his gun in the mill office back in Royalton. A foolish mistake. One he'd been cursing since leaving.

Levi stood. "You can leave," he said to Wilson. "I'm sure Mr. Parks will return your gun once our conversation has been completed." Once the gunslinger had shut the door behind him, Levi said, "Have a seat, Mr. Parks. We need to have a discussion before you are reunited with your sister."

Crofton refused to sit. "Where is she?"

"You seem to have grown awfully fond of a sister you'd never met until a couple of weeks ago."

A ball of fire ignited in his stomach. "You know as well as I that she's not my sister."

"I do," Levi said with a nod. "Don't worry, she's not in danger. Please, have a seat so we can talk." Sitting back down, he said, "I'm not your enemy, Mr. Parks. In fact, I'm the only one willing to make this work."

"Make what work?"

"You taking over for your father." With a slight nod, he continued, "I do offer you my condolences. Your father was a first-class businessman." With a hand, he waved toward a large, framed map of the states. "See all those red lines—those are railroad routes. Santa Fe routes now that we've acquired the SPR, MTK and several other lines. We were the first line to reach Colorado back in seventy-three. Since then, your father played a large part in our expansion."

Crofton gave a nod of acknowledgement. "Along with how you created a demand for your services by selling parcels of the land congress had granted to the railroad."

Levi grinned. "That, too. There's a sparse number of people between Kansas and California. It takes money to build a line, and it takes people to make one work. We need cargo to haul, and people to transport. I've been told you're disappointed we had to pull out of Arizona. The terrain down there is just too much to take on right now. Once we have established regular commissions, we'll look at that possibility again."

Although he wasn't here to talk about the railroad, that was exactly what Levi Lincoln wanted, and at the moment, Levi was the only route to finding Sara. Crofton's jaw tightened. He could search every tent and never find her. These were railroad workers, not lumber-mill workers. Putting on a false front, Crofton sat down. "The ranchers need a way to get their cattle to markets now."

"I may be able to speed that process up, for the right kind of deal."

A knot tightened in Crofton's stomach. "Sara?"

Levi tapped the tips of his fingers together as he leaned back in his chair. "Morton led me to believe you don't care about Sara. It's the money you're after. So you can build up your cattle ranch."

"If I simply wanted money, I would have gone to my father and asked for it." Letting on how much Sara had come to mean to him would make him too vulnerable. The fact he was here already said plenty. Not wanting the man to gain any leverage, Crofton propped one foot on his opposite knee to look less perturbed. "I'm here to make sure my father's business continues on just as he would have wanted it to."

Levi lifted a brow. "And you don't believe your stepsister can do that on her own?"

Crofton let the question stir his thoughts for a moment. In the end, he couldn't lie or belittle Sara. He wouldn't want anyone to do that. "Sara is a very capable and smart woman, with an extremely sharp mind."

"But?"

"But, I'm not convinced anyone will give her the chance. Including you."

Levi leaned forward. "Me?"

"Most everyone seems to believe that Sara is some sort of American princess, sitting in her ivory tower above Royalton embroidering samplers with gold thread and hosting tea parties." That analogy had come directly from one of the mill workers when the man had heard Sara would be passing out the wages. Crofton had let it be known then that insulting Sara would get a person nowhere, and would so again. "My father may have kept her protected from many things, but work wasn't one of them. She knows as much about your contracts as you and I do."

Levi opened his mouth, but closed it. After leaning back in his chair again, he said, "Morton seems to think she doesn't know anything."

"Because he doesn't want her to know, and he'd like to keep it that way. If there is one man who is after Parks's money, it's Bugsley Morton."

"The two of you seem to be in conflict with one another."

Crofton dropped his foot to the floor and leaned forward. "I'm not here to discuss Morton. Tell me what you want, and I'll tell you if it's obtainable."

One side of Levi's mouth curled into a grin. "You are a lot like your old man."

The man was fishing, and Crofton was in no mood to get caught. "I've had worse insults, and I've heard worse lies." When Levi remained silent, Crofton continued, "The mountains of Colorado are far more difficult to build through than the terrain in New Mexico and Arizona." His sixth sense had kicked in strong enough to curdle his stomach. Listening to it, he chose to bluff. "I'd hate to have to fulfill my father's threat. Sara has her heart set on seeing Parks Lumber build the line well beyond the border."

Levi wasn't a large man, but had grown portly from sitting behind a desk and even the drooping jowls beneath his graying beard paled as the man swallowed. He was hiding something dark and deep.

Continuing his con, Crofton said, "As you said, I'm a lot like my father. Just like him, I run a clean business. I won't have schemes or corruption defiling my family or the family name. My father didn't want a pirate at the helm, and I don't, either."

Levi squirmed in his chair before saying, "It's been taken care of, your father saw to that."

He'd like specifics to work with, but Crofton couldn't risk his bluff being called. On a whim, he rubbed the handle of the pistol he'd taken from Woody. "Not all of it. I also won't let anyone take advantage of Sara." As a second thought, he added, "There will be no more accidents. No more people shot in the back."

Levi's eyes widened. "The railroad didn't have anything to do with Winston's accident or the shooting of your friend."

"I can't say I'm ready to believe that," Crofton said, standing up. "But I do know I've had enough, and I guarantee this scheme you and Morton are attempting to pull off will be your downfall. Take a look around because all this finery will soon be gone. You'll be sitting in a jail cell before I'm done. Nothing will stop me. Not you. Not your railroad. And certainly not Morton. Now, where is Sara?"

The way Levi glanced at the door sent a shiver up Crofton's spine as hot as it was cold.

"Think of what my father would have done if something happened to her." When Levi turned his way, Crofton added, "Now multiply it by ten."

Chapter Sixteen

Sara pulled the blanket Josiah Westerlund had given her tighter around her shoulder. Josiah had also added wood to the stove in the center of the tent before he'd left, but the heat wasn't helping the chill inside her. If it meant saving Crofton's life, she'd marry the devil himself. Bugsley promised the marriage was just for the railroad workers, and once everything was settled, he'd provide her with a divorce. So that someday she could marry a man for love.

Love. That wouldn't happen. The only man she'd want to marry, the only one who would meet Winston's standards of the best of the best, was already in love with someone else. Already married to someone else.

Her entire being hurt. The pain wasn't caused by anything physical. It all came from inside her. It just didn't seem fair. Didn't seem right.

She could accept fulfilling Winston's dream, maintaining jobs for so many in Royalton, and running the mill until her dying day, but she couldn't accept taking away Crofton's shares. Married or not, half of all Winston owned was rightfully his.

Grief as solid and raw as when her parents died

washed over her. Why hadn't he told her he was married? Or told Amelia?

Maybe he had told Amelia and the two of them had chosen not to tell her. If that was the case, why had he kissed her like he had last night? That had been more than a peck on the forehead. The memory once again filled her mind, her entire being, until unshed tears burned her eyes.

She took a deep breath and pressed a hand firmly against her rolling stomach. She was still wearing her mother's suit, and though donning it had felt wonderful this morning, now it felt wrong. Like her mother wouldn't approve of what was happening.

Sara closed her eyes while biting her quivering lips together. Mother would never have approved. Neither would Winston.

The sound of men gathering outside the tent was muffled only by the wind that made the canvas billow, and as she listened, a shift happened inside her.

She might not have been Winston's blood daughter, never truly owned the last name of Parks, but in her heart she was Sara Parks. It was time she put to use all the knowledge she had gained from the man who'd chosen to be her father. Chosen to love her.

Turning to Bugsley who sat in a chair near the table, examining the maps lying there, she said, "I can't do it."

"We've discussed—"

"No," she interrupted. "You discussed. You had a rebuttal for every protest I made. Have had since the accident."

Bugsley stood. "Because I've been trying to protect you, just as Winston would want."

Anger built where confusion had sat, and she shrugged off the blanket as she stood. "I no longer believe that, and don't tell me what Winston would have wanted. This is no longer about Winston. It's about me. It's about Parks Lumber. And it's about Crofton."

A gust of wind shook the tent, and as she turned toward the flap doorway that was separating, her heart skipped several beats as Crofton stormed into the tent. The joy of seeing him fused with alarm. His expression was as dark and menacing as his charge forward.

Whatever he said eluded her as he stormed forward and punched Bugsley in the face.

A scream tore out of her throat as Bugsley flew backward, knocking over the table and sending the maps in all directions.

"What are you doing?" she shouted while catching a map before it landed on the woodstove.

"What the hell do you think you're doing?" Crofton shouted in return.

She opened her mouth, but held her words as Josiah and another man picked Bugsley off the floor and hauled him out the door.

The flap hadn't fallen into place when Crofton grabbed both of her arms. "Why the hell would you agree to marry him?"

"I didn't agree to marry him," she retorted, squirming against his strength.

"That's not what I was told."

She didn't have time to respond before Crofton squeezed her upper arms harder. "Lies," he growled. "Why can't you see he's been lying to you all along?"

Suddenly furious, she reacted before thinking. Wrenching an arm from his hold, she slapped his face. With fury raging, she stuck a finger near his nose. "Lies? Don't tell me about lies. Not when you've been lying to me since you arrived."

"I have not."

With no particular place to go except away, she spun around. Heedless of the maps beneath her feet, she shouted, "Yes, you have."

"About what?"

"Your wife for one."

Crofton bounded around the stove and once again grabbed her arms. "I'm not married. What the hell? I get a letter from a woman and the entire territory thinks I'm married?" He gave her a slight shake. "I'm not married to June or anyone else."

Rattled slightly, Sara shook her head. "You aren't?"

"No, I'm not. But even if I was, why the hell would you marry Bugsley? He's twice your age, among other things."

Sara was questioning the happiness exploding inside her when her eyes locked with Crofton's. There was sincerity there, and disappointment. She could feel it more than see it. Regret made her stomach clench. "They told me the workers would revolt when they learned you'd been lying to them. That the only way to stop it was for me to marry Bugsley so he could contest Winston's will."

"I haven't been lying to anyone," Crofton said quietly.

"I know," she answered, fighting back tears.

Crofton's smile was so gentle her throat constricted. "Come here," he whispered while pulling her into his arms.

She went willingly and wrapped her arms around his waist while burying her head in the fabric covering his chest. "I'm sorry. I kept thinking about Winston and my mother, and your friend. I didn't want them to kill you, too. I couldn't bear that."

"Shh," he said, kissing the top of her head. "I'm not going to die. The killing is over. I promise you that."

She bit her lips to keep from sobbing as his hold tightened. His strength was overwhelming. Not just his muscles and brawn, but his powerful presence. It had eased her pain before, and was doing so again now, almost as if he shared his dominance with her, making her strong inside, too.

As she felt it completely filling her, he stepped back and lifted her chin with one hand. "Better?"

She nodded.

He kissed her then. A swift movement that took her by surprise and stole away all rational thoughts. The action was as powerful as him. It too filled her, consumed her, with something more potent than strength. Desiring more, she parted her lips, and the pleasure of his taste, how his tongue teased and encouraged hers to twist with his caused a groan to rumble in the back of her throat. Her breasts tingled, and she pressed them more firmly against his chest. The connection was bittersweet. It filled her with an inconceivable pleasure that was close to being painful in the most spectacular way.

The kiss burgeoned until her head spun and her heart raced. She was lightheaded and breathless by the time the kiss had slowed to the point their lips were merely pressed against one another's. Drawing a deep breath, she tugged her eyes open, but closed them again as he pressed her head against his chest again.

Sighing deeply, she stood there, satisfied, yet yearning for more.

"Mr. Parks?"

Crofton kissed the top of her head once more before he released her and turned about. "Come in, Josiah."

Sara gathered her strength and stepped up to stand beside Crofton as Josiah entered through the flap.

"The men have gathered," Josiah said. "Waiting for the announcement Mr. Morton said Miss Parks was here to deliver to them. Should I tell them to go back to work?"

"No," she said.

Crofton took her arm.

She smiled at the confusion in his eyes, and then at Josiah. "I have something to tell them."

"Sara—"

"Come with me," she told Crofton as she started for the door.

He followed and stood beside her as she stopped near the edge of the wooden platform the tent was built upon.

Taking a deep breath, when she spied Mr. Lincoln and Bugsley near the edge of the large crowd of workers she pulled up a smile. "Parks Lumber has had some setbacks the past few weeks, but you, all of you, working so diligently haven't let any of it hamper your accomplishments. We appreciate that very much, and would like to invite all of you to our annual Christmas party this Sunday."

Silence mingled for a moment, leaving nothing to echo in her ears except the wind. Questioning if none of them would be able to attend, she added, "It'll last all day, so I'm hoping you'll be able to fit an hour or so into your schedule."

Josiah, who stood on the other side of Crofton, said, "We will fit it into our schedule, Miss Parks."

Crofton grasped Sara's hand while glaring at Levi. Even while anger had erupted inside him, he'd never been so thankful to see someone as when he'd opened the flap to Josiah's tent. Nor had he ever been so furious at someone as he had been Morton. And he'd never been so proud of someone as he was of Sara at this moment. Squeezing her hand, he said, "The time will not be docked from your pay, will it, Mr. Lincoln?"

"No," Levi Lincoln shouted over the mumbles that had started. "It will not. Thank you, Miss Parks. Your invitation is a great honor for all of us. The Sante Fe Railroad is proud of our relationship with Parks Lumber and looks forward to it continuing for many years to come."

The crowd cheered, but it was the smile on Sara's face as she looked up at him that filled Crofton with something he may never have felt before. It went beyond approval, beyond satisfaction. The desire to pull her into his arms and kiss her again was as strong as it had been inside the tent. He couldn't do that. Shouldn't have inside the tent. Everyone here thought of her as his sister. Except for him.

"Come," he said next to her ear. "It's time for us to head to town. Before we get snowed in."

The flakes had grown and were falling faster now than before.

"I sent your engine back," Josiah said. "But the worker train is ready to head out."

"Thanks," Crofton said as he guided Sara off the platform.

"I hope you'll be at the party, Mr. Westerlund," Sara said.

"I wouldn't miss it for nothing," Josiah responded. "Thank you for inviting all of us. It'll go a long way with these men."

She nodded, and Crofton couldn't stop the smile that formed, or the pride that continued to grow inside him as they crossed the snow-covered ground.

Levi Lincoln met them at the worker train. "I do hope your invitation includes me, Miss Parks. What I said is true. The Sante Fe Railroad would like to continue our relationship with Parks Lumber for many years."

Sara stiffened slightly, causing Crofton to rub the small of her back where his hand had settled as they'd walked.

"No matter who is in charge?" she asked Levi.

The man nodded.

Crofton didn't miss how Sara's gaze briefly flashed toward Morton, who was standing near Lincoln's private car.

"Then of course the invitation includes you, Mr. Lincoln," she said. "We'll see you on Sunday."

Woody Wilson, who'd been standing behind Lincoln, stepped forward. "Mr. Parks, can I get my piece back?"

Understanding a man's gun could be considered his best friend, Crofton pulled the gun from his waistband. Letting the other man know, gun or no gun, he wasn't a threat, Crofton warned, "Tread carefully, Woody."

Woody nodded and walked away. Crofton escorted Sara onto the train and found a place for them near the small stove at the back of the car. They'd no sooner sat down than a worker approached.

"Can I offer you my coat, Miss Parks?" the man asked.

The flare inside Crofton wasn't surprising, but it should have been. The worker was merely being kind.

"No, thank you, though," Sara said. "You'll need it. The ride will be cold."

"Excuse me," another man said, shouldering his way past the first. Holding out a blanket, he said, "Mr. Westerlund asked me to give this to you, Miss Parks. I'll see he gets it back tomorrow."

She took the blanket. "Thank you. That was so kind of him, and you."

Her smile made the man's cheeks turn red. Ducking his head, the man turned about and scurried to a seat.

Sara spread the blanket over her lap and Crofton's, and he wrapped an arm around her shoulders as the train jostled everyone as it jolted forward. For the briefest of moments, Crofton wondered who was going to catch him. The look in her eyes did more than jolt his insides. He held his breath in order to fight the desire to kiss her, taste her again.

The car's movement became smoother and the clanging and banging grew into a steady rumble as the train speed increased. Her eyes were still locked on him, still glistening with an intensity that stirred his insides.

"I'm not exactly sure what happened today."

Her voice was whispery soft, or merely shrouded by the train noise and the thundering of his heart. Unfortunately, Crofton understood what had happened. Or at least he could no longer deny it. He'd fallen in love with her. Loved her. The flare inside him caused by the man offering her his coat had been jealousy. He hadn't known what it was, what it felt like, until he'd barreled inside the tent and come face-to-face with Morton. He'd been jealous of the man since he'd seen him escort Sara down the mortuary steps. Might have been before then. Knowing Morton had been Winston's right-hand man is probably what had started the jealousy, and Sara's unrelenting trust in the man had fueled it.

"What did you do to Lincoln to make him change his mind?" she asked.

Crofton wasn't sure he could find his voice. His shirt collar was suddenly tight, and worse yet, he was wondering what Sara would say if he asked her to marry him. It was a foolish thought, but, he had to admit, not as out of the blue as he'd like to think. From the moment he'd met her, all the parts inside him that had been numb for years had been rejuvenated.

He couldn't ask her to marry him, couldn't even consider that. People considered them siblings, and a brother couldn't marry a sister—not the blood kind or the step kind. That would cause a scandal these parts had never seen before. Besides, he wasn't ready to be married. His mother had tarnished any and all thoughts he'd had of marriage years ago. It took more than a couple of weeks to undo all that.

"You were right," she said. "I should never have trusted Bugsley."

He silently cleared his throat in order to say, "You've been through a lot the past few weeks. It's understandable why you'd want to trust him."

Letting out a heavy sigh, she said, "But I shouldn't have."

Restraining himself from kissing her forehead, he squeezed her shoulder. "We live and learn."

She wrapped one arm around his waist and rested her head on his shoulder. Nothing in his entire life had felt so good. So right.

"You trusted him because you wanted to," he whispered. "Because Winston had, you wanted to, too."

"Winston would have wanted me to trust you more." Shifting her head slightly, she asked, "You would have told me if you were married, wouldn't you?"

"Yes."

She nestled her head back on his shoulder. "I knew that." Silence lingered for a few moments before she asked, "Have you ever thought of getting married?"

"No," he lied. Not up until lately. "I saw what marriage did to my father."

"You'd think differently if you'd seen him and my

mother. They were so happy," she said wistfully. "So very, very happy."

This conversation and the sensations her closeness caused were dangerous, yet he didn't feel threatened. Instead, he felt peace and thankfulness his father had not only found success in Colorado, he'd found love and happiness. Had lived a life he deserved. Crofton couldn't help but wonder if one day he'd deserve that kind of happiness and success, too.

Knowing she was safe did fill him with thankfulness and he didn't stop himself from planting a small kiss upon the top of her head. As she snuggled closer, all that had happened started playing out in his mind, and a profound realization hit. A picture of Governor Eaton, who had just been voted in, had hung on the wall next to the railroad maps in Lincoln's private car. Eaton was also a rancher. A bolt of understanding had Crofton's eyes snapping open. "That's it," he whispered.

"What's it?" Sara asked.

Although the workers had sat nearer to the front of the car, giving them space, he didn't want anyone to hear the connections his mind had made. "I'll tell you at home," he said.

She lifted her head, and her brows knit together.

"I promise."

The way he winked at her made Sara's heart skip a beat. This time when she wished Winston had never died, it wasn't for herself, it was for him, and Crofton. Winston would have been so proud of him. So proud to have known the wonderful man his son had become.

Once again resting her head on his shoulder, she whispered, "I wasn't prepared for this, Crofton. For my parents to die. To become responsible for so much. To meet you. Bugsley promised to help me, but each time I felt like I'd gained a bit of ground something else happened. You arrived. I fell. The fire." She stopped just shy of saying he kissed her. The contentment his kisses filled her with was so special she didn't want it mixed in with everything else. Couldn't. His kisses made her forget everything else. "So many things happened, and I truly don't know what I would have done without you."

"I'm glad I was here to help you," he said.

"Are you?" she asked.

"Very."

Pure contentment filled her and she closed her eyes. "Me, too."

When the train jostled, she opened her eyes. She hadn't fallen asleep, but she had been in that place where all was right in the world. The whistle sounded and she lifted her head. "We're home."

"Yes, we are," Crofton replied. The air in his lungs felt heavy.

Sara said nothing as the men started rising from their seats when the train jerked to a stop. Crofton assisted her to her feet and waited as she folded the blanket.

A part of him wished the ride had been longer. No, that wasn't true. His wishes were more along the lines of her not being his stepsister. But that would mean he wouldn't be Winston's son, or that Winston had never married her mother. He didn't wish for either of those things. Sara deserved the happiness Winston had given her. His father had deserved that, too. What he himself deserved was what haunted him. A wife. A family. Neither seemed to be in his future. Not the wife or future he now wanted.

"Ready?" he asked.

She nodded and laid the blanket on the bench to be returned to Josiah.

Crofton took her hand and led her down the aisle between the seats. They'd no sooner stepped onto the platform when someone said his name.

"Miss Parks," the man said with a nod at Sara before holding out a hand. "I'm Sheriff Wingard. Just got back into town and it appears all hell broke loose during my absence." With a slight flinch, he looked at Sara, "My apologies, Miss Parks." Looking back at Crofton, he said, "We need to talk."

"Yes, we do," Crofton answered, "but I need to see Sara home first."

"No, you don't," she said. "But can we talk in your office, Sheriff? Out of the cold?"

It was a short walk to the sheriff's office, and even though Crofton had removed his coat and draped it over her shoulders, Sara was shivering by the time they arrived. Crofton led her to stand by the stove in the corner.

"Walter filled me in, as much as he could," the sheriff said as he poured coffee from a pot into three cups, "but I have to admit, I'm not sure where to start."

"I am," Crofton said.

Sara accepted a cup of coffee and sat down as Crofton started to pace the room. "Governor Eaton, who was voted in last fall, has a sizeable ranch in eastern Colorado. A railroad running through Arizona and New Mexico for others to haul cattle to the markets wouldn't be something he'd be in favor of, but he wouldn't want that to be known by anyone. Neither would the railroad. Several years ago a major stockholder company was exposed for the huge profits they were making, and as a result, several politicians lost their seats and many railroad officers lost their jobs."

"I'm not sure what that has to do with all that's happened here," the sheriff said, frowning.

Sara was. The flash in her eyes said so. "Winston said everything turned crooked when politicians became involved."

Crofton nodded. "And he wouldn't have wanted to be involved in it." Turning to the sheriff, he said, "The railroad was set to go south last year. Winston had agreed to provide the lumber, yet as soon as Eaton took office, the contract was pulled. Winston even sent a man down that way to survey it a second time."

"Winston and I spoke about that," Sheriff Wingard said.

"Winston went to Denver several times this spring," Sara said.

"So did Morton." Crofton looked at the sheriff. "Winston wasn't going to let politics govern the routes, but someone else might."

"You think Bugsley Morton's behind all this?" the sheriff asked.

"I'm not completely sure," Crofton answered. "Morton wouldn't chance going to jail for murder. He's smarter than that."

Sheriff Wingard let out a low whistle. "I just arrived in town this afternoon. Let me do some investigating." He nodded toward Sara. "Take Miss Parks home. I'll be in touch as soon as I know anything."

Sara shook her head. "Crofton's friend—"

"I know about that, too," the sheriff answered. "Walter filled me in."

A chill brushed over Crofton's skin. The sheriff knew a lot more than he was saying. There was no doubt the man knew whoever had shot at the buggy at the lawyer's office and killed Mel was still out there. Starting out with his hunch about the governor had been purposeful. Crofton didn't want Sara thinking about all of the other incidents. It appeared the sheriff didn't, either, and Crofton appreciated that.

"We'll see you tomorrow, then," Crofton said. As he set the coffee cup down on the desk, his eyes landed on the newspaper on the table. The one with the headline Prodigal Son Returns.

Chapter Seventeen

Snow had started falling when they walked out of the sheriff's office, and that made Sara lift Crofton's coat from her shoulders. "Here, you'll need this."

"Not as much as you do," he answered before pointing across the street. "There's Alvin."

He took her hand, hurried to the buggy. Whoever had told Alvin to be there waiting for them needed to be thanked. She would see to that, right after she warmed up. Squished between the two much larger men on the small buggy seat, she twisted until one shoulder was behind Crofton's and then, because she was so chilled, she snuggled against him.

The snow was piling up, but they arrived home safely. Amelia met them at the door, and promised a hot meal would be on the table as soon as they both changed into dry clothes. Amelia was full of questions, and explanations of how she and Walter had completed the payout to the mill workers, and invited them to the Christmas party.

Sara voiced her appreciation, but her mind was on other things. Namely Crofton. He'd filled a void inside her. One that had been there even before Winston's death.

That thought lingered as she retired, and whether it

was the sleep, or the dreams that kept her company, she awoke with a smile on her face the next morning. It was a moment before she realized she'd been standing at the altar in her dreams, and the man beside her had been Crofton.

That sent her bounding off the bed. Just because he wasn't married, didn't mean he didn't want to be. Especially to her. It would solve problems, mainly her problems. She could see herself taking care of the house as immaculately as her mother had while Crofton ran Parks Lumber as proficiently as Winston had. Her life would be much like it used to be. The only difference would be that this time her name would truly be Parks. She liked that idea, and could imagine the house once again being full of love and laughter.

After donning a blue-and-white-checkered dress, she made her way downstairs. The ground was snow-covered but a path had been shoveled to the outhouse. She grabbed a shawl from the hooks near the door, and headed in that direction.

Upon opening the door to exit the outhouse, she startled slightly at the sight of Elliott Cross leaning against the corner of the house.

He'd want to know what had happened yesterday, but the front door of the house would have been a far more appropriate place to wait for her.

"Hello, Sara."

His ominous tone turned her insides rock hard in her stomach. Her gaze slipped lower. There was no pen or paper in his hand. Instead the barrel of a small derringer sparkled in the sunlight. The missing link suddenly appeared in her mind. Finally, it all made sense.

He took a slight step backward. "I'll need you to come with me, Sara."

Not about to let that happen, she willed an alternative to come to mind. He was just far enough around the corner that anyone in the house wouldn't see him and the only thing in the outhouse was the broom she used to brush out spiders when needed. Not much, but it would have to do.

The outhouse door was slightly open, her hand still on the frame. Shifting as if to lean against the wall, she slipped her hand through the opening. "Where to?" she asked, knowing that would be expected.

"The mill. There's an issue."

Her fingers touched the broom handle. "I'll need to get Crofton."

"He's busy," Elliott said. "Now, come on."

Panic filled her. "You better not have hurt him," she shouted at the same time she pulled the broom out the door and barreled forward. With both hands on the handle, she whacked at Elliott as if he was the biggest, most dangerous spider she'd ever spied.

His gun went off as he fell to the ground. The sound scared her, but considering no pain filled her, she kept swatting. Elliott attempted to grab the broom, but was also trying to protect his glasses, which made her swing faster and harder.

Snow flew, and he shouted for her to stop, but all the frustration and anger she'd felt over the past few weeks filled her, making her whack harder and faster. "If you've harmed one hair on Crofton's head I'll squish you like a spider! Your own mother won't recognize you by the time I'm done!"

The broom was suddenly snatched out of her hands and two hands grasped her waist. She flayed her arms and kicked her feet, until the voice saying her name filtered through her own screaming. Her entire body went limp as relief washed over her. Then excitement flared. Spinning about as Crofton's hold loosened, she shouted, "It's him. It's been him the entire time!"

"I know," Crofton said, glancing toward the outhouse.

She twisted about. Elliott was still shouting as Sheriff Wingard pulled him off the ground.

So relieved, so happy, Sara spun around and looped her arms around Crofton's neck and without a second thought, she pressed her lips against his. He became the only thing to exist. His lips moved against hers, lightly at first, then faster and firmer. His arms tightened, holding her up against him firmly, wondrously. When his tongue slipped past her lips, all kinds of peculiar and fantastic sensations exploded inside her. An incredible and desert-like heat pounded in her veins as his tongue teased and taunted hers.

The kiss continued until her lungs burned as if she'd just run all the way up the mountain. Crofton pulled his lips off hers, but still held her close. His hands rubbed her back, her shoulders, her hair, and she snuggled her head beneath his chin, still trying to catch her breath.

He was breathing hard, too. She could hear it, feel it, and held on tighter. "I thought he'd hurt you," she said when able to speak. "I thought—" She buried her face into his shirt, unable to say more.

"Shh," Crofton whispered. "I'm fine." His hold lessened, and he placed a hand under her chin, lifting her face. "But are you all right? Did he hurt you?"

"No. He just surprised me when I stepped out of the outhouse."

"I heard a gunshot."

She nodded. "It went off when he fell to the ground. All I had was the broom."

His smile made his eyes light up. "You used it well."

Not sure what else to say, she nodded. "Thank you."

Crofton kissed her again, briefly, before stepping back. "Come on, the sheriff wants to talk to you."

Neither of the men were nearby. "How did Sheriff Wingard get here so quickly?" she asked.

"He and I were in the office. He'd been looking for Cross all night."

"You knew it was Elliott, didn't you?"

Crofton's hand rubbed her back as they walked. "I had a hunch. After you went to bed last night, I went back to town."

"To talk to the sheriff," she said.

"Yes. When Winston put a stop to the scandal before it could gain momentum, Cross decided to give it fuel. He wanted the recognition of breaking the story. Wanted to become famous."

They'd arrived at the house, but she stopped him from opening the door. "He killed your friend Mel, too, didn't he?"

"It appears so. The sheriff has witnesses who saw Elliott talking with Mel right before Mel left to head back to Arizon. He could have easily followed him, and Alvin said Elliott had been in the barn shortly before the accident. Said Elliott claimed his bridle had broken and he needed to borrow an awl to punch a new hole. He could have sawed the brace board before Alvin found him."

"He shot at us, too?"

"He needed to keep the story going."

"And the fire?"

He nodded.

She drew a deep breath and let it out slowly. "So it's over."

He glanced around before meeting her gaze. "It's over, and you were right, Bugsley didn't have anything to do with it, other than being a pawn. Lincoln and Eaton must have thought they'd be able to control him and you if the two of you were married. They were behind the scandal Winston put a stop to. By promising a southern route, they'd started raising money for it, but in fact, never had any intention of building it. They planned on just pocketing the money. The property and mineral rights they'd started to buy up down there were all in their names—not the railroad's. When Winston discovered that, he'd refused to be part of it."

"How do you know that?"

"Sheriff Wingard. Winston had told him about it, in case there was trouble." He glanced at the house before saying, "Wingard was the only one Winston told. If he'd been in town when I first arrived..." He shrugged.

She stretched on her toes and kissed his cheek. "I don't want to think what would have happened if you hadn't shown up when you had."

He lifted a brow but then smiled as he opened the door. "Me, either."

In the office, where Sheriff Wingard had Elliott wearing a pair of handcuffs, the entire tale, just as she and Crofton had deciphered, was repeated. Elliott denied nothing, including how he'd been the one to start the rumor the letter Crofton received had been from his wife.

Once the confession was over and the sheriff led Elliott away, Sara turned to Crofton. "We'd better head down to the mill."

"What for?"

"They need to know what happened, and that it's over," she said.

"I can do that."

She hooked an arm through his. "No, it needs to come

from both of us. They need to know that we are a team, and that they have nothing to worry about."

He shrugged, but straightened and walked beside her down the steps.

Chapter Eighteen

Preparations for the Christmas party had filled her days; Crofton, updating her about the mill, had filled her evenings and dreams had filled her nights. Of the three, it was the dreams that remained with her most of the time. They were full of kisses and weddings, and a future she wanted more and more. Crofton hadn't kissed her again since the incident with Elliott, but sometimes, when their eyes met, she could see the desire that told her he wanted to.

Smoothing the brilliant green gown over her stomach, Sara twisted to check her reflection in the mirror. The gown had been her mother's. One she'd admired, and was delighted it fit her as well as it had her mother. Stepping closer to the mirror, she repositioned the combs holding the hair above her ears, and tugged a couple more ringlets to hang from her temples. Usually not conceited, she had to smile into the mirror. She looked the part. A wealthy young woman. Proud, but not conceited. Sophisticated, but not snobbish.

She let out a breath. These were big shoes she had to fill, but it would be possible with Crofton at her side. He'd be there, greeting the guests as they arrived for the party.

After a final glance in the mirror, she crossed the room to peek out the window at the balcony. The empty bowl and glass saddened her. The sun was shining, but the colder weather had remained, and she hadn't seen the birds. Not once. She'd used her hand mirror to try and look inside the basket, but the hole was too small and she didn't dare move the basket, just in case they were in there.

Spinning around, she hurried to the door. Mother had a tiny mirror in her dresser. Rushing into the hallway, Sara ran directly into Crofton. Her heart went wild when his hands grasped her arms.

"Hey there, slow down," he said. "Where are you off to in such a rush?"

"I haven't seen the hummingbirds the past couple of days. I want to get a mirror to look inside the basket."

He chuckled. "Well, slow down. If you take the steps at that speed, you'll end up breaking your neck."

Not wanting to part from him yet, she reached up and straightened his string tie. "You look nice."

"So do you," he said, stepping farther away. "Go get your mirror. I'll help you look."

"You will?"

"Yes."

"Thank you!"

She flew down the hall and back, finding Crofton on the balcony.

He stood near the basket she'd wired onto the balcony next to the house. "When did you make this?"

"A while ago." She handed him the tiny mirror. "I hoped this would fit in the hole so I could see if they are in there."

She held her breath while he maneuvered a corner of the mirror through the tiny hole. The look on his face when he pulled out the mirror sent disappointment washing over her.

"I'm sorry."

She took the mirror he held out. "It was a silly idea anyway."

"No, it wasn't. It was an admirable one." He took her hand and led her into the bedroom. "Let's go downstairs. I heard wagons arriving."

She set mirror on the dresser. "I heard them, too."

He squeezed her hand as they left the room together. "They'll be back. Next spring you'll have all sorts of hummingbirds."

She smiled at his attempt to make her feel better. "You're right."

They had barely stepped off the last step when the first knock sounded. From that moment on, the flow of guests didn't slow. She had hired the same women from town that her mother always had in order to keep the buffet of food on the dining room table never ending and the dishes clean.

Sara split her time between answering the door and mingling with the guests, just as mother had taught her, and she sought out Crofton every chance she got. He did look very handsome in his suit and standing at his side increased her pride to the point she should be ashamed. But she wasn't.

"Happy?" he asked while closing the door after greeting several railroad workers.

"Yes," she said, looping an arm though his elbow. "It's a fine party."

"That it is," he agreed. "And you are a beautiful hostess." Nodding behind her, he quietly added, "Who is being summoned."

Spinning about to see Amelia gesturing for her, Sara said, "I'll be right back."

Crofton nodded as she parted. He'd concluded a few things the past couple of days, and watching Sara hurry toward the dining room, her skirts rustling, made him sigh. She was so beautiful. So loving and kind and intelligent. And the very reason he had to leave. Staying had grown dangerous. Dodging Cross's bullets had been easier than dodging Sara's star-spangled eyes. Every time she looked at him, his resilience took a hit. He certainly hadn't planned on falling in love with her, but it had happened. There was no denying that. There was just one final matter he needed to settle and then he'd leave.

Oddly enough, his mind no longer thought of the ranch as home. Neither did his heart. The cattle, the land, the idea of success no longer beckoned him. Maybe it never truly had, other than as a way to prove himself to his father. He no longer needed to prove anything. Maybe he never had to. Either way, it didn't matter. The reason he had to leave wasn't for himself—it was for Sara. She was what he wanted. Fully. Forever. Which was exactly why he had to leave.

She had disappeared into the kitchen, and Crofton turned about. He exited the house at the perfect moment. "Morton," he said to the man on the steps.

"Mr. Parks."

"I'd like a word with you," Crofton said. "The barn will work."

Morton didn't protest, and Crofton waited until they were both inside the barn before he said, "I rarely give a man a second chance. The only reason I'm considering it now is because of your history with my father, and let me assure you, I don't want to regret it."

Bugsley shot a wary glance around the barn before he hung his head. "I didn't expect a second chance."

"You shouldn't," Crofton answered.

"Then—"

"Because I believe my father wouldn't have kept you in his employ for so long if he didn't trust you," Crofton said. He couldn't leave without knowing there was someone Sara could depend on when needed. Morton wasn't who he'd choose, but there was no one else. He'd searched the town over, and done his due diligence when it came to Morton. The man had been dedicated to his father, and from what he'd determined, hadn't known what to do after the accident anymore than anyone else. The lawyer, the sheriff, even Walter, were convinced of that. Crofton had concluded one other thing. His jealousy may have blinded him to some of the man's traits. But, forgiving the man for pulling Sara so deep into the mess would not be easy.

"I would have given my life for Winston," Bugsley said. "That's what he hired me for. Not to work at the mill, but to protect him and his family. I failed, and I'm ashamed of that. Ashamed of all that happened. Hell, I'm not even sure how it happened. And I should have known Elliott was behind it. He's the one who started spouting off about how Sara needed to get married right off. I told her I'd take care of everything, and everything seemed to be going smoothly, until you arrived."

Crofton leaned against the wall, letting the man know he was interested in all he had to say.

"When you suggested the accident wasn't an accident, I checked the wreckage. Elliott saw me, and suggested it was the railroad." Bugsley ran both hands through his hair. "That's why I burned it. And why I told Walter to fire shots in the air. I saw Sara in the clearing and didn't want her to see the wreckage. There was some scuttle-butt about a scheme last year, but Winston put a stop to it. I never knew the ins and outs until I went to Denver to question Lincoln, and told him about you. We all thought you were dead. Seems Cross was the only one to know the truth about that, too."

Crofton remained silent, but lifted a brow.

Morton lowered his head and shook it. "When Lincoln and I returned from Denver the other day, Cross was at the station. He not only told me about the letter from *your wife* that he'd just delivered to the post office, he told me that years ago, Winston had received a telegram from a judge out East. A judge who shipped you back to England for thievery. Cross was the one who sent that message back to the judge. He can be quite convincing at times. He led both Lincoln and I to believe that after you robbed the town blind, you'd leave Sara and Amelia, with nothing, and then return to your wife and your ranch, all the richer." Bugsley shook his head again. "I don't know why I believed it all. Why I wasn't thinking clearly. All I was thinking about was how sheltered Sara had always been, and how it was my duty to keep her safe."

"From me," Crofton said, pushing off the wall.

He nodded. "And every other man asking for her hand."

Crofton let it all settle in his mind. Morton seemed sincere, and from what he'd been told, had been as dedicated to Winston as his dog Sampson had been to him all those years ago. Crofton was the one who had been full of distrust. For years and years. Letting that go wouldn't be easy.

"That's why I told Ralph Wainwright, and Sara, there was no need to have the will read," Morton said. "I knew

Elliott would post that in his paper and men would flock in so thick I'd be beating them away with two-by-fours."

"They were thick those first few days," Crofton admitted.

Bugsley offered a half grin. "I have to admit, I didn't mind letting you handle that." He shrugged. "Amelia Long believes I was behind that, Nate's death. I wasn't. I was fighting right beside him when it happened." Blinking quickly, he said, "Held his head on my lap as he took his last breath." He sniffed and wiped his nose. "I saw how close you two are, you and Amelia, that first night at the house. After the funeral. I figured she'd convince you to hate me just as much. That's how it happens, isn't it? You expect a man to be your enemy, and he is. Expect him to be your friend, and it usually works out that way, too."

"It does work out that way at times," Crofton admitted.

Bugsley squared his shoulders. "And a man can always find a reason for doing what he wants to, right or wrong."

Crofton caught Morton's underlying tone. "You aren't talking about Cross."

Bugsley shook his head. "Your father's wife Suzanne once told me that Winston found people at their worst and turned them into their best. He did that. He gave men chances that no one else would have. Including me. I'm ashamed of what I've done, and I'm willing to face whatever consequences you choose in that matter, but, at the end of the day, I was doing what I'd been hired to do. Protect Sara, and that is something I will continue to do. From anyone I feel is not looking out for her best interests."

Crofton knew a threat when he heard one, but in this

case, he wasn't offended. Matter of fact, he appreciated it. He'd put other measures into place, that of Walter running more of the business issues. What he needed was just what Morton claimed to be. A protector, a watchdog for Sara. One she didn't know had her back covered. With a nod, Crofton said, "I believe you will, and I will hold you to that."

"Hold me to that?"

Crofton nodded and gestured to the door. "We best head to the house before we are missed."

Bugsley glanced toward the door, but rather than taking a step, he proved his insights. "Does Sara know you don't plan on staying?"

Crofton questioned answering. A part of him didn't want it to be true. To be what needed to be done. The other part of him knew it was for the best. "Not yet. I'll tell her tomorrow. Right before I head south."

"Why?" Morton asked. "Why leave when you could have all this?"

Crofton shrugged. "I didn't come here to inherit anything from my father. Not his businesses, and not his daughter."

It was Morton's turn to lift a brow.

Pushing the heavy air out of his lungs, Crofton said, "Sara needs time to figure out what she wants. She won't do that with me here. She's too kind, too generous. She'll give in to whatever I want. I can't let her. For her sake, I can't do that to her."

"Your father would be proud of you," Morton said.

"I hope so," Crofton admitted, because leaving Sara might be enough to break him.

Sara had kept one eye on the front door ever since Crofton had walked out of it, and watching him walk in the house made her smile, until she noticed Bugsley following him. Excusing herself, she left the group of women near the table and crossed into the foyer.

"Good afternoon, Bugsley," she greeted, although her smile wasn't easy. Someday, when others weren't looking, she would have a serious conversation with Bugsley.

"Sara," he replied with a bow of his head.

"There is plenty of food," she said, gesturing toward the buffet. "Please enjoy yourself."

The look that crossed between the two men confused her. It wasn't full of animosity. In fact, it seemed like they knew what the other was thinking. "Is there something I should know about?" she asked Crofton as Bugsley walked away.

"No, not that I know of."

She frowned.

"Other than that Morton owes you an apology, and will provide it, but I suggested he waits until another day."

The mystery in his eyes held her attention more than his words. "Why do I get the feeling something is happening that I should know about?"

"Because you have a suspicious mind," he said with a grin and a wink. "Come, I'm hungry and I bet you haven't eaten, either."

"A hostess doesn't eat in front of her guests," she said.

"Says who?"

"My mother."

"And what do you think about that?"

She glanced around before whispering, "That I'm going to starve to death."

He laughed. "I can't let that happen."

Crofton escorted her to the buffet table and handed her a plate and added things she'd missed to it, then he found two chairs in the corner of the parlor, near the large pine tree Alvin had hauled in and set up.

"This is some party," he said.

People had been telling her that all day, but not one of them had made her as happy as his comment. It was exactly as she'd pictured it would be, and as wonderful with Crofton at her side.

She nibbled on her food between visiting with the people who stopped to talk, including Levi Lincoln who promised he and Governor Eaton had no ulterior motives and looked forward to many future contracts.

She smiled at Crofton as Lincoln moved on. Parks Lumber Company, the empire Winston had created would continue on for years to come. That filled her with pride, but she also knew, without Crofton, things would have turned out much differently.

"All's well that ends well," Crofton said.

His tone made her stomach gurgle, and suddenly she knew why. Just like when the link connecting Elliott Cross had connected in her mind, so did this one. Actually, it had been there all along, she just hadn't wanted to think along those lines. Drawing a breath of fortification, she turned to face him. "When are you leaving?"

His gaze never faltered as he stared at her, but it didn't reveal anything, either. It didn't have to.

"When?" she asked.

"Tomorrow."

She sucked up the fear and anger growing inside her. "When were you going to tell me?"

"I've been telling you that since I arrived."

"So you have," she said far more quietly than she felt.

"Bugsley will help you."

"A man you haven't trusted since you arrived," she pointed out.

"I was wrong about him."

Controlling all the emotions tumbling and turning inside her may have been one of the hardest things she'd ever done. It helped to think of her mother, of all her teachings about manners and expectations. Throwing herself at him and begging him to stay in front of a house full of people certainly would not be appropriate. Therefore, despite how it tore up her insides, Sara merely nodded, and smiled at those looking her way.

"I'll check on you periodically."

"Don't bother." She felt a bit ashamed that her tone sounded as cold as she felt. He'd never promised to remain—she'd put that in her head all by herself. She'd put other things in her head, too. Things she wasn't about to admit to. Not to him or anyone else.

She stood and willed her feet to cross the room. People spoke to her and she replied, but didn't slow. After depositing her plate in the kitchen, she took the back stairway upstairs.

"Sara."

She'd barely just sat down on the bed, and shot back to her feet. "Go away."

The door opened. "I didn't leave before now because I didn't want to disrupt your party," Crofton said.

"You didn't," she answered, moving to the mirror to check her hair.

His reflection was there, too, looking back at her even though he stood behind her.

He touched her arm. "I don't want—"

"What?" She spun around. As badly as she'd wanted his touch before, it now burned. Clear through her dress, skin and flesh. Pulling her arm away, she said, "You don't want what? Anything to do with your father? With anything he created? Anything he loved? Fine. Then don't.

Don't bother checking in periodically. It won't be needed. I won't need you any more than your father did."

Holding her head up took all the strength she could muster, so did saying, "Goodbye, Crofton."

Chapter Nineteen

Sara watched from the balcony as Crofton rode away. Her eyes smarted, but there were no tears left to fall. That had happened last night, along with the realization that she'd fallen in love. Completely. Hopelessly. She could even understand why. Just like when Winston had found her and her mother, Crofton had found her when her life was at its lowest. When she'd been scared and alone, and looking for a miracle.

He may have been a miracle, just as Amelia had claimed that very first day, but he hadn't been a lasting one. Because she hadn't needed a lasting one. It had taken half the night for her to come to the conclusion. Lifting her chin, she turned about and headed for the bedroom door. She was a Parks and when a Parks gets knocked down, they get up stronger than before.

She wasn't certain where she'd come up with that, but it fit.

That resolve drove her hard the following week. It turned her hard, too.

"There's no need for you to stay at the mill every night until dark," Amelia insisted on yet another evening that Sara hadn't returned home by supper time.

"Yes, there is," she said, grabbing a piece of chicken off the plate Amelia had kept in the warming oven. "It takes twenty-three hundred railroad ties for every mile of track. When that bridge is done next spring, I want ten miles of ties ready to go, and ten miles after that."

"Men can only build so fast," Amelia said.

"That's why I've called a meeting with Levi, to suggest he have more men ready to go," Sara answered.

"Spring is a long way off," Amelia said. "Christmas is still three days away."

"We've already had our Christmas party," Sara pointed out, and she knew exactly when Christmas was. Exactly how many days it had been since Crofton had left. Eight. Eight days. "You can tell Alvin to get rid of the tree."

"I will not."

Sara truly didn't care either way. "Levi will be here tomorrow, and will join us for dinner. A beef roast will do, with an apple spice cake for dessert. Use the good china. I'll check to see if the silver needs to be polished after I've eaten."

"I'll see to the silver," Amelia said. "You can't run the mill and the house at the same time. I don't see why you don't let Bugsley see to some things. That's what he's there for."

"He is seeing."

"No, he isn't. Not like he should—"

Sara set down her fork with a clatter. "You're as bad as Crofton. A short time ago you hated Bugsley."

"I never hated him," she said. "It's just—"

"It doesn't matter." Sara pushed away from the table. "Bugsley does what I tell him to."

Amelia grabbed her arm. "It does matter, and you're going to listen to me. I didn't like Bugsley because he was with Nate when he died. I wanted to be that person.

I wanted to be the one holding his hand when he died because I loved him. Loved him with all my heart. It didn't turn out that way, and I didn't like it. That's how life is. Things happen that we don't like. Just like you don't like that Crofton left."

Sara sucked in air at the mention of his name. Lately, the mere mention of his name pained her. Left her feeling as empty and cold as when her parents had died.

"He had to leave," Amelia said. "He's too much like Winston not to."

"Just like his father," Sara snapped. "Nothing will stop him from pursuing his dream. Not even his family." She'd thought of that plenty of times lately, as well as how Winston had left his family in Ohio to pursue his dream.

"You aren't his sister any more than he is your brother," Amelia said, "and you know it. Just as you know all you have to do is send a telegram, one little letter, and Crofton will be here in a heartbeat. I've thought about sending that letter myself, before you work yourself into an early grave."

"I'm not in danger of working myself into a grave," Sara scoffed.

"You're not? You aren't trying to do everything Winston did for his business while still trying to do everything here that your mother did?"

"I'm just doing what needs to be done," Sara said, exasperated over the entire conversation.

"Why?" Amelia asked.

"Because I need to," she said. "The railroad needs the lumber. The people of Royalton need the mill. We need a house that is presentable at all times."

"And what about you?" Amelia asked. "What do you need? Better yet, what do you want? Because if you don't want all of this, you're going to come to hate it. Hate your life. Hate it as bad as Crofton's mother hated hers. That's what happened you know. She hated her life so badly she destroyed hers and everyone's around her. Destroyed the last ounce of love that had been left between her and Winston."

Hardened when it came to the idea of love, Sara huffed out a breath. "Love. There's no time for love."

"There's always time for love," Amelia said softly. "You'll see that when you learn to put it first."

Sara had no retort. Her mind flat-out couldn't come up with one.

"You'll also understand why Crofton left, if you'd stop long enough to think about it."

She shook her head.

"He did it for you," Amelia said. "Because he didn't want you trapped into something you didn't want."

Crofton curled his nose at the scent of burnt hair as he stepped back and signaled for Gray Hawk to let the steer bound to its feet. In the days since he'd returned to the ranch, he'd discovered there wasn't much about cattle he liked. There wasn't much about ranch life that he was content with whatsoever. At one time, living so far from town had fit him. He'd been hiding then. In fact, if it hadn't been for Mel's death, he might have never left the ranch.

It had taken him less than a day to figure that all out. How he had been hiding from his father. Over the years he'd told himself he needed to become someone, be successful before searching out his father, whereas he now knew that had been a lie. He'd been hiding from his father. Hiding from anything that would make him feel again. Feel anything except hate and distrust.

Sara had made him see that, and made him feel. Riding away from the house that morning had ripped his insides so open he'd still be gushing blood had it been a flesh wound. Trouble was, he was back to hiding, and it was harder this time. His heart wasn't in it.

"Crofton!"

He turned toward the shout, and dropped the handle of the branding iron onto the ground. Although she'd helped Gray Hawk with all the chores during his absence, since his return, Crofton hadn't seen June leave the house. He wished she would. Eating her cooking reminded him of exactly why he'd missed Amelia's so much over the years.

"You've got company," she said, pulling her horse to a stop that stirred up a fair amount of dust.

The wind didn't need any help. His mouth tasted like dirt all day, every day. It may have snowed in Colorado, but it hadn't here. Dust coated everything. Wiping a gloved hand over his lips, he asked, "Who is it?"

"Go see for yourself," she said. "I'll take over for you."

June and her husband Gray Hawk had moved in with them shortly after he and Mel had claimed the acreage, and after Mel's death, his half became theirs. Crofton had found himself wondering if they wanted his half, too. Telling himself he couldn't desert one family for another no longer resonated with him as it used to. Neither did building up a cattle ranch. Rather than cattle, his thoughts were often on trees and lumber and railroads and, more specifically, one particular woman.

"I left them in the kitchen," June said.

Crofton took the reins she held out and stuck a foot in the stirrup. Whoever it was wouldn't hang around long. June's coffee could chase away coyotes.

Although it was Christmas Eve, he didn't expect any holiday visitors. It was most likely Fred Haberman and his sons. Therefore, Crofton didn't rush to the house. The Habermans owned the place south of his and had opposed the fence he and Mel had erected from the day they'd driven the first post. Namely because the Habermans didn't mind rounding up every newborn calf and branding it as their own.

Rounding the barn, Crofton's thoughts of telling his neighbors the fence wouldn't be coming down disappeared. He recognized the buggy, the horse hitched to it and the saddled one tethered to the corral rail next to the rig.

Crofton dropped to the ground and bolted to the house with all sorts of possible disasters racing across his mind. "Morton," he shouted as he threw opened the door. "What's happened? Is Sara—"

His questions stopped as abruptly as his feet. More beautiful than ever, she rose from the chair slowly, gracefully. The smile on her face was the one he fell asleep to at night. It may have been the one thing he missed most. How the tiny upward curls at each side of her mouth had chased away all the emptiness inside him.

"Hello, Crofton," she said.

The sound of her voice shot through him like a flame. Stung, he turned to Bugsley. "Why the hell did you let her come all the way down here? Do you have any idea how dangerous that trail is? How—"

"Bugsley didn't *let* me do anything," Sara said. "I allowed him to accompany me. Just as I allowed Levi."

Crofton hadn't noticed Lincoln sitting at the table until she pointed toward the railroad man.

"We've come to discuss an opportunity with you," she said.

"Discuss—" He stopped in order to calm his nerves. Excitement at seeing her—damn, he'd missed her—and fury at her traveling along a route that was long, dusty and far from smooth, in the middle of winter, fought for space inside him. "What opportunity?" he finished when convinced he had enough willpower not to grab her, hug her, kiss her.

"The railroad is interested in building a southern route," Sara said with far more poise and dignity than lived inside him at the moment. "Legally, and now, not in the future. It can be built simultaneously with the one going west, they will connect in Utah, and—"

"Will you gentlemen excuse us?" Crofton asked, stepping toward Sara.

Her gaze, locked with his, didn't falter. His didn't, either. He felt the strength she'd gained, and as much as that pleased him, it frightened him. She'd become a powerful woman, and wasn't afraid of that any longer, and therefore, all the more stubborn.

"Gentlemen," she said, while waving a hand towards the door.

As soon as the door closed, Crofton asked, "What are you doing here? Do you have any idea of the things that could have happened to you along that trail? There's barely a road from here to the state line. There are wild animals and roaming Indians and—"

"I just traveled that road, Crofton. You don't need to describe it." She stepped around him, as if needing space. "I came to tell you—"

Not wanting space, he spun and grabbed her arm. "I heard what you said."

She glanced at his hold before looking at him again. "You want a railroad. You want a cattle empire. As your family, I want to help you, so I negotiated a route—"

"You aren't my family." He regretted the words as soon as they left his lips, but it was the truth. He didn't consider her his sister. Never would. "Your name isn't Parks."

The snap in her eyes said his hit had hurt, and remorse struck him deeper.

"You're right," she said, "it's not."

Frustration rolled inside him. "I'm sorry. That's not what I meant."

"Yes, it is. And it's not right." She shook her head. "Me having the Parks name isn't right. I'm not Winston's daughter. I'm not your sister. I don't want to be your sister."

"Damn it," Crofton growled. "What are you doing here, Sara? I don't want a railroad. I don't want a cattle empire."

She pinched her lips together and swallowed visibly before asking, "What do you want, Crofton?"

Not able to admit what he did want, at least not out loud, he shook his head. "Hell if I know."

"Would you like to know what I want?" she asked.

He wasn't sure if he wanted to know or not, yet nodded.

"I want to polish the stair rail with beeswax until it's so smooth a drop of water won't bead on it. I want the silverware to shine when I set it on the table and the china to sparkle. I want the napkins ironed with precise crease marks and starched so they snap when unfolded."

"What?"

She sighed. "Those are things my mother taught me were important. Along with many other things about how to make sure a home is perfect."

"So you are tired of running Parks Lumber," Crofton said, feeling a bit of a gut punch.

She shrugged. "Possibly. I'm grateful for all I've

learned, and am confident that I could continue to run it, but it's not what I want. It's not right."

"What's not right? What's happened? Hasn't Bugsley been helping you?"

"Bugsley does everything I ask," she said. "And nothing has happened, other than the negotiation for the new route. What's not right is that you should be at the helm of Parks Lumber."

He shook his head. "I have my cattle ranch."

"That you don't want," she said. "You just told me that. I want you to have Parks Lumber, Crofton, but if you don't want it, tell me what you do want, what your dream is so I can help you make it come true."

"You don't want to know what I want, Sara," he answered.

She sighed. "I remember asking Winston if I could marry him when I grew up. He was the most perfect man in the world, and I didn't think I'd ever meet another one like him." She closed her eyes briefly before saying, "Until I met you. I love you, Crofton. Once I realized that, I understood why my mother wanted everything to be perfect for Winston. That's how it is when you love someone. I want your life to be perfect, Crofton. I want you to be happy."

For the first time in his life, he'd been knocked speechless.

Afraid she'd gone too far, Sara stepped back. This wasn't how she'd expected things to go. She'd thought he'd be elated about the railroad, so excited he'd have hugged her and kissed her. Shaking her head, yet still wanting his happiness above all else, she said, "You don't have to love me in return, just let me help you. Let me help you make your dreams come true."

"You just did," he said.

Before the words totally settled, he pulled her close. "I love you, too, Sara."

"You do?" she asked, hoping she'd heard right.

"I do. I love you more than I thought possible. You were all I've thought about since I left the house. I've missed you so much I've been downright miserable."

Too excited not to, she looped her arms around his neck. "I've missed you, too. So very, very—"

His mouth covered hers before she could finish telling him how much she'd missed him, and when his tongue caught hers, all of her words were completely forgotten. His kiss grew so vigorous she pressed her length against him, partly to encourage him to continue. The other part was so she could let loose all of the passion, all of the want and desire that had built up inside her like water behind a dam.

A moan escaped the back of her throat as everything she'd been holding back let go. Her entire being quivered at the sensation, but Crofton's hold, so tight, so powerful, let her know it was happiness, pure and unrefined, filling her system. A happiness she'd never have found if not for him.

A true Christmas miracle.

Epilogue

"Good morning, Mrs. Parks."

The arms that slid around her waist made her smile as much as his words. "Good morning, Mr. Parks," she replied, leaning back against him.

"You like the sound of that, don't you? Mrs. Parks."

"Yes, but more so because I'm your wife."

He kissed the side of her neck and then nipped at her earlobe until she scrunched up one shoulder against the tickle. Laughing, he tightened his hold around her and rested his chin atop her head. "I like it, too. Especially the more so part."

They stood there at the balcony for several quiet moments, just watching the sun rising over the mountaintops through the glass panes. It was not only the first day of their married life, it was the first day of the New Year. She thought the date very fitting.

It all was fitting. Her and Crofton marrying. The entire town thought so. It turned out, despite how Elliott Cross's article had attempted to make everyone think of them as brother and sister, no one did. People were very happy to know Parks Lumber would continue with them as husband and wife at the helm.

A flutter caught her attention and she leaned closer to the window. Excitement had her grabbing for the door-knob.

"What are you doing?" he asked as she opened the door. A second later, he ducked, pulling her down with him while tugging the door shut. "What the hell was that?"

Twisting in his arms, she glanced around the room. "My hummingbirds. They're back."

He straightened and looked behind him.

"There," she said, pointing. "On the curtain. They are both sitting up there."

"Well, I'll be," he muttered.

Simultaneously, the birds flew to the dresser. Although she set the bowl feeder out each morning, not wanting the glass to freeze and break, she carried it in each evening and set it on the dresser.

"They're hungry," he whispered.

"Aren't they beautiful?"

"Just like you." He kissed her temple. "They remind me of you."

"Who? The hummingbirds?"

"Yes." Moving swiftly, he scooped her up, one hand holding her back, the other under her knees.

Wrapping her arms around his neck, she asked, "How so?"

The teasing, adorable glint in his eyes sent a surge of heat through her. Becoming his wife wholly and completely last night had been the most wonderful event of her entire life.

He turned, carrying her toward the bed. "Or maybe they remind me of me."

"What are you talking about?" she asked.

"No matter how much they eat, they're still hungry."

She giggled. "You're hungry?"

He laid her down on the bed and separated the front of her dressing gown, revealing that she wasn't wearing anything else. Licking the tips of her breasts, he said, "Yes. For you, my beautiful, loving wife."

Just like all of his kisses, the touch of his lips was bedazzling, and inspired her to want more. Last night, the first time they'd come together, he'd been gentle and slow, introducing her into womanhood with such pleasure she'd been completely boneless. Later, when they'd repeated their union, it had been faster, more demanding, and so consuming her heartbeat quickened at the memory. She wondered which way it would be this time.

He climbed onto the bed beside her. Feeling a bit let down, Sara shifted onto her side so they faced one another.

Crofton ran a single finger under one of her eyes. "Don't be disappointed, my dear wife," he whispered roughly.

Glancing down the length of his naked, glorious body, delight spiraled inside her at his aroused state.

"It's your turn, Sara," he said. "It's time for you to show me what you want."

If there had been any disappointment left inside her, it flew out as fast as her hummingbirds had flown in. Flipping left and right, she tugged her arms out of her dressing gown and then rolled all the way on top of him. Pressing her hands against his shoulders, she arched upward until the tips of her breasts caught and held his attention.

She'd already told him what she wanted, and had it. Him. It was different from what she'd once imagined. She didn't want to just be his wife. She wanted to be his partner. Someone she could be herself around without worry. Someone she could get mad at, argue with and love with all her heart during the entire time, without fear he'd ever stop loving her. Considering she had all that, it took her a moment before she whispered, "I want a dog."

He laughed. "A dog?"

She nodded. "With lots of black hair who will save a boy from drowning."

It didn't seem possible, but his grin filled her with even more happiness.

"We'll get one tomorrow," he said.

Biting her bottom lip to keep from laughing aloud, she whispered, "What about today?"

"Today," he said while circling the tip of one breast with his fingertip, "we have other things to focus on."

"I was hoping you'd say that," she admitted.

* * * * *

COMING NEXT MONTH FROM

ℍ HARLEQUIN®

𝕳ISTORICAL

Available November 22, 2016

CHRISTMAS KISS FROM THE SHERIFF (Western)
Heroes of San Diego • by Kathryn Albright
Schoolteacher Gemma Starling feels like she's been given a fresh start. So she must make sure Sheriff Craig Parker doesn't discover her dark secret...

BOUND BY A SCANDALOUS SECRET (Regency)
The Scandalous Summerfields • by Diane Gaston
The pleasure-seeking Marquess of Rossdale has a plan to survive the Season without a bride—a fake engagement to outspoken Genna Summerfield!

THE GOVERNESS'S SECRET BABY (Regency)
The Governess Tales • by Janice Preston
Governess Grace will do anything to get to know her daughter, even if that means working for the scarred Marquess of Ravenwell! Can this beauty tame the beast by Christmas?

THE SAXON OUTLAW'S REVENGE (Medieval)
by Elisabeth Hobbes
After being abducted by Saxon outlaws, Constance Arnaud is reunited with Aelric, a Saxon man she once loved. They're now enemies, but they can't deny that love is stronger than revenge!

Available via Reader Service and online:

MARRIED FOR HIS CONVENIENCE (Regency)
by Eleanor Webster
Living in the shadow of illegitimacy, plain Sarah Martin has no illusions of a grand marriage...until the Earl of Langford makes her a proposal she can't refuse!

IN DEBT TO THE ENEMY LORD (Medieval)
Lovers and Legends • by Nicole Locke
After her life is saved, Anwen is held captive by her enemy Teague, Lord of Gwalchdu. But what will happen when their passionate arguments turn into even more passionate encounters?

Don't miss Janice Preston's festive conclusion to
***THE GOVERNESS TALES**, a series of four sweeping
romances with fairy-tale endings by Georgie Lee,
Laura Martin, Liz Tyner and Janice Preston!*

Read on for a sneak preview of
THE GOVERNESS'S SECRET BABY
*by **Janice Preston**, the final book in
Harlequin Historical's enticing quartet*
***THE GOVERNESS TALES**.*

I have come this far... I cannot give up now.

She sucked in a deep breath and reached for the huge
iron knocker. Still she hesitated, her fingers curled around
the cold metal. It felt stiff, as though it was rarely used.
She released it, nerves fluttering.

Before she could gather her courage again, a loud
bark followed by a sudden rush of feet had her spinning
on the spot. A pack of dogs, all colors and sizes, leaped
and woofed and panted around her. Heart in mouth, she
backed against the door, her bag clutched up to her chest
for protection. In desperation, she bent her leg at the knee
and drummed her heel against the door behind her.

After what felt like an hour, she heard the welcome
sound of bolts being drawn and the creak of hinges as the
door was opened.

Grace turned slowly. She looked up...and up. And
swallowed. Hard. A powerfully built man towered over

her, his face averted, only the left side visible. His dark brown hair was unfashionably long, his shoulders and chest broad and his expression—what she could see of it—grim.

"You're late," he growled. "You look too young to be a governess. I expected someone older."

Anticipation spiraled as the implications of the man's words sank in. If Lord Ravenwell was expecting a governess, why should it not be her? She was trained. If his lordship thought her suitable, she could stay. She would see Clara every day and could see for herself that her daughter was happy and loved.

The man's gaze lowered, and lingered. Grace glanced down and saw the muddy streaks upon her gray cloak.

"That was your dogs' fault," she pointed out indignantly.

The man grunted and stood aside, opening the door fully, gesturing to her to come in. Gathering her courage, Grace stepped past him, catching a whiff of fresh air and leather and the tang of shaving soap. She took two steps and froze.

On the left-hand side, a staircase rose to a half landing and then turned to climb across the back wall to a galleried landing that overlooked the hall on three sides. There, halfway up the second flight of stairs, a small face—eyes huge, mouth drooping—peered through the wooden balustrade. Grace's heart lurched.

Clara.

Don't miss
THE GOVERNESS'S SECRET BABY by Janice Preston,
available December 2016 wherever
Harlequin® Historical books and ebooks are sold.

www.Harlequin.com

Turn your love of reading into rewards you'll love with
Harlequin My Rewards

Join for FREE today at
www.HarlequinMyRewards.com

Earn **FREE BOOKS** of your choice.

Experience **EXCLUSIVE OFFERS** and contests.

Enjoy **BOOK RECOMMENDATIONS**
selected just for you.

PLUS! Sign up now
and get **500** points
right away!

Earn
FREE
REWARDS
Join
Today!
HarlequinMyRewards.com

MYR16R

REQUEST YOUR FREE BOOKS!

HARLEQUIN®

ℋISTORICAL

Where love is timeless

2 FREE NOVELS PLUS 2 FREE GIFTS!

YES! Please send me 2 FREE Harlequin® Historical novels and my 2 FREE gifts (gifts are worth about $10). After receiving them, if I don't wish to receive any more books, I can return the shipping statement marked "cancel." If I don't cancel, I will receive 6 brand-new novels every month and be billed just $5.69 per book in the U.S. or $5.99 per book in Canada. That's a savings of at least 12% off the cover price! It's quite a bargain! Shipping and handling is just 50¢ per book in the U.S. and 75¢ per book in Canada.* I understand that accepting the 2 free books and gifts places me under no obligation to buy anything. I can always return a shipment and cancel at any time. Even if I never buy another book, the two free books and gifts are mine to keep forever.

246/349 HDN GH2Z

Name   (PLEASE PRINT)

Address   Apt. #

City   State/Prov.   Zip/Postal Code

Signature (if under 18, a parent or guardian must sign)

Mail to the **Reader Service:**
IN U.S.A.: P.O. Box 1867, Buffalo, NY 14240-1867
IN CANADA: P.O. Box 609, Fort Erie, Ontario L2A 5X3

Want to try two free books from another line?
Call 1-800-873-8635 or visit www.ReaderService.com.

* Terms and prices subject to change without notice. Prices do not include applicable taxes. Sales tax applicable in N.Y. Canadian residents will be charged applicable taxes. Offer not valid in Quebec. This offer is limited to one order per household. Not valid for current subscribers to Harlequin Historical books. All orders subject to credit approval. Credit or debit balances in a customer's account(s) may be offset by any other outstanding balance owed by or to the customer. Please allow 4 to 6 weeks for delivery. Offer available while quantities last.

Your Privacy—The Reader Service is committed to protecting your privacy. Our Privacy Policy is available online at www.ReaderService.com or upon request from the Reader Service.

We make a portion of our mailing list available to reputable third parties that offer products we believe may interest you. If you prefer that we not exchange your name with third parties, or if you wish to clarify or modify your communication preferences, please visit us at www.ReaderService.com/consumerschoice or write to us at Reader Service Preference Service, P.O. Box 9062, Buffalo, NY 14240-9062. Include your complete name and address.

HHI5